THE SUMMERVILLE SISTERS

HEATHER DIXON

Copyright © Heather Dixon, 2024

The moral right of the author has been asserted.

Ebook ISBN: 978-1-80508-318-4
Paperback ISBN: 978-1-80508-320-7

Cover design: Sarah Whittaker
Cover images: Getty Images

Published by Storm Publishing.
For further information, visit:
www.stormpublishing.co

ALSO BY HEATHER DIXON

Summerville Series

Last Summer at the Lake House

The Summerville Sisters

Burlington

For all the hockey-playing girls I know—the ones with wild hair and big smiles.

ONE

If you drive through the center of town in Summerville and blink, you'll miss most of it. Along the edge of the road on one side is the flat, glassy stillness of a blue-brown Shadow Lake. As you wind your way into town a little further, you'll find small shops that look like they can only survive in summer; a store that rents boating gear and sells water skis; a shop dedicated to souvenirs and T-shirts. There's one fish and chip spot, two decent grocery stores, one tiny bakery, one place to get good shoes. No mall or movie theater. You have to drive further out for that.

It wasn't the most exciting of towns to grow up in, and Claire could see it might become an issue for her twelve-year-old daughter. Lilah could get so bored. Claire knew that boredom led to trouble. When Claire was Lilah's age, there were the kids who did everything they weren't supposed to just for kicks, and then there were the kids like her: too nerdy to feel the urge for danger. She had always liked the safety of the quiet in Summerville. Lilah, on the other hand, had a little gleam in her eye that made Claire nervous.

As she navigated her way through town now, thinking about her daughter made her even more eager to get home, but the roads were busy, like they always were in July. The summer tourists slowed her, not to mention her car was as old as dirt and falling apart, which meant it wasn't the most reliable way to get home quickly.

At the red light, Claire put her head back and closed her eyes for a second.

She had seen her mother again today.

Even though she knew it was impossible – knew it was grief playing tricks on her – Claire had kept seeing her throughout the last week since her death; in a reflection in a window, a person walking up ahead.

Today had felt different. It was her final day of seeing clients at the clinic before she took her leave of absence. Claire had requested time off for bereavement, which wasn't easy as a midwife, due to the unpredictable nature of the job, but her partners at the practice had said they would cover for her. She hated to let down the mothers she'd got to know so well, and would never want to put her colleagues under more pressure. It wasn't like her to even take time off. But she knew she couldn't be responsible for the arrival of a new life into the world right now, not when she was so deeply sad about her mother leaving it.

That afternoon, as Claire had walked out of the midwife clinic, she'd glanced up and seen a woman across the street, leaving a shop. The woman had straight, sandy-blonde hair that was cropped in a bob around the middle of her neck. She was dressed sharply in an oversized black V-neck shirt that settled onto her frame perfectly. She looked to be about the same age as Claire, somewhere in her forties. She was average height, average build. There was nothing extraordinary that would make her stand out in a crowd.

Except for the fact that she had Claire's mother's face.

Claire had watched the woman for a moment, a chill winding its way up the back of her neck, but then someone bumped into her and she was jostled out of position. She had glanced sideways at the passerby and mumbled an apology for standing in the middle of the sidewalk on a busy street filled with summer visitors, and when she had looked back, the woman was gone.

Claire had headed to her car and tried to shake the feeling off as she drove home. It was just grief messing with her brain. Her mother had only been dead for a week; the pain and loss were still fresh.

Now, at the traffic light, a honk came from behind her. Claire opened her eyes and saw the light was green. She waved an apology at the driver behind and made her way home.

When she got to her house, her shoulders softened slightly. This was her oasis. Her home was cozy and familiar—the outside painted a bright blue with white trim, surrounded by a garden of flowers blooming in oranges and pinks next to bright green shrubs. The inside was open and airy, with wooden beams that ran across the ceiling, floors covered with warm, honey-colored wood and oversized windows on the far wall which allowed a spectacular view of the lake. For a moment, it was possible for Claire to imagine her life hadn't changed, her mother was still alive and would soon walk through the door after a single knock, the way she always did when she came to visit. But the moment was fleeting, and with a shiver Claire was brought back to reality. Her mother was gone.

Claire put her keys on the table next to the front door and set her bags on the floor.

"Lilah?" She made her way through the living area, opening windows to allow the summer breeze through. She went out back to the covered porch, which Greg had built when they were still married and living together. The vaulted ceilings made out of maple sat over the top of an open space big enough to hold a table in the middle, a couch decorated with colorful pillows on one side and hanging lamps overhead that gave off a warm glow in the evenings. It was one of Claire and Lilah's favorite places to hang out. Her mother had loved it, too.

Today, it was empty.

Claire pushed the screen door open and took a step back inside. "Lilah? Are you home?"

"I haven't seen her." Greg's voice startled Claire, and she jerked around to look out through the open doorway. He stood on the porch now, his dark blue eyes gazing at her, his square, handsome face pointed in her direction.

"Oh—you scared me. What are you doing here?"

"Nice to see you, too," Greg said.

Claire tilted her head and placed a hand on her hip. He was joking, she could tell by the slight smile at the edge of his lips, but she shot him an exasperated look anyway.

"Was she home when you got here?" Claire asked. She didn't mind when Greg popped by unannounced, but only because they knew one another so well. Still. She didn't want the extra company right now; she wanted to talk to Lilah.

Claire had no rational way of explaining how she felt to Greg, anyway. There had been something inside her, a deep, indescribable need, telling her to get home and make sure her daughter was okay. It was a gut feeling, based on nothing except for the fact that she and her daughter both missed her mother. Cancer was horrible and Lilah hadn't talked much about it yet. Death was a strange and confusing thing when you were young. Claire had learned that firsthand.

"No, I haven't seen her," Greg said.

"So, why are you here?" Claire moved to one side to let him in the house and shut the screen door behind him. She tried to hide the sigh in her voice when she spoke, but Greg must have detected it; it was his turn to tilt his head at her.

"This used to be my place, too," he replied. And then, in a gentler tone, "I needed to borrow some gardening tools. I thought it was okay that I dropped by like this?"

Claire nodded. "It is. Yes. Of course. I've got a lot on my mind."

"Anything I can help with?" He took a step forward, crossing his arms over his chest. His forehead creased and he frowned, suddenly serious. He studied Claire, his eyes not moving from her face. Claire was reminded that he was often thoughtful in this way. He made being separated both easy and hard on her just by being him.

"No, but thank you."

She wasn't ready to tell Greg what she was experiencing, or what was running through her mind. It didn't make any sense the way the worry gripped her until she felt like it was hard to breathe, but it was there.

"You sure?"

"It's fine." Claire turned her head, looking out the back window to avoid his gaze. Avoidance had been her move with Greg for a while now. It felt easier. Besides, when it came to Lilah, there was something unspoken between the three of them—an understanding that Lilah would always come first for Claire. Maybe that was part of the reason she and Greg didn't make it. Claire couldn't help it, though. It was her nature to be a protective mother bear. She had learned from the best.

After a moment of silence, Greg said, "I'll go look for those tools."

Claire watched him go as she pulled her phone from her purse. Then she let her head fall back and gazed up at the ceiling for a second, taking in a deep breath. She didn't want to be like this, she wanted to let him in, but sometimes she couldn't help herself.

Claire brought her gaze down to the phone. The screen flashed with notifications—a promotional email from the local library, an update on the weather—but nothing from Lilah. She dialed her number and waited. After what felt like a dozen rings, it went to her daughter's voicemail. It often struck Claire as odd, hearing her daughter's still young-sounding voice asking her to leave a message, telling her she would call back as soon as possible in such a grown-up manner. She hung up without leaving a message.

The house was so quiet—an empty kind of quiet that Claire didn't like. It served as a reminder that something—someone—from her life was missing. Lately, whenever she had a quiet moment like this, Claire's mind went to her mother and all of her good qualities—the things she so desperately wanted to hold onto. There was a lot to remember: the way she would pause and give Claire all her attention when Claire spoke. The way she had the uncanny ability to make anything she cooked taste better than if Claire had made it herself. The way she loved Lilah.

When Lilah was a baby, Claire was careful with her, as new mothers are. She took extra caution with her neck and head whenever she picked her up. She made sure Lilah was always dressed warm enough, her tiny limbs and feet covered with layers. Despite this, Claire's mother made it seem like she could never be careful enough. Like Lilah was the most precious. Her mother would overreact when Lilah tumbled or fell over; she pleaded with Lilah to be careful anytime she was close to anything even remotely dangerous; and she scolded Claire for allowing her out of her sight. At first, Claire thought it was a case of just Veronica being Veronica—overprotective because she didn't know how else to be. Eventually, she came out of her new mother fog and connected the dots. Of course, her mother was this way. You would naturally be scarred for the rest of your adult life when you'd lost a child. Especially a child who was so young. Now Claire felt she couldn't help but be like her mother. It was in her genes to be cautious when it came to her child.

Claire clicked on Lilah's name on her phone screen and typed out a new message.

Call me please.

Then she waited. She went into the kitchen and wiped down the already-clean counters with a cloth. The kitchen was the only downside to her otherwise beautiful cottage-style home. It was too small for Claire's liking. The counters were barely wide enough to hold her blender and the fancy coffee maker she'd splurged on last winter. Lilah was always leaving a book or her headphones lying around which added to the clutter. Claire couldn't stand clutter. Everything had a place, and she preferred things to be orderly. Besides, how many times had she told Lilah that the kitchen was not a storage spot for her things?

Greg came into the room. He held up a shovel. The skin around his eyes crinkled, revealing fine lines when he smiled. "Thanks for this. I'll bring everything back next week."

Claire nodded. She chewed at the fleshy inside of her lip.

"What? You're not telling me something." Greg was looking at her intently again. "We haven't really talked about your mom. It felt like she was sick for a while but then gone so quickly. Are you doing okay?"

"I'm fine. I thought Lilah would be home. That's all." It was nice of him to ask, but Claire was agitated in the moment. She couldn't unpack how she was feeling about her mother when she was so focused on Lilah.

As if on cue, Lilah walked through the door. She had on her favorite pair of jean shorts, a baggy T-shirt she had been given at one of the hockey camps she went to in the summers and those high-top Converse running shoes she never went anywhere without. She stopped in her tracks when she looked at Claire. Her arms, with wrists covered in bracelets made from rainbow-colored threads, dangled at her sides.

Lilah looked from Greg to Claire, her father to her mother, with a hint of alarm in her expression. "What happened?"

TWO

"Nothing. Everything's fine. I just hadn't heard from you, so I wondered where you were," Claire said to Lilah.

That wasn't true. Everything wasn't fine. She wasn't herself, but how could she be? She had never known life without her mother until recently, and now she felt like she was losing her mind; seeing her everywhere, even though that was impossible. Claire looked down and pretended to study something on the counter so Lilah wouldn't see her expression. She didn't want to get caught in a lie.

When Claire lifted her gaze back up, she caught Lilah shooting a look at Greg and Greg shrugging in response. Claire's neck prickled. They had their own way of communicating that Claire felt on the outside of. She couldn't understand the father-daughter relationship because she had nothing of her own experience to base it on.

"Lilah," Claire said, but she didn't know how to continue. She wanted to talk to her daughter about her grandmother, yet she knew she would have to be delicate. For the past week, they had been trying to figure out how to grieve together. A part of Claire had wondered if Lilah would need her more, after the death. Only for a brief, fleeting moment did Claire desire that. Then she had pushed the thought away, ashamed that she could think any good could come out of her mother dying.

"What?" Lilah said, her tone edging on exasperated. Her dark brown eyes were wide, her thick, untamed eyebrows high on her freckled forehead. She ran a hand through her short, curly bob, even though Claire told her not to touch her hair too much when it was dry. Claire had the exact same head of curls and knew from experience that touching it too much would make her hair big and frizzy. Lilah didn't care how big her hair was. She had a strong sense of self, a confidence. Claire wasn't quite sure where it came from—it certainly didn't come as naturally to her—but she admired the hell out of it.

"Are you ready for camp? You don't think it's too soon to go?" Claire leaned her hip up against the edge of the kitchen counter. Two weeks at a sleepaway camp felt so long.

"Playing hockey will be a good distraction for me. My friends will be there," Lilah said. She looked from Greg to Claire. "What are you going to do all day without me and without work?"

Claire forced a smile. "I'll be fine. You don't have to worry about me. I'm going to get things sorted out at Grandma's house and then I'm going back to work."

A few days after Veronica had died, Claire had known she needed a break from work, as much as she loved it. She would miss not being there for the birth of babies. Bringing a brand new being into the world and placing them on top of their parent for the first time was an indescribable privilege. But she had realized quickly that she wasn't coping, and there was just too much to do; she was the only one who could take care of her mother's things. Bank accounts needed closing, her mother's house had to be emptied, her things saved or stored away somewhere before they could sell them. The amount of work there was to do after someone you love dies was exhausting. Claire hadn't expected it to be so much. And she would need to give herself time.

Losing her mother was like losing a part of her. When she was growing up, it had always been just the two of them. They had spent an inordinate amount of time together, not only because they only had each other, but also because one of her mother's most favorite things was to be with Claire. She told her that often.

Now it was Lilah's turn to study Claire's face. She held her gaze for longer than usual and then gave one shoulder a shrug. "Okay," Lilah said. "You can write to me, you know."

Claire's chest expanded. She tried not to react visibly, but could feel a warmth in her face. It was big when Lilah let her in. As she got older, Lilah was slowly slipping away. Even when she was in front of Claire, like she was now, Claire couldn't help but feel somewhat desperate, because Lilah always had her attention somewhere else, her eyes directed downward, her body language telling Claire she wanted to leave the room. Claire had read all the parenting books and articles, so she'd known this was coming. It was normal for a twelve-year-old girl to want to pull away from her mother, but it was still new to Claire. It was still raw.

"I'd like that."

"I have to run," Greg said. He leaned over and kissed the top of Lilah's head and then brushed his hand over Claire's arm. "Everything good?"

"All good." Claire waved at him on his way out.

Now would be a nice time to pour herself a small glass of wine and sit out back on the little rickety dock right down by the water's edge to watch the lake. It was a beautiful, peaceful spot to sit in the early evening. The water was still and flat, and she could look clear across to where a row of cottages sat.

Claire and her mother loved watching summer vacationers from there. Her mother would comment on the kids, and how they showed their joy so easily and often, jumping into the lake and yelling and laughing while they bobbed up and down in the water. Veronica had loved kids—and not just her own. Her face always brightened whenever she saw a toddler or heard the sound of a child laughing. Claire usually noticed the adults when they sat out watching the lake. She liked the way they lounged on their docks watching the sunset, or talking, always so much talking and laughing out on boats, or on the docks, wading in the water, in large hats and colorful bathing suits. It used to please Claire that her hometown made people so happy, but now it felt different. It seemed wrong to sit out there and relax with a crisp glass of white wine without her mother.

But she also knew she had to create some normalcy in her life. She had to keep doing the things she used to do until they felt right again. She picked up her wineglass and was heading toward the back of the house when there was a knock at the front door.

"Did Dad forget something?" Claire asked Lilah.

Lilah shrugged.

Odd. And Greg wouldn't knock, anyway.

Claire went to the door and opened it up, her breath catching when she saw who was standing there. It was the woman from town today. The one who looked so much like her mother.

Claire froze, her hand still holding the open door, and tried to make sense of this moment. What reason could there be for this woman to show up at her house? And who was she?

The woman's body was turned slightly away, as if she wasn't sure if she wanted to be standing there or if she wanted to leave, but then she turned to Claire and looked directly into her eyes. It was a shock to see her mother's face again; the resemblance was uncanny.

"Hi," the woman said. "I was looking for Veronica Brown and someone told me you're her—" She stopped.

Claire couldn't speak, she was so caught off guard. What on earth could this be about? Was she a lawyer, maybe? Someone from the bank?

"You're her—" The woman stopped again. Her lips twitched, like she was too overcome with emotion to speak.

Claire's eyes narrowed slightly and she stared intently, as if that would help her understand the woman better. This didn't make any sense. "I'm her daughter," she said. "I'm Claire. Sorry, you are?"

The woman went pale and put a hand out to steady herself against the side of the house. Claire felt an urge to help her, but she also didn't know if she should—if she could trust this woman who was so strange and so familiar all at once. And then the woman said in a soft voice, "I think I'm her daughter, too."

There was a rushing sound, a whooshing in Claire's ears. Had she heard right?

"I'm sorry, you must be mistaken. My mother didn't have another child. Only one who died a long time ago when she was a little girl." Claire's voice shook. She wasn't sure why she was explaining all of this to the stranger. This woman didn't need to know details, she just needed to know that she was wrong.

Later, Claire would wonder if the feeling she'd had earlier, the urge that drove her home to check on Lilah, had been a sign. Maybe she was developing an extra sense. Maybe more signs were to come. For now, she looked back at this stranger and confusion swirled within her.

"I'm Audrey," the woman said.

THREE

Claire's skin flushed and her body went hot. She held a hand up to her forehead. What kind of a sick joke was this? Who was this woman standing on her doorstep claiming to be Veronica's daughter—her sister? Her head was foggy; so much so that she could barely concentrate on what the woman said when she spoke again.

"My father told me that my mother lived here, in this town, and when I went to her house, a neighbor gave me your address." She looked down at her feet and cleared her throat.

Claire shook her head. *No.* None of this made sense.

"Why are you here?" She needed to know why this woman was at her house. What would possess someone to lie about who they were, to hurt someone in their moment of loss? What could this person want? "My mother is gone. She didn't have money."

The woman stiffened, her expression pained for a moment, then she shrugged and gave a shy smile. "I totally understand why you might think that. But I'm not here because of money."

"Then why? And who are you?" Claire hoped Lilah was upstairs or out back by now. She didn't want her hearing this.

"I know this is a lot to take in, but I think I must be your sister."

Claire studied her. She had round eyes that seemed to be shining. Her blonde hair softly framed her angular face. She had the kind of look to her that Claire could only think of as warm or inviting. Familiar, even. A hint of a smile appeared on her face.

Claire stiffened. "I don't have a sister," she said. But even as she said it, she felt a sense of shame. It wasn't true. She had *had* a sister.

Claire remembered her name. Audrey.

When Claire was a child, they didn't talk about her younger sister. It hurt her mother too much. She knew she'd had blonde hair, but she couldn't remember anything else about her. Her mother had kept some photos of Audrey in a box up in her closet, but she wouldn't allow Claire to take them down and look at them. After a while, the box of photos had disappeared. Audrey's only lasting presence on them was reflected in her mother and how she would cry. She cried a lot for a long time, and she did her best to hide it, but Claire would often walk into a room and see her mother's back turned, her shoulders shaking. She was usually sniffing, but the actual crying was always silent. As if the sound was the only thing that would upset Claire.

Claire only knew what she had been told in bits and pieces: one moment she had a sister two years younger than her, and the next Audrey was gone. She had overheard her mother tell other adults a few details. A car crash. Their father had made it out alive, but Audrey didn't. Her mother and father couldn't come back from it; it tore their marriage apart. It bothered Claire at first that she couldn't remember her father. When she asked about him, her mother would only say he was gone, too, and not to expect him to come back. It was harsh, but at least her mother didn't beat around the bush. Claire eventually grew to learn she shouldn't expect to have a father in her life, and that would be fine. She would be fine.

Now, back on the front step, Audrey frowned and ran a hand through her hair. "This is very confusing, I realize. It is for me, too. I never knew I had a sibling till now."

Why? It was all Claire could focus on. Why would this person think she was Claire's sister? Or, if this wild claim was somehow impossibly true, what had happened to Audrey all those years ago? Had there really been a car crash and Audrey had survived? But why hadn't she come to see Claire until now? Did her mother know? Or—and this was even harder to fathom —had her mother lied to her?

She didn't know how to react. "I need time," she managed to say.

"Of course. I understand. I'm, uh—I'm staying here in town for a few days. At the Summerville Waterfront Suites. Here's my number." She handed Claire a piece of paper. "When you're ready, maybe we could have coffee? I have a lot of questions."

She had questions? Claire was dizzy. She shivered even though it was a gorgeous, cloudless day in July.

"Mom?" Lilah's voice came from behind her.

Oh no. Not now.

Audrey's eyes widened. They searched for the source of the sound behind Claire, but Claire stood taller, shifted her body to try to take up most of the open space in the doorway.

"Oh, hi," Lilah said when she appeared next to Claire.

"Hi." Audrey's voice went quiet. She smiled. "Is this—"

"Okay, well, thanks," Claire said. She gripped the piece of paper with Audrey's phone number, even though she had no intention of using it.

Audrey opened her mouth, but Claire shifted, turning her back to Audrey and lightly nudging Lilah away from the door, pulling it slightly behind her so that she could speak to her privately.

"I need a minute here," she said to Lilah. She waved her hand to gently shoo her away.

"Who is that?" Lilah bent her head forward and whispered.

"I don't know," Claire answered just as low, so Audrey couldn't hear.

"You don't know?" She folded her arms over her stomach and her head jutted forward slightly.

"Can you give me a moment here?" Claire used her firm voice, the one she had to use when Lilah would push and push, rather than accepting Claire's first answer.

"Okay..." Lilah's voice trailed off as she said it, like Claire was acting odd for no good reason. "You're being so weird."

"I know, but we can talk about it later." Claire knew that as a mother, you had to shield your children but also be as honest with them as you could. It was often a delicate, impossible balance.

Fortunately, Lilah seemed to accept the answer. She shrugged and went toward the living room.

Claire turned back to Audrey. "Sorry."

Only, she wasn't exactly sorry. She wasn't sure what she felt. It wasn't every day someone showed up at your door and told you she was your long-lost sister—the sister you'd believed was dead for forty years, the sister that your mother told you had died. Claire stood, shaking with nerves, or adrenaline, and then put a hand to her forehead. Her mind was whirring with thoughts. Her mother couldn't have been lying to her all this time. Could she? No, this woman had to be wrong. What was she supposed to do now? What was the appropriate response when someone revealed that what you thought to be true for your entire life might be wrong?

Claire studied Audrey's face again. There was no denying that this woman looked like her mother. Enough that it had caused Claire to pause and take notice in town earlier. The shape of her lips, the way she ran her hand through her hair, just like her mother used to. Watching her do this now, Claire could tell she was nervous.

"I was wondering..." Audrey started, fumbling over her words. "I know you need time, but I thought you might want to know a little about our father."

Our father. Claire took a step backwards. All of this was too much to process. She knew nothing about her father at all, other than the fact that he had left them when Claire was young, when she thought her sister was dead.

"I can't. Not yet." Claire gave a wave and said, "I'm sorry," and she closed the door, leaving Audrey standing on the front step. She knew it was rude to shut the door on her like that, but she couldn't help herself. Her heart was racing. She hoped Audrey would leave. She didn't know who this woman was, let alone anything about her father. She was sure of nothing at the moment.

For the next few minutes, Claire moved around her home— from the kitchen to the back porch to the living room—on shaking limbs, trying to calm herself, thinking about what she should do next. She went and peered through the window near the front of the cottage to check the stoop where Audrey had been standing. She was gone. Thank goodness.

In the kitchen, Claire took out cleaning products to scrub the kitchen sink. It wasn't dirty, but it couldn't hurt to give it another good clean. She scrubbed at the stainless steel until her fingertips went white and her shoulder hurt from the exertion while her mind worked over what the hell had just happened. When that was done, she went to the laundry room and took Lilah's clothes out of the dryer. Who knew how long they'd been sitting there? Then she went to Lilah's bedroom.

"Here." Claire put the basket down on the bed, where Lilah was stretched out with a book. "Put these away, please. And don't let them sit there for days getting wrinkled."

"Okay. Jeez," Lilah mumbled in response to Claire's sharp

tone. Claire couldn't help it. She always got short and sharp when she was stressed.

After a while, Claire grabbed her purse and car keys from the table at the front of the house. "I'm going out for a little bit. I need to run some errands," she called to Lilah. She had to get out of there. What if Audrey came back again? She wasn't going to talk to her until she was ready. "Don't answer the door while I'm gone!"

Lilah shouted back that she wouldn't.

Outside, the cicadas emitted a low buzzing as Claire made her way to her car. She stopped and listened. It was so quiet and peaceful here. If she closed her eyes, she could hear the trees, the gentle whooshing of their leaves in the summer wind. Birds called to one another. In the distance, children yelled with delight and splashed in Shadow Lake. It was calming and beautiful and Claire should have been able to enjoy it, the way she always had, but it was different now. Her mother was gone, and this woman had showed up, and what she suggested... Goosebumps sprang up on the back of her arms.

Claire fiddled with her keys until she found the right one. Inside the car, she turned the key in the ignition and listened to the car come to life. She drove down narrow roads, passing tourists and locals wandering the streets, looking as aimless as she felt. She had no idea where she was going, which unsettled her even more, but, before long, found her car pulling into a parking lot near the locks.

It was one of her favorite spots. She came here often growing up. The best time to see the locks was when the sun began to set, when the sky was a pinky-orange, and the water was still. The big boats trudged slowly, passing through the waterway from one lake to another and looked like they were cutting glass, they glided so smoothly through the water.

Claire got out of the car and made her way to a patch of grass on a sloping hill. How many times had she come here to sit and watch the boats? Too many to count. Most of those times were when she was a kid, which meant it was just her and her mother, sitting with knees touching, having an ice cream. Her mother would always get vanilla, nothing else, not even French vanilla, and Claire would tease her about her choice. But everything had changed. Her mother was gone. She was still struggling to process that fact. And now, she had something even bigger to process.

Claire ran her hands over the soft grass and pulled at a few strands, letting them wrap around her fingers. If Audrey didn't die in a car crash as a toddler, where had she been all this time and why hadn't she come here before now? She supposed that what actually mattered was that there was a chance her sister might be back now.

Her sister. It couldn't be. Could it? No, it was way too impossible to believe.

Another thing that was impossible to believe was the idea that Veronica didn't know about Audrey. Maybe she did. Claire's stomach tightened. She didn't want to believe that her mother could have been lying to her. If only she could talk to her one more time. Clear all this up. Find out what was real. It struck Claire that she would never get the answers she needed from her mother. An emptiness, a desperate type of feeling, settled into the base of her stomach.

"Claire?"

The voice startled her. She turned to see Sam, one of her former clients, standing above her, a chubby baby hoisted up onto her hip.

"So good to see you! How are you?"

Claire attempted to smile. So many well-intentioned people asked that question casually in conversation all the time. She should answer that she was fine and ask Sam how she was, how her daughter was doing now. How long ago had it been that Claire had delivered Sam's baby? Time didn't feel linear right now, but more of a jumbled mess she was trying to make sense of. "I'm good, thanks. How about you?"

"Yeah, I'm doing well, thanks. Busy, a bit sleep-deprived, of course. I'm sure I don't have to tell you." Sam laughed. The sunlight shone through her curly hair. She looked great, despite the lack of sleep. Claire was happy for her.

A lightness developed in Claire's limbs, and she stood to greet Sam. She remembered now. She had delivered that very sweet baby Sam was holding just a few months ago. It was fascinating to see who those tiny newborns became.

"So you decided to stay here then?" Claire asked, recalling that Sam had been a temporary visitor back when her baby was born. Her mother lived in Summerville, but she hadn't been a permanent local.

"Yes, I love it. I want to raise my daughter here. It's perfect for kids, isn't it?"

Claire nodded. There was so much hope in Sam's eyes. Not that long ago, Claire would have agreed that everything in Summerville was as close to perfect as it could get. She had been happy delivering babies, taking care of new mothers like Sam. Then there was her mother's diagnosis and, what felt like so soon after, her death and the tidal wave of grief. Everything had changed. And now there was this. Nothing about home felt right for her. The confusion took Claire's breath from her momentarily.

"Anyway, how have you been?" Sam asked, bringing Claire back to the present. "You were so great with me. I can't thank you enough for taking such good care of me, getting me through labor... I've been telling everyone what an angel you are. It feels strange to have seen you for the entire pregnancy and be so close, and now nothing. I feel like I should be checking in with you." She grinned.

"Thank you," Claire said. "But that's the way it goes. We help bring in adorable babies"—she waved at Sam's daughter—

"and then you take over for the rest of their lives." Claire noted how strong and assured her voice was when she spoke about her work. However muddled she felt right now, Claire knew she was a very good midwife. She excelled at it because she loved it, and she had put so much time and dedication into it. She worked so hard, and it felt satisfying for a moment to recognize her own ability and skill.

"But we don't get any kind of instruction manual," Sam laughed.

Claire gave a warm smile. She had always liked Sam. "No manual. Yet somehow, we all figure out how to be parents."

Sam shifted her weight to stand upright and moved her baby from one side of her hip to the other. "And you? You're doing well?"

Claire looked down, clearing her throat. That question was difficult to answer, though she knew she should only respond in a way that wouldn't make Sam uncomfortable. She shouldn't tell Sam that she felt consumed by her grief, and that it was unbelievably hard to lose the only parent she had ever known. That was too raw. And she shouldn't say she felt guilty at the same time for wanting to return to work because she loved it so much and it was a huge part of who she was. Most of all, Claire knew she shouldn't tell Sam that she was thinking about Audrey, actually considering that she could be who she said she was, and that there might be a tiny sliver of something new fluttering within her. Something that reminded her of hope. It was too confusing though, so Claire pushed that last feeling away.

"I'm good," Claire said instead, a simple, uncomplicated platitude.

After Sam said she had to go, gave Claire a quick hug and left, Claire pulled the piece of paper Audrey had given her out of her pocket. She held it between her fingers and stared. As much as she didn't like it, she knew she could never go back to not knowing. The only way was forward.

FOUR

Greg was outside his cottage, working in the garden on his hands and knees, when Claire arrived. His back was toward her, but she could already guess at how his face looked: creased with deep concentration. She knew him well after all the time they were married, even though they had been separated for three years now. She didn't need to see his face to know what he was doing. It was one of the nice but also confusing things about their relationship post-separation. They were familiar and comfortable, and knew one another better than anyone else. None of that changed. The confusing part was that they should have worked, but they somehow didn't.

It had been a slow, gradual separation. They had drifted apart in a meandering kind of a way. As they had got busier with parenting and life in general, they had seemed to have less time for one another. There were fewer moments to spend talking, to hold hands and go for walks. They went from telling each other all about their days to sending short texts about groceries they needed. One day, Claire woke up and wondered what had happened. Greg asked her about separation soon after. She was devastated at the time—she never imagined her marriage breaking down and she still loved Greg. It hurt that he was the one who decided they were too far gone to fight for.

"Hey," Claire called to him after she got out of the car. She liked the place Greg had bought and moved into after they separated. It was at one side of Summerville, where the town seemed to stop abruptly. The road he lived on came to an end after a series of little resort cottages that lined the street and Greg's house sat next to the marina.

Greg turned his upper body. "Hey. What are you doing here? Everything okay?"

Claire opened her mouth, but knew it was too late; she was about to cry.

As soon as she burst into tears, Greg stood quickly, brushing the dirt off his jeans and rushing to her side. "What is it? Is Lilah okay?"

"She's fine," Claire said.

"What is it then?"

Claire considered how to answer this. How to put into words what had happened. Perhaps it was easiest to just tell it like it was. Claire didn't see the point in beating around the bush most times. Especially with family. If you couldn't say whatever you wanted, however you wanted, to your family, who could you speak to that way? And Greg was still family, even in their complicated way.

"Someone showed up at my door and... she said she's my sister. She said she was Audrey."

Greg's eyes widened. His arms dangled at his sides for a moment before he moved an inch closer to her.

"Claire." He hesitated, only briefly, before he reached for her. The pause was likely because they didn't touch all that much anymore. It was the only thing she could see that caused awkwardness between them. They knew how to co-parent

Lilah, they knew how to listen to one another, but the physical part was tricky. Nobody explains how to handle that when going through an amicable separation, especially when you were still very much in one another's lives.

Claire folded herself into his arms. She needed his touch right now, needed to feel his solid, strong arms around her body.

"What do you think?" he asked. He knew what this might mean to her. Claire had spoken to Greg about Audrey before. Over long, deep conversations early in their marriage, Claire had told him how her mother never provided much in the way of information about her sister. Only when Claire had asked and asked would her mother throw her a tiny morsel, likely so Claire would leave it alone.

Her name was Audrey.
She had blonde hair.
She was quiet, like you.
She loved raspberries.

Then she would tell Claire to stop asking, it was all she could remember, it was too painful.

Claire would spend hours and hours alone on weekends or after school, finding ways to entertain herself, reading books— she read so many books growing up—painting or doing other crafts. It soothed her and it passed the time. She was content with her life, but she spent most of her childhood thinking about how wonderful it would have been to have a sister. Someone to play with, to swim in the lake with, to stay up late talking to, to share her thoughts and worries and good news with. Claire had noticed girls at school who had sisters and, most notably, a set of twins in her class. The O'Grady twins were known around school as only 'the twins,' instead of their first names, almost like they were one. There was something untouchable about them: a bond that Claire wished she could experience. They were never without one another, and Claire had wanted that so much when she was younger. She wanted someone who loved her in a way that even your best friend couldn't.

Eventually, as she got older, she stopped asking about Audrey. She stopped longing for a sister, because she knew it wasn't going to happen. This was her life, and she accepted it. Besides, she didn't want to hurt her mother. She was the only person Claire had left. Audrey was gone. Or so she'd been told.

"I don't know what I think." Claire wiped at her eyes with the tips of her fingers.

"Where is she now?" Greg asked.

"I told her I needed some time," Claire said. "She gave me her phone number, but then I asked her to leave. I'm trying to process this."

"Yeah." Greg sighed, and then pulled back. His face was serious. Someone might have thought he looked stern, but Claire knew how to read him. It was his thoughtful face. He often thought about things for a while before speaking, whereas Claire usually said what was on her mind the minute it came to her. Her opinions rarely came from a place of impulse, so she thought it was best to simply tell it like it was. "What are you going to do?" he asked.

"I'm not sure. I have so many questions. I guess it makes sense to talk to her."

"You think so?" Greg's head tilted to one side. "You only just met her. Are you even sure she is who she says she is?"

"Well, no." Claire had wondered the same, but there was something about Audrey. Maybe it was her expression, or the way she had run her hand through her hair just like her mother used to. Maybe it was because something inside Claire wanted Audrey to be who she said she was.

"The timing is odd. She could be out to scam you or something. You're inheriting your mother's house..."

Claire stiffened. Her head had also gone there, but what else was she supposed to do in a moment like this? She had to know more. There was absolutely no way she could let something as monumental as who this woman was hang in the balance. What if she actually was Audrey? The thought caused the very pit of her stomach to flip. Claire didn't want to admit it to herself just yet, but the idea of a sister—her sister—even after all this time, was quite thrilling. But she had to focus. "There's a lot I need to find out."

"Okay, but please be careful," Greg said. He ran a hand down Claire's back and then pulled away. He cleared his throat and looked at the ground. Another familiar thrill went through Claire at Greg's touch, but that also confused her, so she decided to ignore it. There was only so much she could concentrate on in the moment.

"Can you keep this between us?" Claire asked. "I want to talk to this woman first before I tell Lilah anything." Claire's approach to parenting had always been to protect first. It was easy when Lilah was little; a young kid didn't need to know all the details about adult life. As Lilah grew up and got older, however, Claire had to navigate and figure out when she could let Lilah in on some of the adult things in her life. It was nice to have those kinds of conversations with her daughter, but also unnerving to speak to your child in a more grown-up way. Today's experience was completely different. This was big and complicated. Claire never knew what might potentially screw up the way her daughter saw the world, but she suspected telling Lilah that her dead aunt wasn't actually dead and had showed up on their doorstep might do it. She wouldn't roll those dice. Not until she knew more.

"Sure. Of course," Greg said. "Let me know if you need me." He smiled at her in a somewhat sad way and ran a hand over her arm.

Part of Claire wanted to stay there with him where she felt

comfortable and safe, but another part of her knew what she had to do.

Back in her car, Claire drove to one side of the marina, where it was usually quiet, so she could be alone. She parked. Then Claire took a deep breath, dialed Audrey's number, and waited.

FIVE

The café's patio was set up like a tropical getaway, with vibrant blues and reds painted on the outside walls, umbrellas in yellows and bright greens. There were large leafy planters making a border around all the tables and waitresses bringing charcuterie boards and platters of pulled pork tacos and sandwiches out to guests. It was loud and buzzing with people and music and conversation. The perfect place to blend in. Nobody would notice Claire if she started crying or had other big reactions when she and Audrey spoke.

Claire had known she wouldn't be able to concentrate on anything else, let alone sleep, after Audrey's appearance at her house. She was relieved when Audrey seemed keen to meet straightaway, and had made her way to the café and taken a seat at a table in the corner. She arrived early intentionally to calm herself, ordering a glass of water and an almond milk latte while she waited. She liked to be early for everything. It threw her off when she was late; showing up a good ten minutes early felt perfect. She glanced at her watch, but couldn't see it very well because of the shade cast over her. She was glad at least to be out of the hot sun.

Audrey arrived right on time. Claire didn't want to admit to herself that she liked that. She didn't want to feel anything for Audrey yet. She wasn't convinced this woman was who she said she was. Or she didn't want to allow herself to believe this was her sister if there was a chance she actually wasn't. Claire wasn't sure she could handle losing a sister twice.

"Hello," Audrey said. She was smiling warmly, but paused before sitting, like she was waiting to be invited. She had on a simple top and leggings, but she looked fashionable and put-together. Claire could see Audrey's hair was cut nicely and highlighted, her clothes and even her shoes—a stylish pair of sandals—gave her a certain look. As if she was from a big city. She definitely didn't look like she was a resident of Summerville.

"Hi." Claire remained motionless.

Audrey pulled out a chair and sat.

When the waitress appeared, Audrey smiled and set her eyes directly on the waitress' face when she spoke. She ordered water and a glass of white wine. "Thank you so much," she said to the waitress.

Claire thought you could tell a lot about a person by the way they spoke to others. As Audrey turned back to face her, she gave her a quick smile.

"So. Where do we start?" Audrey asked, her voice bright, despite the circumstances.

"Good question," Claire said.

"I have so many questions." Audrey shook her head.

Claire's pulse quickened. "I bet I have more than you." There was a touch of bitterness to her tone that she regretted; she didn't even know who she was upset with. It didn't make any rational sense to be angry with Audrey in this moment, and Veronica wasn't here. She couldn't bring herself to think about her father—Audrey's father—yet, and what it meant if he had been parenting Audrey all this time. She really shouldn't direct her anger at anyone, but she couldn't help it.

Audrey frowned. "My entire life has been upended recently, too." Her voice shook when she spoke. It softened Claire, but only a little.

"Why don't you start with how you got here?" Claire said.

Audrey sat back in her chair and her shoulders lowered, like the muscles were loosening. "I live about three hours south of here. In Elora. It's where I spent my entire life, raised by my dad."

"Do you have siblings?" Claire asked, trying to stifle her shock at the thought that she had lived so close by all this time—and her father, too.

"No. Only child. You?"

"Same. Only child," Claire answered. "My mother's heart was broken after she lost—" She couldn't bring herself to finish.

"Oh." A flash of pain crossed Audrey's face. "I'm sorry."

Claire nodded.

"I used to wish I had a sibling," Audrey said. "It was always only me. I felt like I really missed out on something special." Her voice was filled with sadness.

Claire's breath hitched. It was how she had felt, too. Like there was something—*someone*—always missing from her life. She nodded in response.

Audrey cleared her throat and continued, "Anyway, when I was little, I used to ask my dad about my mother all the time, but he always avoided the topic. He did for as long as he could, until I finally wouldn't accept that any longer. That was when he told me that my mother—Veronica—left us when I was just a toddler. He said she didn't have it in her to be a mother." Audrey's voice was like lead. She paused and fiddled with her napkin. "He said that after she left, he took me and moved us to another town. A short while later, he told me my mother had died in a car crash."

"You were told your mother died in a car crash?" Claire's pulse quickened again. The back of her neck prickled.

Audrey nodded.

"I was told you died in a car crash," Claire said.

Audrey must have noticed Claire said "you" this time. Her eyes shot to Claire's. Then she continued, "After he told me my mother died, I was in shock, but I had no reason to search for anyone. There was nobody to look for. Or so I thought. I mean, I had no reason to think he wasn't telling me the truth. He was my father. I trusted him."

And Claire had trusted her mother. She frowned and then said, "Is there any way you can prove what you're telling me?"

Audrey's head jerked back. "No, I can't. It's what my father told me, though. Like I said, I trust him."

Claire had so many questions buzzing in her head. If he was their father, why would he and Veronica separate Audrey and Claire? Why would he want to keep them apart from one another? How did parents choose one over the other? The thought was incomprehensible to her. But she wasn't about to allow herself to wonder why he chose to stay out of her life and remain in Audrey's. That was much too painful. And, Claire suddenly realized, Audrey must feel the same about their mother. "Why wouldn't he tell you I existed?"

"I have no idea." Audrey rubbed her hands down the tops of her pant legs. "Maybe he wanted to make sure I would never go looking for anything."

Claire took a sip of her latte and placed it in front of her, studying the foam on top, thinking and absorbing everything she was being told. An ache in her throat had developed. She couldn't imagine being denied a mother for your entire life. Her eyes went to Audrey's face and a pang of sympathy stabbed at her. "But why would he want that?" Claire asked. It didn't make sense that he wouldn't want his daughter to know her mother or find her sister. It struck Claire that if Audrey was telling the truth about all of this, it was exactly what her mother did to her.

Audrey shook her head. "No idea."

"So how did you end up here?" Claire asked.

"Veronica called my father right before she passed away."

Claire's heart lurched. "She knew where you were?"

Audrey frowned. "I guess she tracked us down. Maybe she knew where we were all along? I don't know. Things have been confused with my dad recently, but when he told me that she wasn't dead, as I'd always been told, and broke the news that she had called, I knew he was telling me the truth. Maybe she wanted to reach out to me right then. Why else would she call?" She stopped and looked away, shifting in her seat. Then she looked directly at Claire, and Claire saw so much sorrow in her eyes.

"Did you talk to her?" Claire asked.

A flash of pain crossed Audrey's face. She shook her head. "I wish I had. But I didn't get the chance to. He didn't tell me about the call straightaway."

"What? Why not?"

"He forgot." The pain in her expression was replaced by a shadow and Claire wondered if it was something she'd said.

"He forgot?" How could you forget something like that?

"He has Alzheimer's," Audrey said. She looked down at the table and frowned.

"Oh. I'm so sorry." Claire had heard about how awful that disease could be, and how hard it was on loved ones. She felt another pang for Audrey, despite wanting to stay hardened. But this was all so awful. Claire looked around at the cute café; they were surrounded by color and vibrant noise, and here they were, discussing such heavy things, their faces creased with frowns.

"It's okay. We're finding a way to manage. Anyway, at least I found out eventually," Audrey said, her voice shaky. She picked up her drink and took a sip before continuing, "He had been acting odd for a while, his behavior had changed, and it felt like something different from the Alzheimer's. I kept asking him what was going on. It took him a while, but he finally remembered the phone call. That's when I learned that my mother had been alive and living here. Although he still left out the part about you."

A pained look crossed Audrey's face again and Claire wondered how much a person could take. They had both had so much confusing information thrown at them so quickly. Despite Greg's warning, and despite everything within her telling her to be wary of this woman, Claire couldn't help but feel a connection. They were going through the same thing—they each grew up without a parent in their lives, they had lost or were losing their only parent, and now they were discovering there was a possibility they might be related.

Claire shifted in her seat. "Did he say why he lied about her being dead?" How could someone do that to a child? How could her own mother have done the same thing?

"He said she wasn't a good mother." Audrey's voice went quiet, like she was apologetic. "He didn't want her in my life because he said she wasn't stable."

"That's not true," Claire snapped, feeling a flash of protectiveness towards her mother. She couldn't look directly at Audrey. This was too much; she knew nothing about Veronica. "You didn't know her. She was an excellent mother."

Audrey tilted her head back, her eyes flicking upwards. She didn't say anything for a while. When she eventually spoke, her voice was wobbly. "I know. I didn't know how to react when I first heard. I sat on it for a couple of weeks, trying to decide how I felt, what my life meant, who I was. I wouldn't speak to my dad, I didn't ask for Veronica's number. I wanted to process it in my own time. And then I found out she was gone. I was too late. I'll always regret that."

Audrey's body rounded in on itself. She looked so small and sad, Claire almost reached out toward her to place a hand on her arm. She couldn't help but feel for Audrey in that moment, even though she didn't necessarily want to. Lilah always teased Claire about her softness. Claire cried at anything even remotely emotional. Now, her mind raced and she felt a fluttering in her stomach. If it was true, her father was still alive and she might be able to meet him. She shifted in her seat. She felt so hot now. Queasy, too. How could you explain a mother and a father separating siblings? How could a mother and a father both not want their own child? Claire could never in a million years live without Lilah.

"I'm trying to figure things out," Audrey continued. "I know your life is being upended, and I know it's a very confusing feeling, but I wanted you to know that I can sympathize. It's happening to me, too. If this is all true, it's a terrible thing to find this out about my mother."

Claire bristled again, feeling defensive of Veronica's character. "What's terrible?" she asked.

"To find out your own mother doesn't love you enough to stay with you."

Claire sat back in her chair, drained. It was true, what Audrey said. She was feeling the same. In fact, Claire had wondered most of her life why her father didn't want her. Again, she noticed how much she shared with Audrey.

She put her hands in her lap and considered everything she had been told. Audrey's story seemed legitimate, and Claire couldn't think of a reason why she would be here lying about this now. She looked at her, this woman with her mother's face, who she just knew somehow was her sister. And yet, something made Claire pause. Maybe it was her cautious nature, maybe it was because she never did anything risky, or maybe she just wanted one solid answer.

"Did you tell him you were coming here?"

"Yes," Audrey said.

"So then why did he still not tell you about me?" Claire asked.

Audrey hesitated.

"What?" Claire said.

"He said he lost touch when Veronica left us, he wanted to cut himself off from that old life. He didn't want anything to do with her. After Veronica's neighbour told me about her, and who you were and where you lived, I called him to ask what was going on and he said he wasn't even sure how to find you. I guess he didn't think you'd be living here and so easy to find." Audrey shrugged. "So, where do we go from here?" she asked tentatively.

Claire hesitated. She picked up her glass of water and took a sip to cool her flushed, warm body. "I think we should take a DNA test."

Audrey frowned. "I suppose that makes sense."

It did to Claire. She liked data and facts, and she needed answers. Besides, part of her was steeped in skepticism. She wanted to be careful.

"I don't know how to move on," Claire said. And then she surprised herself in the moment by breaking down. Right in front of Audrey. Deep, heavy sobs that Claire thought she might choke on.

Audrey's eyes widened for a moment, and then, as if they had always known each other, she leaned in close and put her hand on Claire's arm. "It's okay," she said soothingly.

It wasn't okay, but Claire was touched by Audrey's kindness. This woman who only knew that Claire's mother might have also been hers. Claire wanted to say something kind back. Instead, she cleared her throat and went to shift in her seat, which meant she had to draw her arm away from Audrey.

Audrey's mouth made a small downturned bow, the way Lilah's did when she was sad, and Claire was struck by the familiarity of the gesture. She couldn't allow herself to believe it fully, though. She needed to know for certain first.

SIX

A couple of days later, Claire stood inside Veronica's house, listening to the silence. She fought for air in the emptiness. It felt like she couldn't breathe, so she went to the back of the house and pulled open the sliding door and clicked the screen door shut. There. Now a cross breeze coming up from the lake could cool her skin and air out the room at the same time.

If she allowed herself to stand here alone for too long, the grief and confusion would threaten to overtake her. Claire needed to move. She went up the stairs and into her mother's bedroom. All of Veronica's things were still there: her clothes thrown over the back of a chair, two books on her nightstand. On the wall were three paintings by Veronica's favorite local artist. Claire couldn't remember who the artist was, but his painting—landscapes in bold, bright colors—always reminded her of her mother. Veronica was known for having an eye for unique art, it was what made her so good at her job selling it.

All the things in Veronica's bedroom reminded Claire that she needed to get a handle on this. There was so much you were supposed to do after someone died. She made a mental note to do it soon, although time was disorienting to Claire. It didn't feel like it was that long ago that her mother had first told her the news.

The call had come on a Thursday afternoon. Claire had been on her way home from the clinic when her mother phoned her. Veronica's voice had been so quiet, Claire had to ask her to speak up.

"Cancer," her mother had said. "It's… in my pancreas."

But Claire had thought she'd heard somewhere that pancreatic cancer wasn't an immediate death sentence. In this day and age, it wasn't outlandish to think someone could have it and recover. Especially if they caught it early.

"I didn't want to tell you," her mother had said. Her voice had wobbled, like she was trying to be strong but was scared. "I've known for a few weeks now. I had symptoms for a long time, I just didn't realize it."

Claire had pulled her car over at the side of the dusty road, while she processed the words her mother had spoken. It was typical of Veronica to try to keep her safe, to not tell her about her symptoms and try to shield her from anything even remotely stressful. She was always trying to protect her.

When Claire was younger, Veronica wouldn't let her out of her sight until she was at an embarrassingly old age. While her friends walked to school in pairs or groups without parents, she had to endure her mother trailing behind, pretending she was merely walking the dog, when in reality, she was always watching. It wasn't until Lilah was born that Claire began to understand her mother's protectiveness.

"I'll be right over," Claire had said into the phone. Why hadn't her mother told her she was going to the doctor? She looked at herself in the rearview mirror and noticed how deep a line was carved between her eyebrows.

"No, no. I'm fine," Veronica had replied.

Claire went anyway, and Lilah insisted on going. Lilah knew something was up and didn't want to be kept in the dark. Kids often just wanted to be told the truth; Claire could see that in her daughter.

When they had arrived at Veronica's house, Claire leaned in and hugged her mother. After she pulled back from the embrace, she saw her mother's eyes were red and glassy.

"Don't cry, Grandma. Then I'll cry." Lilah had tried to lighten the mood, bless her. It didn't work. All three of them were sniffling and wiping at their eyes.

It was Veronica who broke the ice and laughed. "We're a mess. But it's okay. I'm here right now." She had shifted in her seat and went to push herself up to standing. "Can I get you both something to drink?"

"Sit," Lilah had insisted. She motioned for her grandmother to stay where she was. "I'll get us something." She disappeared into the kitchen, leaving Claire standing over her mother.

"Did you go to the appointment alone? I could have gone with you."

"It's fine. I wanted it that way."

"What did they tell you?"

"I have surgery scheduled for next week. After that, my doctor said I could do a round of aggressive chemo combined with radiation, but it's stage four."

Claire's breath had hitched. Stage four. She already knew it was bad, but hearing the words made it seem much more real.

"Are you going to do the chemo?"

"It's aggressive, Claire. That means I would be really sick and weak. It would be awful."

"But the alternative?" Claire's voice was rising. "You would rather do nothing?"

"The doctor said if I do nothing, I could have up to six months. Can you imagine? That long? She said I wouldn't be as sick. Eventually, my body will shut down, but she says usually it's not too painful. I'll just lose consciousness until I'm gone."

Claire's limbs had tingled and then gone weak. She rubbed at her forehead. It was dizzying to hear this, her mother sounding so matter of fact.

"I'm dying." Veronica's voice was gentle now.

Lilah came back into the room. Veronica had shot Claire a look of warning before she turned to Lilah and tried to smile.

"I heard the last part," Lilah had said, her face pale. "You don't have to pretend around me. I'm not a little kid."

"No, you're not. You're right. Where has the time gone? I remember when you were a chubby little baby. And you were as bald as could be until you were a toddler." Veronica had laughed.

Lilah had tried to smile in return. "So now what?" Lilah's voice was quiet. There was a hint of a crack in it, as if she would break like a dam if she had to keep talking.

"I don't really know. This is all new to me, but I think it's time for me to rest," Veronica had said. "I need a nap."

"Let me help you." Claire had stood and held out a hand to her mother.

"I can do it."

"You're going to have to allow us to help you. I'm not letting you do this by yourself," Claire had insisted.

A look of relief had washed over Veronica's face. She had placed her hand into Claire's and squeezed it.

Upstairs, and after she was settled into her bed, Veronica had said something that Claire had paid no attention to then.

"There are some things we'll eventually have to talk about." Veronica had shifted under the covers.

Claire had gone to the bathroom to find her mother's brush. Her hair was so messy, and she saw for the first time how thin she had gotten—it made Veronica look unlike herself, like she was disheveled and weak. How had she not noticed this before now? Claire felt the need to at least brush Veronica's hair out until it was smooth.

"Claire?" Veronica had said.

"Later." Claire's shoulders were tight around her ears, already holding so much tension. This was hard. All of it. Every single moment they shared would be difficult now. The tightness radiated down one side of her neck. She had touched her mother's hand, run her fingers over the top of her smooth skin to let her know something—what? That she was there. That she would help her get through this.

Now, in her mother's bedroom once again, Claire went back into the en suite bathroom to find the hairbrush. Her mother's hair was twisted into it, in a ratty nest. It was odd to Claire, to see something that had once been a part of her mother after she was gone. Something that her mother had touched, was a part of her body at one time.

Claire pulled the hair out of the brush and took a wad of toilet paper off the roll, then placed the bunch of hair into it and folded the toilet paper over the top. Claire was nothing if not rational and sensible, and she knew this would be the best way to get an answer. She liked facts, and she knew science and DNA would give her a fact that was undeniable. Maybe then she would allow herself to feel something deep for Audrey, but for now, it was very confusing, and Claire was trying hard not to get ahead of herself.

She went back into the bedroom next and stood in front of her mother's closet. Even though she knew it hadn't been there since she was a little kid, Claire looked through the small space for the box she had once seen. The box she wasn't allowed to look through because, if Claire's memory was right, it contained photos of Audrey. Veronica had said it was too painful whenever Claire had asked about it, but now she wished she had paid more attention to it so she could remember some details. She wanted proof, something tangible that would tell her all of this was real, so she pushed through her mother's clothes, moved an old jewelry box to see what she could find, but came up with nothing.

Next, Claire went to her mother's drawers and pulled them open, sifting through her socks and pairs of pajamas. She didn't have a clue what she was looking for, she only knew that she wanted to find something that might give her a hint about her past.

Audrey had been like a heavy curtain in Claire's life growing up. She felt the weight of her now, of who she could have been in their family. The idea of Audrey was present for so long in Claire's life, in the background. It had been like losing someone you so badly wanted to speak to one more time. Except, Claire didn't know who Audrey really was.

The sound of her phone ringing came from downstairs, so Claire left the bedroom and went to answer it.

"Hi. It's me, Audrey."

"Hi." There was a pause. Claire didn't know what to say. Would they always be this awkward with one another?

Audrey said, "I just wanted to say it was great meeting you. I had a nice time."

"Thanks," Claire answered. Another pause. She had, too, but for some reason, she didn't say it. She was still guarded, still wanted to be careful.

"Anyway, I've done the test."

"That's good. I'm collecting some of my mother's hair to use as a sample now." Claire's words sounded clinical as they came out of her mouth. She didn't like it. "I'm going to send it in today."

"Well, good luck," Audrey said.

"Thanks," Claire responded. Although, she wasn't sure what the luck was for.

They were silent for a moment.

"Claire?" Audrey eventually spoke.

"Yes?"

"I hope this—I hope it's true."

Claire's insides felt like they were vibrating. What did she want? She would need time to think about it. For now, she answered Audrey with what she realized was honesty.

"Me, too."

SEVEN

Over the next few days, Claire waited for the results from the DNA test. After she had swabbed her cheek and included her mother's hair in the DNA collection kit, she had mailed it back. It was that easy. She had shaken her head when she first opened the kit and had seen how simple it was. Imagine determining something so monumental as who your parents were with a kit you could do at home and send through the mail.

Once it was done, Claire had felt small slivers of hope radiate through her. Most of the time, her shoulders and neck were tight with tension. When she tried to think straight, all she felt was confused about what she believed and what she wanted. But every now and again, when she allowed herself to grasp the enormity of this situation, she could identify the swirling feeling in the middle of her chest as hope.

The sky that evening was dim. As far as Claire knew, Audrey was still staying at the inn in town, but they hadn't spoken since a few days ago. Claire had said she needed space and Audrey was giving it to her. But now, when she felt that feeling in her chest again and she truly imagined what it would be like to have her sister in her life, Claire knew she needed to call Audrey.

"Hi," Claire said stiffly.

"Hi," Audrey answered.

"I just wanted to let you know that I did the test a couple of days ago."

"That's great," Audrey responded. "I suppose now we wait."

"Yes," Claire said. It was hard to know what else they should do. Claire felt weird knowing that Audrey was here, in town, both of them waiting to find out their fate.

"Would you—you wouldn't want to meet up for coffee or something again, would you?" Audrey's voice was low and shy.

Claire froze. She wasn't sure she was ready to get together with Audrey again. But then she remembered the swirling within her. The hope. "Sure."

"Really?" Audrey's voice had an excited, surprised lilt to it. "Great. Should we meet at the same coffee shop in town?"

"That works." Claire was about to suggest a time and end the call when she remembered her car had refused to start last night—such an old heap of junk—and she had to have it towed to the repair shop in town this morning. It wouldn't be ready until tomorrow. "Wait. I just realized I can't. I'm expecting a call from the repair shop. I had car issues and I'm stuck here without it until I hear from them."

"I could come get you?"

"Oh. Um, that's really nice of you." She hoped she sounded convincing, but it felt awkward. Still. She decided to roll with how things were unfolding. "Sure, thank you. See you soon then?"

"Okay," Audrey said, her voice bright.

After she hung up, Claire went through the kitchen, putting dishes away, and then headed upstairs to brush her hair, find her purse. She scribbled a quick note to explain to Lilah that she was out but to call or text her if she needed anything when she got back. She didn't expect to hear from Lilah, however. It was her night with Greg.

When her phone buzzed, Claire looked at the screen and saw Greg's name.

"Greg?" Claire said. "How are you? Everything good?"

"Hi, yes. I'm good," Greg spoke in a rushed tone. "But I got caught up in Port Perry."

"Port Perry?" It was a town an hour away. "What are you doing there? I thought you were picking up Lilah from the movies."

They had a plan. Lilah went to the neighboring town to see a movie at the theater there, Greg was supposed to pick her up and they were going to spend the evening together.

"I had to see someone. They were selling a car part I needed."

Greg was always fixing something himself—his car, his plumbing, even his electricity. Claire should have asked him if he could take a look at her car, but they didn't live together anymore. She didn't like to ask too much of him.

Claire glanced at the time, her stomach just starting to churn. "The movie finished already, didn't it? When can you make it there?"

"I have no idea," Greg said. "There's traffic here and I'm at least an hour and a half away already. That's why I'm calling. I can't pick her up. Can you?"

"My car's in the shop. I'm stuck," Claire said. "She's at the movies with Ava, right? Could you call her parents?"

"They picked Ava up already. Lilah and I made plans for her to wait around because I said I would be there about ten minutes after the movie ended."

Claire's pulse sped up. "So now what? She can't stand there for an hour or longer."

"I know. I'm thinking."

Claire's mind whirred with thoughts of who she could call. Normally, she would ask her mother. There was nobody else she could think of who would likely be available at a moment's notice. "What are we going to do?" Claire asked. She knew her voice had a panicked edge to it. The thought of Lilah standing there alone for who knew how long... She was only twelve.

"She has her phone, she'll be okay," Greg said.

Claire grimaced and pulled the phone away to look at the time again. Her muscles tightened. "No, Greg—" she began, but there was a knock at her door. "Hang on. I'll call you right back."

Claire hung up the phone and went to open the door to Audrey.

"Hi. I'm not ready, sorry. I'm dealing with something." Claire wished she didn't sound so sharp, but it was always her initial reaction to stress.

Audrey didn't seem fazed. "Not a problem. Are you okay?"

"Yes. Well, no. Not exactly. My ex was supposed to pick our daughter up at the movies, but now he can't and she's there alone. I'm trying to figure out what to do."

"Right, because of your car," Audrey said.

"Yeah."

"We could use mine?" Audrey suggested.

Claire thought about it for a moment. This was absolutely not ideal, but what other options did she have? The panicked feeling overtaking Claire's body told her to go now, not to wait any longer. When something unexpected like this happened and it involved Lilah, Claire didn't want to wait for an ideal situation. She wanted to fix it.

"That would be great. She's in the town next to here," Claire said. She gathered up her purse and keys. Once she had locked the front door, she turned to Audrey who was standing there, waiting. "Thank you."

"No problem." She smiled at Claire.

In the car, Claire texted both Lilah and Greg to let them know she was on the way.

"Thank you again," Claire said. She tried not to sound awkward.

"Of course." Audrey focused on the road in front of her. "Let me know where to go."

The roads were clear, thankfully, and the drive would be quick. Claire could sense Audrey turning toward her as if she were going to say something a couple of times, but then she looked back at the road in silence. Claire supposed she could have tried to spark up a conversation, but she was too focused on Lilah. She texted her again while they drove.

> We're almost there

> Who are you with?

Claire paused. She rubbed her eyes. They were sore lately. Allergies, maybe. Or maybe it was the weight of the situation.

> The woman who came by the house the other day.

Three dots appeared for a second before Lilah's message came back.

> What???? Why???

> I'll explain later. When we're alone

"Everything okay?" Audrey's eyes shot down at the phone in Claire's hand before going back to the road in front of them.

"Yes. I'm telling Lilah when to expect us," Claire said.

"Lilah? That's her name?"

She hadn't told Audrey Lilah's name yet. She hadn't planned on telling Audrey anything much at all until they had answers. Yet, now here they were, in close quarters, and Audrey was helping Claire out with something that mattered a lot. Her pulse slowed into a steady rhythm at the thought of talking about her daughter. It was something she loved to do.

"Yes, Lilah."

"That's a beautiful name," Audrey said.

"Thank you. I think so," Claire replied. "Sometimes she likes it, and sometimes she tells me it's way too old-fashioned sounding."

"Lilah? That doesn't sound old to me."

"Right? I don't think so either. But Lilah sometimes says it sounds like an old lady name."

Audrey's face twisted into a confused smile. "Old lady?"

"I think she's thinking of Delilah. Remember that song? *Hey there, Delilah*... It came out when I was about sixteen or seventeen years old."

Recognition flashed across Audrey's face. "That makes it an old lady name? Back when we were teens?" She laughed.

"I'm afraid so." Claire smiled.

"I guess at some point, we become old ladies." Audrey laughed again. "But when does that happen? I still feel so young."

"So do I. But my gray hairs tell another story."

Audrey glanced over at Claire. "You don't have any gray, do you? I can't see any."

"You're being kind." Claire laughed despite herself. This kind of banter wasn't something she had much of in her life. Aside from her coworkers, Claire didn't have many close girl-friends. Most of her friends growing up had moved out of Summerville as soon as they could. And with Claire's unpredictable work schedule and raising Lilah, she hadn't had much free time to develop friendships. Any friends she had were ones she would see once in a blue moon, when the stars aligned, and everyone had a rare free evening.

If she was honest with herself, this moment was exactly how she imagined having a sister would be. Someone close by to chat with, to laugh with. It struck Claire that she felt oddly comfortable right then. It was a familiar kind of a feeling that didn't make sense; she had only just met Audrey. But it was there.

"Do you mind if I ask what you do for a living?" Audrey glanced sideways at Claire.

"I'm a midwife."

"Really? That's so interesting." Her chin lifted a little. "I'm assuming it's a tough job."

Claire considered this. It was hard, but it was also such a rewarding career. Claire had always wanted to do something that might make a difference. "It definitely has its challenges, but I love it. There's nothing like it."

"That's a good feeling," Audrey said. A smile settled onto her face.

In her lap, Claire's phone buzzed with a text message from Lilah again.

Are you almost here?

Two minutes away

She put her phone in her lap and pointed at the road ahead. "Take a right here."

When they arrived, Lilah was standing with her shoulder leaning up against a wall. She looked bored and tired, but her eyes squinted and flicked from Claire to Audrey as soon as she saw them.

"Thank goodness you're okay," Claire said when she got to Lilah's side.

"Of course I'm okay. Why wouldn't I be?" Lilah asked.

"Never mind." Claire hugged Lilah and pointed in the

direction of the car where Audrey was standing. "Let's go. I'll explain later."

As they approached, Audrey's face brightened. Her eyes widened and she smiled at Lilah in a genuine way, like she was happy to see her. Claire liked that quality about a person. Her mother used to smile like that all the time when she would see her and Lilah, even though they lived in the same town.

"This is Audrey," Claire said to Lilah. She turned to Audrey. "And this is Lilah."

"Nice to meet you." Audrey smiled.

Lilah nodded and gave a tiny smile. Claire was used to filling the awkward silence usually left by Lilah in conversations with adults, but she didn't today. This was all she was able to offer at the time. After a moment, Lilah got into the back seat of the car.

The drive home was mostly silent, with Claire and Audrey only making small talk. Claire was focused on how she was going to explain this to Lilah—because Lilah would definitely have questions—and how much she would have to tell her.

The next evening, Claire was alone again. Lilah and Greg had rescheduled to spend time together that night and were out at dinner. Claire had avoided discussing Audrey with Lilah after Audrey had dropped them home, and somehow Lilah knew not to push. Now, Claire had time to think about it all. This past day, she'd had a lot of time to think about how Audrey had helped her out of a bind at a moment's notice. Claire wondered why someone who barely knew you would be so helpful, but decided to try not to overthink it. She was good at that; she could overthink anything. Instead, she picked up her phone and made a call.

"Hi," Claire said when Audrey answered her phone. "I, uh

—I wanted to thank you again for yesterday. You really saved us."

"Don't mention it. I was happy to. I'm sure you would do the same for me."

There was an awkward silence after Audrey spoke. Would Claire do the same? Audrey seemed sure of who Claire was.

Claire shifted her weight from one leg to the other and pushed ahead with the reason for calling. "We missed out on our coffee yesterday, so I was wondering if you wanted to come by, maybe? Evening right by the water is so nice." Claire was aware of how awkward she sounded. She was also aware of the way she sucked in a breath after speaking, as if it was a big risk to ask Audrey this. She wanted to do the right thing, though. And Audrey had been so kind and helpful yesterday, it was only right to thank her. They had missed their opportunity to chat, and now, Claire was alone again. It seemed like a good time.

"That would be nice." There was a shyness to Audrey's voice. Maybe she felt the same way Claire did, awkward and uncomfortable, but willing to give this a try.

Claire and Audrey agreed on a time and then Claire sat back in her chair and waited. She sipped her peppermint tea. After a moment, she stood and went to the kitchen to fill a glass with water. She headed out to the patio overlooking the lake and placed her glass down on the table. Actually, a pitcher would be better. She should bring a pitcher of water out and another glass in case Audrey wanted one. Claire moved back and forth between the kitchen and the back patio until she told herself to stop. There was no reason to get so flustered. All of this would be fine.

If she were being completely honest with herself, there was a very good reason to get flustered. Did she just invite someone cho barely knew over to her house to have tea? Was she entertaining the idea that Audrey might be the sister she never had?

She was. It was the hopeful side to her that made her want to believe in the possibility.

When the doorbell rang, Claire's hands went clammy. She answered and let Audrey in.

"Hello again," Audrey said. She tucked her hair behind her ear and ducked her head forward. The gesture was so familiar, Claire froze in place. It was something about the way she did it, so similar to how Claire did, it was like Claire had passed a mirror and saw herself for a fleeting moment. There was another swirling in her chest. "Are you okay?" Audrey asked.

"Fine, thanks," Claire answered. She pushed her shoulders back and gave her head a quick nod. "Follow me."

They went through the house and out to the back patio.

"This is gorgeous," Audrey breathed.

"I know. My ex built it."

Audrey's eyebrows raised and she smiled. "Very nice." She glanced around.

Claire offered Audrey a glass of water. "I also have tea. Or I could make you a coffee?"

"Tea is great, thanks."

Claire nodded and went to get it. They were both being so polite. The formality was due to the situation and the fact that they didn't know each other yet, but it bothered Claire. This was stiff and awkward, not comfortable like in the car yesterday, and not at all what she pictured it would be like to have a sister.

When Claire was a kid, she would imagine what it was like to do regular family things, like go to a grocery store with a father and a sister. She only did things with her mother. It was always the two of them, and Veronica had a certain careful, strict way about her. With a sister, things could have been much lighter and more playful. Now, when she saw Audrey take a sip of water, or shift in her seat, a wave of sadness washed over Claire at all they had missed out on. Every small gesture and big moment.

Claire stopped moving around the kitchen with Audrey's tea. What was she thinking? They didn't even have the results of the test yet. But then again, even though Claire's feelings were all very complicated, she couldn't help but get swept up in the idea of a sister. Audrey was right in front of her. She couldn't ignore what this might mean. At the same time, she tried to forget any of the negative thoughts of Veronica. She was still grieving her mother and didn't want to consider the questions she had in this moment. Claire took the mug of tea and went back outside to join Audrey.

"I'm surprised you asked me to come over," Audrey said.

"You are?"

Audrey nodded. "I thought it might take a long time before we could get to this."

Get to what, Claire wondered. Where were they? If she told someone what she was doing—*I'm having a cup of tea with someone who might be my long-lost sister who I thought was dead but actually never was and has come back to find me*—it would sound like it was straight out of a movie. But this was real life. Claire had to face it.

"There's a chance we are sisters," Claire said with a shrug. She held onto herself, crossing her arms and rubbing at her forearms with her thumbs. "And there's so much I don't understand."

"Oh, me too," Audrey said. She sat upright in her seat and leaned forward. Claire found it odd how Audrey seemed so... Eager, that was probably the right word. Did she not have as many doubts about this as Claire did?

"Where do we even start?" Claire asked.

"The first thing I keep wondering is what you've been doing all these years," Audrey said.

It was a simple question, but it took Claire a moment to decide if she was going to be open to this—to letting this woman in.

"I've been living here all my life," Claire said. Yes, she was going to do it. She would allow herself to acknowledge the hope swirling in her chest and push down the doubt and get swept up in this moment right here, right now. "It's always been just me and my mother in Summerville. I like it here, so after I finished school, I came back home and met my ex, Greg, and had Lilah."

Audrey smiled when Claire mentioned Lilah.

"What about you?" Claire asked. "What have you been doing?"

"I grew up in Elora, and I still live there. I moved away from home to go to school and then went back and now I'm a teacher, living a few neighborhoods over from where I grew up. I loved where I lived as a kid, too, and I missed it when I was away at school, so I decided to go back and make it home."

Audrey was a teacher. That fitted, and it made Claire smile; she seemed like she'd be good with kids.

"Is it okay if I ask about... her?" Audrey's voice went quiet and small.

Claire knew she meant Veronica. She cleared her throat and tried to even out her voice when she spoke. "What do you want to know?"

"What she was like, I suppose. Who she was. Any memories you feel comfortable sharing?" Audrey looked down at her lap and then back up at Claire. She chewed on the inside of her lip.

Claire gulped for air. Her mind flashed with memories of her mother, and she felt protective of them, like she wanted to keep Veronica to herself. But after a moment, she composed herself enough to speak. Audrey should know her, too.

"She was a really good mother. Very loving, very protective," Claire said. She thought about what else she could say. "She was creative—she worked in the art industry, and she was also a good singer."

Audrey smiled, so Claire continued.

"She was beautiful. It was a kind of beauty that seemed to come with being at ease with getting older."

"That's so lovely," Audrey said.

"I thought so. Anyway, she didn't have a lot of friends and she was single for as long as I can remember, but she always told me she was happy with her life. She liked that we had each other. I think it was all she needed."

Audrey's mouth turned down at the edges for a moment. Her neck went red and splotchy.

Claire shifted in her seat and looked away when she realized what she had said. Of course, that would be painful for Audrey to hear. Claire should try to be careful. This was tricky to navigate.

It was the truth, though, and Claire wasn't sure how else to put it. Her entire life had been the two of them. They had no other family; her mother was an only child and her parents had died when she was in her twenties. She only casually dated here and there, and she never introduced anyone new into their lives. There were men who were interested in Veronica over the years, but she never seemed interested enough to do anything.

"You're all I need to focus on," Veronica would say. "You have me, and I have you." When Claire was young, this satisfied her. She didn't want to share her mother. But as she got older, Claire tried to encourage her mother to get out more, to meet someone. She wanted to know her mother wouldn't be alone after Claire grew up and moved out and had a family of her own. Veronica had her best friend Fatima, but Fatima led a busy and full life. She wouldn't always be around for Veronica at the drop of a hat.

Yet, as far as Claire could tell, her mother was being honest with her when she said she wasn't lonely and didn't feel deprived. She had Claire, she had her work, which was flexible enough for what she needed and also gave her enough income from commissions to raise a daughter on her own. She was content. It was almost as if Veronica didn't want to rock the boat, because things were going well.

Until she got cancer.

Back when Claire still thought Audrey was dead, Claire had wondered if, during those last few days, her mother had made peace with dying because it meant she would get to see Audrey again. Claire was logical, so she wasn't quite sold on the afterlife and meeting up with loved ones. She wasn't sure what she believed about death. The only thing she thought she did know was that if her mother could have somehow escaped cancer's terrible grip and stayed healthy, everything would have been fine. Only, she supposed if that had happened, Claire wouldn't be here now. With Audrey.

"I'm sorry," Claire said.

"No, it's okay." Audrey shook her head.

"What was your life like growing up?" Claire asked to shift the focus.

"I had a good childhood. It was just me and my father for a while, but then he eventually met my stepmother, Julie. I loved her. We were lucky to have her." A flash of pain crossed Audrey's face. "She passed away a year ago."

They were both silent for a moment, a shared pain between them.

"I'm so sorry."

"It's okay," Audrey said. "It happened fast. I don't know if that's better or worse."

Claire leaned back in her seat and considered this. It had happened fast to her mother, too. After the surgery to remove the cancer, her mother had recovered reasonably well, and then, almost like it was the next thing she knew, Veronica was deteriorating right in front of Claire's and Lilah's eyes. Claire had arranged for an in-home nurse because she knew she couldn't offer her mother the kind of care she needed, but she would visit every day to check in, talk to her about Lilah, refresh her mother's water, help her to the washroom.

That was the first sign, actually. How little Veronica was urinating. Her pee turned from a pale yellow to a dark orange so quickly. Next, her mother's feet turned blue. The at-home nurse told Claire it was called mottling. She said people usually had about a week left after it started happening.

Fatima visited daily, too. She wanted to be with Veronica, to talk to her and try to make her laugh. Claire was more grateful for Fatima than she knew how to say.

One morning, four weeks after Claire had first heard the news from her mother's lips, while Claire was at a nearby hospital bringing a baby into the world, Veronica had been asleep when Lilah was there with her. Her eyelids had fluttered. Lilah later told Claire that Grandma's breathing had grown deep and raspy. A rattling noise came from her throat. And then she was gone.

After Lilah had called Claire sobbing, Claire rushed to be with them. She had told herself that she was determined to let the fact that her mother wouldn't accept treatment go. Existing on what ifs and maybes would only cement the ache into her body. She couldn't be weighed down with pain, she had a daughter to take care of.

For several days after that, Claire had watched Lilah when she moved around the house, making herself toast with peanut butter and banana in the kitchen, sitting with a book out on the porch. She studied her daughter for signs that she wasn't okay. How could you be when you were only twelve years old and you had watched a person you love die right in front of you? How could you be when you were an adult and you lost your only family?

Audrey shifted in her seat, bringing Claire back to the present. "I miss my stepmother, but the three of us had a great life together. Now I'm trying to learn how to navigate my father's illness. It's very hard."

"I can't even begin to imagine," Claire said. A prolonged illness like that must be so difficult.

Audrey shook her head. "I don't mean just the illness. That's tough, of course, but it's even harder because I'm losing my only family." Her voice broke at the end. "Sometimes I feel like I have nobody."

A heaviness formed in Claire's chest, as if she had to breathe deeply in order to get enough air. She had some under-standing of it now, after her mother, but she still had Lilah and Greg.

She gave Audrey a minute. Then she said, "And now you're dealing with all this." She gestured to herself. "That's a lot on your shoulders."

Audrey smiled. It was small, but it settled onto her face and softened her features. "What do you think we should do now?" she asked.

Claire wasn't sure if she meant in this immediate moment or not. "I don't know." Claire looked out across the water. "I suppose we wait for the test results."

Audrey frowned, as if the test results were a negative thing. Claire could understand Audrey's expression. She both wanted to know the answer and didn't. If Audrey was her sister, Claire could move forward with a plan. If she wasn't, then what? Would this all be over and done with? She supposed it only made sense that Audrey would leave, and they would carry on with their lives as if this never happened. All of this emotional upheaval would be for nothing. Claire frowned at the thought.

"Do you think you'll tell your daughter more about me? I noticed you didn't really explain in the car," Audrey said.

Claire stiffened.

Audrey must have noticed Claire's body language. "I didn't mean to impose," she said. She looked down at the floor and her hair fell around her face. When she looked up again and tucked her hair behind an ear, her forehead was creased. "I'm sorry. I don't know how to handle this."

"Neither do I," Claire agreed. It would take time, but who knew how long? There were no instructions for working this out. They would have to figure it out by gut and instinct until they had something real to back it up with.

EIGHT

Several days later, Claire poured herself a glass of red wine and went out, barefoot, to the edge of Shadow Lake. On the dock, she took a seat on one of the chairs and leaned back into it to allow her body to relax. She put both feet on the edge of the seat and sat with her knees up, watching the water. Someone fishing in a canoe passed by slowly. A loon landed on top of the water before letting out an eerie, lonely cry. The vacationers had gone inside for the day, likely to get a reprieve from the July sun, to take off damp bathing suits, have a shower and put on warm clothes for the evening.

"What are you doing out here?"

It was Lilah's voice, coming from behind Claire. Lilah was leaving the next morning for sleepaway camp.

"I'm having a glass of wine," Claire said. "What about you?"

"I don't know." Lilah shrugged in her twelve-year-old way. She took the seat next to Claire and directed her gaze out to the lake.

Claire glanced at her. Her expression was difficult to interpret. She was neither smiling nor scowling, she could have been thinking any number of things. Claire would normally watch her for a moment, wishing she had some insight into what was running through her daughter's mind. Today, she turned her eyes back to the water.

"Are you going to finally tell me what's going on?" Lilah asked.

"What do you mean?" Claire already knew exactly what Lilah was talking about. She placed both of her feet back down on the dock and shifted in her seat.

"Mom. Come on," Lilah said. "Who is Audrey?"

Claire pinched at the bridge of her nose. When she closed her eyes, they were heavy. She took in a deep breath. "She says she's my sister."

Lilah's head snapped sideways. "What? *That* Audrey?" Her eyebrows were high on her forehead. "But I thought your sister died when she was little. She can't be your sister. Can she?"

"I don't know. She might be." This was still new for Claire, to speak to Lilah this openly. As she got older, Claire found talking to her daughter less and less like a little kid only helped their relationship, but this was an entirely different topic to navigate. "We took a test to find out. We're still waiting for the results."

"When?"

"About a week ago." Had it already been that long? No wonder Claire was exhausted. Her entire body had been weighed down with the enormity of the situation for a week now.

Lilah placed her hands on the armrests of the chair she was sitting in and looked out at the lake, too. "Wow. That's... that's just, really... wild." She barely moved.

"I know," Claire said. "She came over the other night when you were at Dad's."

"She did?" Lilah turned her entire body to face Claire. "What for? Are you just, like, hanging out now? And why would Grandma say she was dead if she wasn't?"

So many questions. Claire suddenly felt very tired.

"We're still trying to figure all of that out. It's a work in progress."

Lilah shifted her body again and stared outwards at the horizon. Claire could see her daughter's mind working. It was hard enough for Claire to understand; she couldn't even begin to imagine making sense of all of this as a twelve-year-old.

"But I don't understand about Grandma. How could she have a daughter who didn't live with her?"

"I don't really have any answers yet, but when I do, I promise I'll let you know." Claire took the last sip of her wine and placed the glass down before she stood up. She went to the very edge of the dock and bent her head to study the deep bluey-brown of the lake. "Want to jump in with me?" She turned her body and smiled at Lilah. Any attempt to distract her from further heavy questions.

"What? Right now?"

"Sure. We're not doing anything."

"My bathing suits are packed," Lilah said.

"Let's go in our underwear." She pulled at the edge of her tank top. "I don't want to change. Besides, we can leave our tops on." The lightness that suddenly appeared in Claire's chest was refreshing after the last week. She was rarely ever spontaneous, so it was no wonder Lilah looked confused. But Claire didn't want to think or process right now. She wanted to do something. To feel something. "Come on," Claire coaxed. She peeled her shorts off and then turned back to the water and jumped in.

The cold water shocked as it wrapped and swirled around her entire body, between her toes and under her arms. She came up for air and took a deep breath in, then blinked and swiveled around to look for Lilah.

"No way," Lilah shouted, but there was a smile on her lips, a tiny, excited flash in her eyes. Her face was relaxed, and it almost made Claire want to cry. Those moments when Lilah allowed herself to be a kid were few and far between now.

"Suit yourself," Claire said. She started to breaststroke away when she heard a thumping on the dock behind her and then a pause before a giant splash. Claire smiled.

"It's so cold!" Lilah shrieked.

"The sun is going down." They were bobbing up and down, treading water next to one another, only their heads above the surface, and Claire wondered what they looked like from afar. Maybe less like mother and daughter and more like two adults, two friends.

"Remind me why we're swimming again?"

Why did they come out here? Claire could tell Lilah it was because she was desperate to hold onto her, because Lilah was the only thing Claire was certain about right now, but Lilah would look at her funny. "I don't know. For fun."

"Who's that?" Lilah's brows were squished into a line. She gazed back at the shore and lifted one hand out of the water to point at something.

Claire turned and saw a figure approaching. Someone was walking around the outside of her cottage and heading down toward the dock. It took a moment, but then the person got close enough for Claire to see.

"Audrey?" Claire said. She forgot how much your voice carried across the lake.

Audrey stopped for a second and held a hand over her eyes, bending forward at the waist to try to get a better look. "Claire?"

Claire's stomach sank. She didn't want to stop swimming with her daughter at dusk on the eve before she left, but she couldn't very well ignore Audrey.

"What's she doing here?" Lilah asked. She squinted to try to see better and then her face went serious, contemplative. Claire could tell her daughter's mind was whirring already.

"I'm not sure. Come on." Claire swam toward the dock.

When she got there, she heaved her body up onto it and wrung out the edge of her tank top. She stood, then held one hand out to help Lilah up.

"Sorry to intrude," Audrey said.

"It's fine," Claire said, but in truth, she felt a snip of resentment. Lilah came up next to her and stood watching Audrey.

"Hi, Lilah." Audrey's face lit up in a way that felt genuine again. She smiled broadly and nodded at Lilah but didn't say anything else. Points to her for not asking her questions or trying to make small talk.

Lilah nodded back but didn't speak. She attempted a tiny smile, but Claire could tell it was mostly to be polite.

"Do you want to go and get changed?" Claire asked.

"No, I'm okay," Lilah said. She crossed one leg in front of the other and folded her arms over one another. She was likely chilled, but she clearly wasn't budging. She wanted to hear whatever it was Audrey had to say.

Audrey gave Claire a look, as if to ask if it was okay to keep speaking in front of Lilah. Claire nodded and hoped she wouldn't regret it.

"I got my results from the DNA test," Audrey said, her voice almost breathless. She pulled a piece of paper from her purse. "Do you have yours?"

Claire's leg muscles twitched and quivered. She wasn't sure if it was from the swimming or the news. "I haven't checked the mail today." The words came out choked. She had been checking her mailbox every day that week, unsure if she would be happy to find the answer inside or not, but she hadn't had a chance to look yet that day.

"I can check," Lilah said. She looked at Claire, waiting with her body now poised to move, to go back to the house.

Claire hesitated. "Okay," she said eventually.

Lilah left instantly, moving rapidly up the slight hill to the stairs that went up to the open porch at the back of their cottage.

Claire shivered. She wrapped her arms around her body.

"Want to know?" Audrey asked in a hurried tone. She held up the paper.

"Sure. Yes." Claire fumbled over her words. Did she really want to do this here? She supposed she did.

"My father is my father. The probability of paternity is 99.99999999%." Audrey looked down at the paper as if to remind her and then showed Claire. "And Veronica is my biological mother." Her eyes lit up and then swelled with tears. Her face flushed with color. She smiled broadly at Claire.

Claire froze. A light-headedness came over her. She put a hand out to steady herself against the Adirondack chair. Her sister. Audrey was her sister. They had the answer. Claire needed to sit. She was numb and this was all so much to take in.

"Isn't that the best news? I hoped, but to know now that I have family..." Audrey paused and smiled at Claire, her eyes rimmed with red already. "To know I have you."

Claire felt hot and stuffy, like it was hard to breathe even though they were outside.

A sister.

Audrey moved an inch closer to Claire.

Claire opened her mouth to say something and started to lift her arm—for what? A hug, maybe. What was appropriate for that moment? Before she could do or say anything, Lilah came down the steps, moving as quickly as she had been when she left. "Here," she shouted. She held up an envelope. Claire's head was muddled and foggy while she watched Lilah get closer.

When Lilah got to her mother's side, she handed Claire the envelope. Claire slid her finger under the flap and ripped open the top. The paper was covered in numbers. Columns and rows of numbers. It didn't make sense. She scanned until she came to the bottom, where the summary was.

It was then her vision narrowed. She stumbled backwards. Her skin tingled. It couldn't be. It couldn't.

"What?" Audrey said. Her voice sounded so far away.

"Your father isn't my father." Claire's body swayed. "And Veronica isn't my mother."

NINE

Claire needed space and time. She couldn't think. Not standing here on the dock, not with Audrey in front of her. Lilah didn't say a word. Her eyes went back and forth between Claire and Audrey.

"I need to be alone," Claire managed to say. Her voice was hoarse.

Audrey's head dropped and her body seemed to fold in on itself. Claire could tell Audrey wanted to be there with her. Or maybe she was processing the news, too. It didn't really matter. Claire knew she needed Audrey to go. It was too painful to find out they weren't sisters and incomprehensible to think her mother wasn't her mother. Nothing felt real. Not the three of them, standing here on the dock. Not the letter with the results. Nothing.

"I need... some time," Claire said. She looked down at her feet, just to have something real to focus on. The paper dangled at her side in her hand. It had to be wrong. There had to be a mix-up at the lab.

"I understand. But then maybe we should figure this out together," Audrey said.

"Not yet. Please." Claire closed her eyes. She felt unsteady. She didn't trust Audrey in the moment. Audrey, who was not her sister but was Veronica's daughter.

Eventually, Audrey spoke. "Okay." Her voice was so quiet, Claire almost couldn't hear. She opened her eyes again and found Lilah staring at her, eyebrows bunched up and forehead creased.

"Mom." The confusion in Lilah's voice made Claire's heart ache. This was too much.

"Please," Claire said to Audrey. "Go."

Audrey slowly turned and left the dock, walking back up to the front of the house and disappearing.

Lilah took Claire's hand.

"We should go and get changed," Claire said.

They went to the house together, side by side and silent.

At quarter past eight the next morning, the bus was late. Lilah couldn't seem to stand still. She kept turning her head, studying Claire. Claire could see Lilah's movements out of the corner of her eye while she watched the road in front of her for the bus. It was supposed to have arrived fifteen minutes ago to take Lilah to hockey camp.

Lilah shifted her hockey stick from one hand to the other. She put it down on top of her hockey bag in front of her, pulled at the front of her T-shirt, adjusted her hat.

"Mom?"

"Yes?" Claire faced Lilah. She tried to soften her body language. Every muscle felt impossibly tight since yesterday, but it wasn't Lilah's fault.

"Are you going to be okay?"

"I will. I promise," Claire said. It surprised her, how convincing she sounded. There wasn't an ounce of Claire that knew anything at the moment. "Are you? I know this is a lot for you to take in right now, too."

Lilah's mouth was thin, stretched across her perfect face. The freckles she sprouted every summer seemed to be multiplying across the bridge of Lilah's nose. She folded her arms over her chest. "I'm not sure."

Claire's chest seized the way it did whenever she worried about her daughter. This was huge. Lilah must be reeling from the news that the woman she thought was her grandmother wasn't her grandmother at all. They didn't have time to process it, though. The first day of camp was here, and there was no way Lilah could miss this. It was paid for, and besides, this camp was the highlight of every summer for her daughter.

"Lilah!" A voice came from across the parking lot. Charlotte, Lilah's friend, waved an arm in the air.

Claire's body relaxed. Lilah would likely be fine while she was away. She had her friends for distraction. They had hockey and swimming and canoeing and staying up late by the fire. Two weeks of carefree independence were ahead of them. It was just what Lilah needed. Staying at home to wallow in the news wasn't the right course of action.

After the bus arrived and Lilah's bags were loaded onto it, Lilah came to Claire's side. She reached her arms straight out in front of her for a hug the way she used to when she was a toddler. Claire melted into her, relishing the rare opportunity.

"I'll miss you," Claire said.

"I'll miss you, too." Lilah squeezed Claire a little tighter. "You can call the camp if you need me, you know."

Claire's eyes dampened at the thoughtfulness of Lilah. "I thought that wasn't allowed."

Lilah pulled away to look into Claire's eyes. "They would let you this time. This isn't normal."

Claire had a hard time discerning what was normal

anymore. She didn't even know who she was or who her mother was.

"Okay," Claire said. "That goes for you, too. You can call me anytime if you need me. The timing for you to learn all this isn't the best. But I promise, I'll be fine, and we'll sort things out together when you're back."

"Promise me you're not going to change your mind about work. You're going to take care of yourself, right?" Lilah's tone was laced with concern. Her bottom lip quivered the way it did when she got emotional.

"I will. You don't need to worry about me. Do I need to worry about you?"

"No," Lilah said.

Claire held Lilah's eye for a moment, studying her daughter's face to look for signs that this knowledge was too heavy a burden. Lilah stared back at her, her face hard to read. Yet, Claire knew that camp with friends and keeping busy was probably the best place for Lilah right now.

"Okay. You should go. Charlotte's waiting." Claire nodded in the direction of the bus.

Lilah turned her head to see Charlotte madly waving again, this time from the back of the bus. She grinned and laughed before holding up a hand to motion to her friend to hang on.

"Go," Claire said again, a small amount of relief washing over her at the sight of Lilah's reaction to her friend. She would be okay. "Have so much fun."

Lilah gave Claire one final hug. "We'll always have each other, no matter what any tests say about Grandma."

Claire looked down so Lilah wouldn't see her face crumple.

After the bus had pulled away and parents dispersed, Claire got into her car and put both hands on the wheel. She couldn't go back home. She couldn't walk around her empty house, wiping down kitchen counters, sitting by Shadow Lake with a glass of wine, surrounded by everything familiar. It all reminded her too much of her other life. Her life with her mother—who wasn't her mother.

Bits of memories flashed through her mind. Like when she was young and they went on vacation to Prince Edward Island, the two of them. It was the only far vacation they ever took, and they drove there for days. They listened to oldies in the car; Mom loved Gordon Lightfoot and his voice lulled Claire into a calm state, even back then when she was too young to appreciate really good music.

Another flash, this time of her teen years, when she was so angry at her mother. Over what? She could never recall specifics, just that they had fought. Claire was up in her bedroom sobbing and sobbing, her body heaving. Her bedroom door had swung open, and Claire thought her mother had come to yell at her again, but instead, Veronica had opened her arms and walked forward, wrapping Claire into a tight hug. They had sat on her bed and cried together until neither one of them had anything left.

Claire shook her head as if the memories could dissipate like fog. They made her stomach tighten and her skin hurt. She couldn't face going back home, where the memories of her old life were suffocating, so, instead, she drove. She drove and drove, first down Main Street and past the shoe store in Summerville, and then past wide-open fields and farms with cows grazing. She got on a busy highway and opened her window a crack so she could listen to the wind whipping and the cars zooming by. So different from the sounds of home.

After driving for a couple of hours, Claire eventually ended up in the city. Toronto was the kind of place that was as different from Summerville as she could imagine. She almost instantly regretted the decision to come here when she had to navigate her way through one-way streets and cars honking aggressively. There was a hotel up ahead, and on instinct Claire turned into the parking lot rather than drive any further.

Inside the lobby, Claire smoothed down her T-shirt, as if that would help her look any less out of place. She knew she was disheveled. She hadn't blow-dried her hair that day, and she didn't generally wear makeup in summer. She had found it hard to care what she looked like these past few days, anyway, and opted for loose, baggy T-shirts and athletic capris that were at least fifteen years old.

There were only a few rooms left. Claire booked one for one night and went upstairs to the eighth floor to let herself in. The room was pristine and cool, almost too cold, and quiet. Extremely still. She needed this.

After Claire read the DNA test results yesterday, she was unable to quiet her mind. She had been certain the results had to be wrong. There must have been some mistake made with the samples she sent in. She had been so convinced, she had called to question them.

"There's been a mistake," Claire had said into the phone. Her entire body vibrated. "The results I received can't be right."

When the woman on the other end of the call had checked and then checked again, confirming that the results were, indeed, correct, Claire had felt sick. She had hung up and gone to the bathroom to throw up as quietly as she could so she wouldn't alarm Lilah.

Now she was alone and could react however her body told her to and not worry about her daughter seeing, but she felt uncharacteristically calm. Claire took a long shower and then put on the robe she found inside the closet. She sat on the bed and realized for the first time in a couple of days that her stomach was aching from hunger. She would need something soon.

The last thing she wanted to do was leave the hotel room. Toronto had seemed like a good idea in theory. Now that she was here, Claire could admit to herself that this place made her nervous. It was odd and unfamiliar. Maybe she would order room service. Could she do that though? Pay forty dollars for a burger and fries?

Claire caught a glimpse of herself in the giant mirror that sat over the desk in the hotel room. Her face was chalky and her skin also blotchy. She recognized that person; those eyes, the curly hair, the pale skin, but she didn't know who she was. A part of her was lost, or possibly even disappearing, now that she had the knowledge about her mother. The person she thought she was seemed to be fading. What would she have left?

Her phone buzzed. Claire looked at the screen. It was the fifth time Audrey had called. She would have to rip the bandage off eventually, and there was probably no better time than now when she was here, alone and away from Summerville.

"Claire?" Audrey's voice was loud through the phone. "Oh my God, Claire! I thought you were never going to talk to me again. Are you okay?"

"I don't know," Claire said. "I mean, I'm okay, I guess. I left town."

"You left?" Audrey asked in a stunned sort of voice.

"I dropped Lilah off at the bus for camp and then I just started driving."

"Oh, Claire." Audrey went quiet.

"It's fine," Claire insisted. "I'm not flying off the handle. I just needed to get away for a while. I needed space. It was suffocating being at home." Although, she already knew being here wasn't the answer either. The city was too loud, too busy.

Audrey only wanted to be close to Claire to help, Claire could sense that. Even though her gut reaction was to be wary, there was nothing backhanded or sinister about her. She just wanted to be there, with Claire. It wasn't possible, though. She couldn't be in the same room as Audrey, couldn't listen to her speak without seeing her mother staring back at her.

Anyway, Claire had Lilah. Yesterday, Lilah's concern had gone into overdrive, and it broke Claire's heart a little, the way she could see her daughter trying to take care of her mother. That's not the way it was supposed to be. Thank goodness Lilah was able to get away to camp, where she could just be a kid for a few weeks.

Last night, Claire had notified work that she would need to take a longer leave than she originally expected. There was no way she could do her job well right now when her head was so muddled. She felt like she was having an out-of-body experience, and she was watching herself learn that her mother was not actually her mother. It was so dreamlike, it couldn't be true.

"What are you going to do?" Audrey asked through the phone.

"I don't know."

Sleep. That was one thing Claire hoped she could do here. It was too hard at home. Being in the same place where every little thing reminded her of her old life was difficult. She couldn't take a mug down from the kitchen cupboard without remembering the last time her mother had used it, or how calm and normal life had been back then.

Normal was something Claire had thought about a lot these past few days. When was the last time her life had felt completely normal? How long ago had that been and what had she been doing in the moment? Claire couldn't remember.

"Do you think you'll want to look for some answers?" Audrey spoke in a low tone, like she didn't know how to navigate the subject.

Claire closed her eyes. How did one proceed when they learned their mother wasn't their mother? Where would she even begin? She had no idea.

Since yesterday, things kept coming to Claire. Memories that didn't make sense until now, like the fact that there were no baby photos of her. Her mom had said they didn't get around to buying a camera back then. They didn't get one until she was older. Why did Claire believe that? Why had she not questioned her further? It was one of those small details that she merely accepted as fact because Veronica told her that was the way it was. She had asked why there were pictures of Audrey but not her, but never got a straight answer. Her mother told Claire it hurt too much to talk about Audrey, so Claire left it alone.

There were the differences, too. Everyone used to ask her mother where Claire's wild, curly hair came from when Veronica's was dead straight. Veronica always shook her head and laughed it off, saying she had no idea.

Every detail that Claire had let go before could be called into question now. She worried that if she dug too deep, she would find there was hidden meaning behind everything, and she wouldn't like what she found. If she went searching for answers immediately, she would have to ask herself who she actually was if she wasn't Veronica's daughter. Who was her real mother, and where were her real parents? She wasn't sure she would like the answers.

"I don't know," Claire said to Audrey now. "At some point."

There was a pause. Audrey cleared her throat, but in a timid manner, like she was unsure.

"I thought I would stay in Summerville for the rest of the month. Maybe even into August. I don't have to be back at work until a couple of days before school starts. I would like to help you," Audrey said. "I think we could help each other if you're willing."

The tenderness in her voice unexpectedly brought tears to Claire's eyes. It seemed impossible to think they could help one another. It was too raw, wasn't it? And Audrey wasn't her sister. Claire wanted to believe there was a concrete reason for them to remain connected, but there wasn't.

"I have to go," Claire said. She didn't trust herself to keep speaking. Her voice was bound to break any second. She wanted to be quiet now. To sleep. She only wanted to think

about what she was going to do immediately after she hung up
the phone, not what to do for the rest of her life. Minute by
minute, day by day. That was how she would survive this.

After a long, deep sleep, Claire woke to the low hum of the
room's air vent. It was dark, but a sliver of light was shimmying
its way through the narrow crack in the curtain's opening. She
craned her neck to lift her head and look around. There were
her clothes, strewn across the chair that sat in the corner of the
room. On the table next to it were leftovers from last night's
dinner: a piece of hamburger bun, a couple of cold fries. A glass
with only a little beer left pooling in the bottom.

Claire got up and splashed water on her face, then rinsed
her mouth with the mouthwash provided by the hotel. She tried
to tame the frizz on top of her head and then got dressed. She
clicked on her phone and found the welcome email from the
camp Lilah was at. They had a link to a page where you could
look at photos of the kids. You had to scan through hundreds of
photos with no guarantee your child was in any of them, and it
had only been one day, but Claire still needed to check.

She opened the link and moved her thumb slowly from the
bottom of the screen upwards, scanning each photo, searching
for a glimpse of her daughter. There were kids in shorts and T-
shirts, baseball caps on their heads and towels slung around
their necks as they walked across a sandy patch of land, smiling
at the camera, holding up two fingers in a peace sign. Kids on a
dock, with life jackets on, about to step into a boat; kids gathered at a campfire, sitting close, smiling at a counselor piling
sticks into a tent-like formation in front of them. They all looked
so happy, already having done so much.

After she had scanned each photo and hadn't seen Lilah,
Claire went through them all again, squinting her eyes to look
closely at the background of each shot. No Lilah.

Claire's pulse sped up. There had to be a reason why there were no photos of Lilah. She must not be okay. Something had to be wrong. Claire knew it. Something must have happened to Lilah and the camp hadn't let her know.

She went through the photos again, this time scrolling even faster, frantic to find a glimpse of her daughter's face. When she saw nothing, Claire fumbled with the phone with shaking hands until she found a phone number for the camp. She called and waited, her chest thudding.

"Hello, I'm calling to check on my daughter." Claire's voice came out in a rushed, harried tone. Even she could hear it, but she couldn't help it.

"I'm sorry?" The voice on the other end was confused.

"Lilah Jones. She's not in any of the photos on the website. Something must be wrong," Claire said impatiently.

There was a silence on the other end. Eventually, they spoke again. "One moment please."

It felt like Claire waited forever. She stood and went to the hotel room's window to look down at the roads. Her mind worked over how quickly she could get to camp if she needed. With every minute she spent listening to only silence on the other end of the phone, Claire's breathing sped up. If they didn't come back on the line and answer her, then what? Her head throbbed.

The line clicked.

"Hello?" Claire practically shouted.

"Hi, Mrs. Brown, my name is Melissa. I'm one of the head counselors here. Lilah is doing great and having a good time. She's out on a stand-up paddleboard right now."

Claire's shoulders dropped. She almost asked to speak to Lilah as proof, but realized Lilah would be mortified. It hit her like a wave that she was losing it. She needed to calm down. Everything would be okay if she just took steadying breaths and tried to relax.

After thanking Melissa and ending the call, Claire sat still for a while, trying to calm her racing mind with long, deep breaths. Then she had another thought. She opened up a screen and typed her mother's name into the search bar. A few images came up—none of them her mother. A profile of a Veronica Brown from a crafting website was the first link. The preview said she was born and raised by a sheep-farming family in southern Patagonia. Definitely not her mother. There were social media pages of women who shared her mother's name, even an obituary of a Veronica Brown from a small town in British Columbia. But nothing about her mother.

It struck Claire that she didn't know a lot about the background of the woman who she thought of as her mother. They had gone their entire lives living together, just them against the world, and now Claire couldn't think of what kind of search she could try to find more details.

She closed her phone and slid it into the back pocket of her capris. She grabbed her things and left the room behind.

Downstairs, Claire went directly past the front counter without checking out. She wasn't fully convinced that leaving was what she wanted to do. She didn't particularly want to stay here either, without any clothes, with only her phone and wallet, but she had no plan. So instead, she decided to walk. A walk around the city might help her clear her head and give her some direction.

After fifteen minutes, Claire realized she hadn't seen a single thing around her. Her mind had been too focused on everything she knew for a fact up until that point. Her mother wasn't her mother, she didn't know who her real parents were, and she thought her long-lost sister had returned. Instead, it turned out that Audrey had more claim to Veronica. Audrey was Veronica's. Claire was nobody's. She had no identity.

She turned a corner and ended up on a street lined with stores and restaurants and filled with people milling about. It buzzed with the energy and noise of summer on a Saturday afternoon. There was a sign on a lamppost that said Yorkville. Two men were sitting on a bench having coffee, women with big sunglasses were going from expensive-looking shop to expensive-looking shop, with boxy, white and black shopping bags. Cyclists locked up their bikes. Couples went into a restaurant, while others sat at a rooftop patio, sipping drinks and people watching. Claire caught sight of the store names—Dolce & Gabbana, Gucci, Prada, Louis Vuitton. Where on earth had she ended up? It was about as far away from Summerville as you could get.

She turned on her heel, ready to head back in the direction of the hotel, when she was almost hit in the face by a man's shoulder.

"Sorry," they both said at the same time.

The man stepped to one side and put an arm around the shoulder of a mini version of himself. A little boy. Next to him was a girl who looked only slightly older. On the other side was another man, his husband, Claire assumed. They smiled at one another before continuing on their way, walking in a line, four across the sidewalk. Their hands were linked now.

There was a thickness in Claire's throat. The tears that sprang to her eyes embarrassed her. But it was the sight of them —the perfect little family, hand in hand—that made Claire feel so lonely. It was a feeling that could bury her if she allowed it to.

Lilah's face sprang to her mind. This wasn't just about Claire. It was also about her daughter. Claire might not know who she was, but it struck her that Lilah wouldn't know either. Lilah wouldn't know where she came from or who her grandparents were. She would know nothing, unless Claire did something about it.

Claire picked up her pace so she could get back to the hotel before her checkout time. She got to the front desk, paid for her room and went down to the underground parking lot. Inside her car, Claire paused for only a brief moment, steeling herself to drive through the busy city streets again. She would do it, though. She would do it so she could get home and figure out how to find answers.

She would do it for Lilah.

TEN

At four o'clock in the afternoon, Claire arrived home. The house was silent and still without Lilah. She went through the place opening windows so she could at least hear the breeze in the trees. The whir of a motorboat floated up from the lake. This was much better than the city. Now that she was home, Claire had no idea what had got into her or why she thought leaving would be a good idea. Summerville was her safe place, despite everything that had happened.

She had a proper shower, changed her clothes and cooked a few eggs with some rye toast. She took it out back to the covered patio and sat at the table so she could look out at the water in front of her.

Her phone rang and Greg's name lit up the screen.

"Hey. How did things go with Lilah's drop-off?"

They often started conversations this way, about the one thing they could both talk for hours about—Lilah.

"It was good. She was excited," Claire said.

"I'm sorry I missed it."

"It happens. She understands you have to work."

"I know, but still." Greg's voice was heavy. He paused and

Claire thought the conversation was already coming to an end. She'd texted him about the DNA results the same day she received them, and he'd called immediately. Claire had answered him mostly with one-word answers and then gave the phone to Lilah. She knew she would have to talk to him in more depth eventually. "How are you doing? You disappeared after you dropped her off?" he asked.

Claire tipped her head to one side. "How did you know that?"

"I went by the house yesterday after work. You weren't there. I swung by later on in the evening, too."

"Oh," Claire said. "I went for a drive and ended up in Toronto, and then stayed in a hotel overnight."

"You?" Greg said, the tone of his voice a bit higher than usual. "You went to Toronto? Like, downtown? You hate places like that."

"I know. I wasn't thinking."

"Are you—" He paused, as if he was thinking about how to be delicate. "Are you going to be okay? I'm worried about you."

"I really don't know," Claire said. It was the most honest answer she could give. She continued on so he wouldn't over-worry. "But I'm sure I'll figure it out. I just need some time to myself. I've taken a leave from work, so I should be good." A subtle hint. *Please don't come over. I need to be alone.* As much as she found his presence comforting, she wasn't up for a visit.

"Have you found anything out? I can't believe this. It's so surreal."

Claire picked at a piece of dry skin on her bottom lip. Her muscles ached, even though she hadn't done anything physical.

"I know nothing." It was the truth.

"If she wasn't your biological mother, why was she raising you like she was? Have you looked into whether you were adopted?" Greg asked. He was thinking out loud, and Claire could tell he didn't mean to upset her. But he did.

"Not yet."

"And where is your real mother? Where has she been all this time?"

"Stop," Claire snapped. "Please."

"I'm sorry," Greg said, his tone careful. "I want to help if I can. Promise me you'll call me if you need me, alright? This is a lot for you to absorb."

"Thank you." She was lucky to have Greg in her life. Even though it hadn't worked out for the two of them together, she could still rely on him. That much was clear.

After she finished eating, Claire sat back in her chair and sipped her coffee. She stared at the lake for what felt like ages before she finally stood and carried her plate and mug into the kitchen. She made her way to the front of the house, picking up her keys and slinging her purse over her shoulder along the way.

There was still the issue of her mother's house and all her things. Claire knew it made sense to sell the house, but she had been in no rush to go through years and years of clutter, deciding what to keep and what to get rid of. It wasn't like her to delay a task, although now she was thankful that she hadn't started the process yet. It gave her the chance to go over there and search again. If she took another look, she thought she might find something she had missed the first time. Anything that might give her an answer.

She closed the front door and locked it before making her way down the long dirt-and-gravel covered driveway to the car. The sound stopped her—the crunch of pebbles under a set of tires.

Claire turned just in time to see Audrey. All the tension left her body, her limbs went light, and her jaw softened, which surprised Claire. She realized she was happy to see Audrey again

"Hey." Audrey reached an arm out of her car window and

motioned at Claire. She put her car into park and turned the ignition off.

It's too soon for her to be here. Claire looked down at her feet, then over at Audrey's car. It *should* be too soon, but Claire couldn't deny that relief washed over her. Audrey was someone who understood what Claire was going through. Someone Claire could talk to.

"I'm sorry to just show up like this," Audrey said as she approached. "I'm really sorry. But I didn't know what else to do. I feel like I could really use your company and I was hoping you might feel the same? We might need each other right now."

Claire was struck by Audrey's words. She mostly needed answers. But Audrey was here, and she was trying, she was a connection to Veronica. Claire knew Audrey must need so many answers, too.

"I'm having a hard time," Claire admitted.

"Me, too." Audrey held a hand up to her chest. She watched Claire intently, almost in a desperate kind of way.

"I just don't know how to handle this." Claire wanted to know how to handle this. She wanted to be in control, but she wasn't. "I'm trying to hold onto my family."

She meant Lilah and even Greg, but she also meant her memories of her mother. Of what they had. She was only being honest again, so Claire couldn't understand why Audrey flinched.

"It's nice that you have family to hold onto. That's all I want."

Her voice was so sad and low, Claire softened in spite of herself. It was all everyone wanted, she supposed. To be loved by family. Audrey's father was sick, her mother who she never knew was dead. No wonder she felt like she needed to hang onto Veronica somehow. And even though Claire thought she should be wary of Audrey, she couldn't help but be drawn to her.

"I'm heading over there now," Claire said. "To my mother's house. I could use some help with sorting things out. You can come if you'd like." The heat radiated down from her forehead to her neck after she said it. *My mother*.

Audrey's head pointed down and her mouth pursed into a small bow on her face, like she was trying to hide the emotion. Her voice was thick with it, though. "I would love to go with you."

"Okay."

There was something about the way she looked at Claire, so honest and vulnerable. She was the kind of person you could tell would accept any answer you gave her, no hard feelings. Maybe Claire shouldn't trust her so easily, especially after learning Audrey wasn't her biological sister, but there was already a closeness there. It had been developing ever since that day in the car.

"Follow me." Claire opened her car door and got in.

When they arrived, Claire went into the house first and opened windows again like the last time she was here, like she always did.

"I'm going to start upstairs," Claire told Audrey.

Audrey stood silently, eyes wide and head slowly panning around the room, like she was seeing something strange or deeply interesting.

Claire didn't wait for an answer and instead grabbed one of the cardboard boxes she had brought over right before the funeral and hoisted it up on her hip. Maybe Audrey needed a moment alone. Claire could give that to her.

Upstairs, Claire went straight for her mother's room. She put the box down on the bed and stood in front of the closet. Sweaters and T-shirts in blues and greens hung in front of her. There was a belt and some folded slacks set neatly on the shelving unit. Below that, pair after pair of shoes: rubber flip-flops, fancy sandals with jewels along the straps, old running shoes, a pair of high heels. When did her mother ever wear high heels? Claire's eyes went to the top corner of the shelving unit, where she half-expected to see the box she wasn't allowed to look in. The box of Audrey's photos. She could only imagine how Audrey might feel if they found them.

Nothing from back then made any logical sense. Why would a mother not raise her own daughter? Why would she not take care of both Audrey and Claire? Claire couldn't even begin to imagine how she had ended up with Veronica. She had heard of people finding out they were adopted as babies when they were fully grown adults. There could have been adoption papers hidden somewhere under the same roof Claire grew up in—all this time.

A sound came from just outside the room. The creak of the old floor.

"Can I come in?" Audrey asked.

Claire nodded.

Audrey walked around the room, studying everything closely. Claire watched for her reaction at seeing it all for the first time; her mother's moisturizer, the brush she used, the clothes she wore, everything that made Veronica who she was. Claire wondered what Audrey was thinking as she took it all in.

"Nothing makes sense to me," Audrey said. Her eyes were rimmed with red.

"I know." Claire touched the arm of a gray cardigan her mother used to wear all the time, now flung over a hook in her closet. She took it off the hook and put it in the box of things to keep. "What has your father said about everything?" Claire asked. "Has he been able to give you some answers?"

"Not really."

Claire turned to face Audrey. "But he must know. Why would he take you and my mother take me? What happened to my birth parents?" It was impossible to imagine what it would take for a mother to leave her biological child behind. Her mother's shaking shoulders flashed in Claire's mind. She used to cry so much.

"I'm not sure he can help us. He wavers between frustration and anger and sadness these days over how much he can't remember. He's not well." Audrey's face was drawn. She looked exhausted.

"Sorry," Claire said. She almost forgot. All of this must be so hard for her, just as it was for Claire, but in a different way.

"It's okay." Audrey's voice wobbled. "He sometimes doesn't know me at all, so it's been hard to get any kind of answer from him. I only got little bits about all of this."

They stood in silence, not looking at one another. If they couldn't get answers from Audrey's father, what were they supposed to do? There were so many questions. It was almost impossible to know where to begin.

"Do you have any of your paperwork from when you were a baby? Your birth certificate?" Audrey asked.

Claire had one, but she had no idea where it was. She couldn't recall seeing it much as a kid. She had only needed it a handful of times, but she had one somewhere. "Somewhere downstairs, I think. In her old files." When she had left home and moved out, she had only moved a short drive away from her mother, so she didn't bring everything with her. "I don't know how it'll help though."

Audrey's eyes connected with Claire's. "Wouldn't it have both your parents' names on it?"

That was something Claire *could* remember. The birth certificate had Veronica down as her mother and, now that Audrey asked, it triggered Claire's memory. It also listed Audrey's father, Robert Adkins, as her father. But after the results from the DNA test, none of that mattered. Veronica wasn't her mother, despite her name being on the certificate, and Robert wasn't her father.

"It has Veronica and your father on it. There might be something else in her files that could be useful."

Audrey shrugged in agreement.

They went down the stairs into the darkness of the den. In the corner of the hallway that led to the laundry room was Veronica's office. Claire went through the filing cabinet, looking for the folder with the important documents. The ones they rarely ever looked at. She flipped through insurance papers, leases, the mortgage, until she saw it. Her birth certificate. There was her name, her date of birth, birthplace, a registration number. It all looked familiar and normal.

"Here," Claire said. "Veronica's name and Robert Adkins." Not her birth parents. Who knew who they were? She held up the paper and Audrey took it, glanced at the front and then flipped it over. She ran her fingers over it and then handed it back to Claire.

"Can I look through here?" Audrey asked. She motioned to the closet next to Veronica's desk. It was used for storage and held old boxes of Claire's artwork and report cards from when she was in school; some of her mother's files from work were in there. She even stored Claire's wedding dress at the back.

"Sure. There's not much though."

Audrey opened the doors and took a step inside.

Claire turned back to the filing cabinet, trying to decide what she would keep and what could be shredded. There was so much to do when someone died. So much to empty out of a house.

"What's this?" Audrey's muffled voice called from the back of the closet.

"What's what?"

Audrey backed out of the closet, one hand holding her phone with the flashlight turned on, and the other holding a key with a piece of tape stuck to it. "I found it taped to the back of the closet. High up in the corner."

"I've never seen that before," Claire said. "Why would it be taped to the back of the closet?"

"And hidden away so high up."

They locked eyes for a moment, and then, as if they both knew what the other was thinking, scanned the room, searching.

ELEVEN

When the water went still right at dusk, Claire thought it was about as close to perfect as you could get. The lake had always been one of Claire's favorite spots to be alone, in a kayak or a canoe, gliding across the glassy surface. Shadow Lake was particularly gorgeous at the end of the day. Most families were done swimming and had gone inside to change out of wet bathing suits, opting for comfortable jogging pants and hoodies in anticipation of the cool night ahead. It was quiet and Zen-like, even though Claire wasn't the yoga-loving, Zen-like type. She was, however, at her happiest out in nature. Especially in mid-July.

Early that Sunday evening, the day after having Audrey over to her mother's house, Claire pushed the paddle she was holding straight down into the water and then pulled back, propelling herself forward. She worked her arm muscles over and over until she could feel the breeze sliding over the skin on her face, her exposed shoulders, her arms. She had no idea where she was going, but she didn't really need a plan. She could navigate these waters blindfolded by now.

When she got clear across the lake, past the tiny island she had named "Gull-poop Island" as a kid, past the small bridge, Claire stopped. She placed the paddle in her lap and reclined an inch back into her kayak seat. She hadn't realized she had been tensing her muscles, but her thighs relaxed, her hips loosened.

Now what?

It was the question on her mind most often since Audrey showed up on her doorstep. From the moment she had met her, she had wondered what she should do next until she got to this point in her life, where she was no longer comfortable and didn't know how to react to anything.

After Audrey had found the key, they had both looked around the room for something with a lock. There was nothing unusual in her mother's office, though. There was her desk, with drawers filled with pens and loose sheets of paper, a box of unused envelopes. There were books on the filing cabinet, there were things in the closet to go through before she could sell the house. There was no box with a lock on it and the key didn't seem to fit in any desk or drawer. It likely unlocked something Veronica didn't want found. Claire thought of the possibility of adoption papers again. Maybe it was a sign that they couldn't find what they were looking for. Nothing good could come of opening a Pandora's box that belonged to Veronica Brown. Claire should leave it all alone.

But she knew she couldn't keep living her life as if she didn't know everything up until now was a lie.

She placed her paddle into the water to turn the kayak around. She had been drifting too far to the right and was about to go under the bridge.

"Claire?"

She looked up. Greg was standing on the bridge above her, shopping bags in his hands. His eyebrows were scrunched up into a tight knot and his mouth was open slightly, like seeing Claire on the water in a kayak was an odd thing to witness.

"What?" she called up to him.

"What are you doing?"

"I'm kayaking," she said.

"No, you're not. You're floating."

"Okay." She looked around her. What was wrong with floating a little?

"Are you okay?" he asked.

That question again. Greg asked her often, as if she was going to break any minute. He looked at her the way Audrey had.

"I'm fine. I'm just out here to think."

"Where are you going?" he called down to her.

"Nowhere. Just around. In a circle."

Her own words brought Claire up short. Where was she going? What was next? She didn't know, but she did know that fighting it wasn't working. Audrey was here. The DNA test wasn't lying. These were plain and simple facts that she would have to accept. She needed to keep looking for some solid answers so she could move on, no matter how painful those answers would be.

"Can I pop by in a bit?" Greg asked.

"Why?"

"I just want to talk."

"Okay. Yeah." Claire wasn't sure why it had to be now, but she liked having Greg around, and he meant well, so she waved up at him and told him she was heading back home, placed her paddle in the water again and turned the kayak around.

She pushed and pulled through the water without stopping until she got back to her dock. When she got out of the water and put the kayak away, she headed into the cottage to look for her phone. She never brought it out on the lake with her. Too risky.

Once she was inside, Claire opened her phone and clicked on the link to the camp photos again. It had been updated since she had last looked and there were over three hundred photos to scan. She was about to browse through them when she heard a sharp knock at the door and then it opened.

"It's me," Greg's voice called.

"What's going on?" Claire came around the corner of the kitchen and got a better look at him now that he was up close. He stood there in dark jeans and a black T-shirt, both a little dressier than usual. His arms were down at his sides, and Claire couldn't help but notice how tanned and relaxed he looked.

"I've been worried about you," Greg said.

"I'm fine."

"You always say that." He smiled at her.

"I will be, eventually," Claire said. "What can I get you to drink?"

"I can help myself. I remember the lay of the land." He went to the fridge and pulled a beer out. Then he turned to face her. "I'm also here to help you." He moved a step forward. There was a slight hesitation, like he was about to reach for her and wrap her in a hug, but stopped himself. Claire wished he hadn't.

She moved toward him, too. His face was covered in day-old dark stubble peppered with flecks of gray. He was so handsome. That had never been part of the problem. It was hard to know in moments like this what it was that had caused them to fall apart.

Greg stood up straight and took his hand out of his pocket. His face registered surprise at her coming closer to him.

"Thank you," Claire said. It could have been how kind he was being, or it could have been that Claire was overwhelmed by everything, but something made her want to melt into him. She stood next to him and rounded her shoulders in on herself so she could settle herself into the grooves of his body. She closed her eyes and enjoyed the warmth, the familiarity.

Greg wrapped his arms around her and placed his chin on

the top of her head. "Mmm," he murmured. "It's been a really long time since you've let me do this."

Claire opened her eyes. "What do you mean?" She wasn't sure why she felt defensive, but she did, and she suspected by the way his body tensed ever so slightly that Greg heard it in her voice.

"You wouldn't let me hug you for the last while we were married," he said. "Or, if you did, you always pulled away quickly."

Claire fought the urge to pull away now and prove him right, but it overpowered her. She took a step back and looked up at him. "What? No, I didn't."

Greg looked tired. His mouth turned down at the edges. "I'm not criticizing you. It's just a fact."

There was truth to what he was saying, and Claire knew it. When she thought about his comment, little memories flashed through her mind. Memories of Claire being irritated by Greg's inability to see when she was too tired or busy to stand in the middle of the kitchen and hug. Memories of her pulling away from him, not just once or twice, but often. In this moment, she was no longer irritated, but instead felt ashamed. What was wrong with her? What kind of a woman didn't want her partner, who she loved very much, to hug her? No wonder they didn't work out. A large part of it had to be her fault.

Claire moved away. "I need to check this," she said, holding up her phone. "Can we talk about things another time?" She didn't wait for his response and instead stared down at the phone so she couldn't see Greg except in her peripheral vision.

He put his beer on the counter. "I'll call you later." His voice was quiet. Then he turned and left through the front door without saying anything else.

She brushed the tears from her eyes, relieved that he seemed to understand she needed space. She wouldn't be able to explain to him why she was so sad about them right then, but she was.

To distract herself from the swell of emotion, she went to the kitchen and sat on the edge of one of the chairs and opened the link to the camp photos again. She scrolled through all of them, stopping suddenly when she caught a glimpse of Lilah. Finally.

She was stand-up paddleboarding, in her black one-piece bathing suit. Her hair was wild, so big and curly, like she hadn't washed it or used conditioner since she'd left. There was someone next to her, another camper Claire didn't recognize, smiling directly at the camera, her mouth open wide and her hand up in the air, waving at the camera. Lilah had both hands on the paddle and was directing her attention in front of her, concentration in her expression, but also a genuine smile on her face. She looked like she had maybe just been laughing and now was righting herself, focusing so she wouldn't fall.

Claire's eyes went glassy again. Her mouth twitched. She put a hand up to cover it, even though nobody was there with her. Lilah was happy.

She scanned the rest of the photos and found another one of Lilah, this time in a big group, sitting on benches and smiling directly at the camera. After she got to the end of the photos, Claire closed the tab and pressed on Audrey's number.

"Hello?" Audrey said.

"Hi. Do you want to meet at Veronica's house again? I thought we could take another look."

"Oh. Yes. Okay, sure," Audrey fumbled.

"Meet you in fifteen minutes? I can bring some takeout. Do you like seafood?" She hadn't eaten yet and her stomach felt hollow suddenly.

"That would be nice," Audrey said. "I'll bring wine."

Claire said goodbye, ended the call and hoped she wouldn't regret this.

TWELVE

They started with the food. The takeout from Just for the Halibut, the local fish and chip place in town, was world-famous and they were both hungry, so Claire ordered them the salt-and-pepper calamari, scallops and shrimp sautéed in white wine and garlic butter, a garden salad, as well as a plate of halibut and chips to share.

In the kitchen, Audrey opened a bottle of white wine and poured two glasses. They took all of it out back, to Veronica's dock overlooking the lake.

"This is gorgeous," Audrey said. She stood gazing out at the water.

"I know. Lilah and I both loved coming here for dinners in the summer."

Audrey took a sip of her wine. She was quiet for a while. "What's it like to have a daughter?"

"Do you want kids?" Claire realized they had gone this long and she hadn't asked Audrey much at all about her personal life so far. How rude of her.

"I haven't found the right person yet. I've dated off and on, been in love a few times, but I didn't meet anyone I'd want to share my life or have kids with."

Claire moved the conversation on. They talked more about Audrey's life. She loved her job and being around students every day. "Being a teacher becomes more and more challenging every year with all the demands, but there's nothing quite like setting up the room at the start of a new year and thinking about all the unique and creative ways I might be able to engage a young mind."

"I love hearing that. As a mother." Claire smiled.

"Thanks. It's been hard with my father's health, especially until he had regular care, but I'm managing."

Something quiet and sympathetic moved through Claire. "That sounds so hard."

"It is. But I know he receives great care, and my friends have been so supportive." A wistful smile crossed her face. It wasn't much of a surprise to Claire that Audrey had great friends. Audrey was warm and genuine, the kind of person everyone would like. "Anyway," Audrey said. "Tell me more about being a mom."

"I only have Lilah, so I'm not overly experienced, but motherhood is interesting," Claire said. "It's hard." She thought of Veronica.

They were both silent for a moment.

"I don't know if I could be a good mother," Audrey said. "I had nobody to show me how."

Claire's throat ached. She couldn't imagine her childhood without her mother, or adulthood without Lilah. Even though this was odd, sitting here eating takeout and having wine with someone who was her mother's daughter, Claire knew she was lucky. She was the one who was raised by a loving mother. Despite all Claire had learned in the last few days, she still believed Veronica's love for her was genuine and real.

Claire leaned forward in her seat. "I bet you'd be great at it. You'd figure it out in your own way as you go."

"Is that what you do? Figure it out as you go?" Audrey asked. She picked up her fork and stabbed half of a scallop onto it.

"That's all I can do. Things are always changing with Lilah."

"What do you mean?"

Where to even begin? Raising Lilah had been the best, most rewarding thing Claire had ever done, while also being the single most difficult part of her life.

"Lilah is almost thirteen, so she wavers between loving me the way she always has and being incredibly annoyed by my mere presence," Claire said.

Audrey laughed. "Really? Already?"

"I know. It's a bit sooner than I expected, but she is definitely hormonal and definitely annoyed by me often. Sometimes I think I can't get anything right, that she'd just prefer I leave her alone rather than even say hello to her, and then there's times when she'll allow me to hug her, or we'll have these really great, long chats."

Claire thought of the swim in the lake the other day. Any time Lilah chose to spend with Claire felt special. You never knew which Lilah you were going to get that day, and when it was the Lilah who enjoyed her company, Claire grasped onto it with all her might.

"I don't remember being particularly annoyed by my dad," Audrey said. "Maybe it's different with mothers and daughters. But, again, I have no idea. No frame of reference."

Claire reached out for Audrey on an impulse. Before her brain really knew what she was doing, she put a hand on Audrey's arm and held it there for a moment. Her way of saying she was sorry for the way things had gone, for having to live an entire childhood without her mother. Audrey stopped what she was doing and smiled at Claire.

"I was that way with Veronica," Claire said. "Guess I'm getting my payback now." She laughed and Audrey did, too. Claire realized she enjoyed this time here with Audrey. It was comfortable, like they were meant to be friends. Was that even possible? After what they knew now, Claire wasn't sure if she would be able to get past the baggage, but this was a start. "Veronica used to tell me I was giving her more gray hairs than was fair." Claire sipped her wine in between bites of dinner. She had to be careful, or it might go to her head. She hadn't had anything to drink in a while; it only took a couple of glasses before she felt it.

"Ugh, the gray hair." Audrey ran her hand over her head. "That reminds me of our conversation in the car. I'm still convinced you don't have any, but I sure do."

"No way. I can't see any?" Audrey's hair was a gorgeous shade of blondish-brown, and all of it was that way. It wasn't peppered with silver the way Claire's was, mostly at the temples. She needed to get a box of hair dye soon.

"I get it done frequently so they don't show," Audrey said. "But have you ever thought about why we do that? Try to cover all signs of getting older? I should stop. I don't mind it."

Claire took another sip of wine. "You don't mind getting older?"

Audrey shook her head. "Nah. I've earned the right to grow older. It's a privilege. I don't need to hide it."

What a mature way to see the world. Claire wished she had that kind of outlook. "I'll say I don't mind it, and then I'll find a new sign I'm getting older and suddenly I can't pretend it doesn't bother me anymore," she said.

Audrey chuckled. "What signs?"

"Have you ever looked at your neck in a mirror that shows it really close up? Like those magnified types they have in hotel rooms? I did and I thought the skin looked like crepe paper."

Audrey burst out laughing. "Oh my God! I thought I was way too young to get wrinkly already, but I'm not. Or my legs. Why are my veins showing up all of a sudden? That can't be right."

"And the random hairs. One day, I sprouted a hair out of this mole." Claire placed her finger on the mole on her jawline. "Not so bad, I just pluck it every now and again. Except the other day, I plucked the hair and it was white."

"No!" Audrey gasped and they both laughed. Claire's sides were starting to hurt from laughing. Audrey refilled her glass and leaned back into her seat, her face flushed from laughter and wine.

"I'll give Veronica credit, ageing was one thing she was comfortable with. She did it well," Claire said. "You have that in common."

Audrey's eyes brightened. "We did? I'd love to know more about her."

Claire stiffened for a second. She tried to recover, but Audrey must have noticed.

"I'm sorry," Audrey said. "I never know how much is too much to ask about. This is hard to navigate."

"I know." Claire cleared her throat. "Why don't we head inside? Maybe seeing her things will help you learn more about who she was. And there's a room we didn't check out the other day that might have a spot for that key in it."

When they stood, Claire felt a little light-headed. She stumbled over her foot and then giggled. Who the heck was she? Giggling. It was ridiculous.

"The wine?" Audrey asked. Claire nodded and Audrey laughed. "Me, too. I can't handle it like I used to when I was younger."

"Another joy of getting older," Claire remarked.

They went through the sliding screen door and into the kitchen.

"Oh, I forgot to put the dessert out," Claire said, remembering.

"We could have it with some coffee after we're done looking around?"

"Sure. It's only a small dessert anyway. I made raspberry bars." Claire felt a flush creep across her face and neck. "I remember my mother telling me you liked raspberries when you were a kid."

Audrey put her plate on the counter in front of her. A shy smile bloomed on her face, like she was trying to stop it from getting too big. "I do. I love raspberries. That's so thoughtful of you."

"It's no problem." Claire smiled back, pleased that Audrey still liked them, and then motioned for Audrey to follow her upstairs. "I haven't done much clearing out of her stuff yet, so I momentarily forgot about this place." At the end of the hall, they went up a set of five stairs.

"Do you want more help when it comes to clearing out and selling?" Audrey asked as she trailed behind Claire. "I'd be happy to do it."

"That would be nice." Claire meant it, which surprised her. It could have been the warmth she felt from the wine, or it could have been that it was true emotion over Audrey, and the realization that Claire really liked her.

They came to a stop at the top of the stairs inside a tiny room. It had low, angled ceilings and was so small you could barely turn around, so neither Claire nor Veronica went in there much. It was mostly used for storage.

"I'll start over here," Claire said. She pointed to one corner of the room. She crouched on her knees and scanned the boxes sitting on the floor. Nothing out of the ordinary, but there was so much stuff here. Everywhere she looked, she saw things that would need to be sorted and organized and cleared out.

She opened one box with the intent of deciding if it would need to be organized, or if she could take it out of the house as it was and put it into recycling or the garbage. Inside were some old cloth tablecloths Claire had never seen before, white and trimmed with lace. There were a couple of frames with no photos in them. Buried underneath all of that was what looked like a jewelry box. It was bulky and relatively large: another thing Claire had never seen before. How was it possible that her mother had things in her house, where Claire had lived most of her life until adulthood, that she still hadn't seen? Then again, she supposed there was a whole side to Veronica that she hadn't seen or known.

She ran a hand over the top of the box and down the front of it. There was something jagged and cool there. Claire looked closer. A lock. She tried opening the lid, but it wouldn't budge.

"Audrey."

"What is it? Did you find something?" Audrey asked.

Claire pointed to the box. "Maybe this is what the key unlocks."

Audrey came over to where Claire was kneeling. Claire pulled the key from her pocket and put it into the lock and turned. When it clicked in place and the lid popped up a millimetre, Audrey's eyes shot to Claire.

Claire's pulse sped up. There must be a reason this box was locked. She pushed the lid open and looked inside. A photo of a baby's face was staring up at them. The baby was sitting up on a floor and had on a soft gray shirt with flowers on the front. She was smiling and touching the wisps of hair on the top of her head.

"Oh my God," Audrey said. "It's me."

This had to be the box of photos Claire remembered seeing once or twice when she was a kid.

Audrey picked up the photo and touched it gently with her fingers. Her eyes welled up with tears. "I used to ask my dad why there weren't many photos of me as a baby. He never had a good answer. We only had a couple. This is definitely me."

Underneath were more photos of Audrey. A close up of her in a highchair, eating breakfast, then one of playing on the floor. She looked so happy and well-loved. Claire looked closer at the background of the photos. She didn't recognize the house.

Claire picked up another photo. It was her mother holding Audrey, standing next to a man.

"That's my father," Audrey said.

It looked like any typical family photo. A father and a mother, holding a baby, their biological daughter. They were standing in a driveway, in front of an old car, smiling at the camera. They looked happy. It was so confusing. When did this phase of their life end? It was hard to imagine what could have caused them to separate and disappear, pretending the other didn't exist.

A pressure built in Claire's chest. She had accepted the fact long ago that she didn't have a father in her life, didn't have two parents at home, and that was fine. That was her life. But looking at this photo of Veronica and Audrey's father and Audrey was painful. She felt nothing but loss. A loss for something she never even had.

Something in the background of the photo caught Claire's eye. She took another closer look. The walls of the room closed in on her, the floor felt like it would drop out from under her at any moment. She went cold, from the top of her head, all the way through her limbs. Audrey must have noticed the shift in Claire.

"What?" Audrey asked.

Claire pointed. In the background of the photo, there was a house next to her mother and Audrey's father's house. The grass was overgrown, and the front of the house looked rundown. Paint was peeling, and some of the wood looked like it was rotting. There was a toddler out front, with dirty clothes and messy hair, holding a teddy bear. A teddy bear Claire could remember holding and loving and sleeping with as a child.

She touched the photo. "That's me."

THIRTEEN

In the car the next day, Claire tried not to think about all the things she had left behind. The lights at her house were all turned off, the doors locked. She could check those things off, at least. They had left Summerville so early that morning, after the visit to Veronica's house the night before, she felt a bit frazzled. It wasn't her way to do anything in the spur of the moment, but it seemed like that's all she did these days.

Audrey drove. Her face had a pinched look to it. Stress, maybe. Claire couldn't tell because she still didn't know Audrey all that well. What she did know, however, was that she needed answers.

After they had found the photo, Claire's head throbbed with questions. Why was she in front of that house next door instead of in her mother's arms? Why did she look so wild and uncared for? Audrey had all the same questions, too. She didn't know any more than Claire.

"Shouldn't be too much longer," Audrey said. She had both hands on the steering wheel and Claire thought that couldn't be comfortable for as long as she had been holding them there.

They were almost at Audrey's house. For the past three hours in the car, they spoke very little. Now Claire's throat was dry and scratchy. "Okay," she said.

When they arrived, Audrey got out of the car and came around to Claire's side, like she wanted to help her somehow. Claire supposed she was going to be pitied now. Audrey was only trying to be kind, but Claire wasn't sure how to take it.

"Let's go put our things down and then I'll call to see if he's able to have visitors today," Audrey said.

Claire followed Audrey into her house. It was small and clean, a townhouse with open rooms and big windows. The walls were blue and a pale gray. There were lots of framed photos everywhere. Of Audrey and so many different people. It seemed like more than you would usually put on display, but what did Claire know? She didn't have this many people in her life. Claire studied a couple of photos on a bookshelf while Audrey moved through the room, placing her keys down, putting the mail on a table. She stopped and glanced at Claire.

"Most are of me and my friends," she explained.

"You have a lot of friends."

Audrey laughed. "Not really. Only a few are really close to me."

"So why do you have so many on display?" Claire asked.

Audrey looked at one of her and a tall man. "They make me feel less alone. Being surrounded by memories and people who have been in my life at some point is comforting."

Claire nodded and tried not to let a flash of pity cross her face. But she did feel sorry for Audrey in that moment. Everyone wants to feel like they belong and are valued. Claire had always felt it because of Greg and Lilah. She was lucky.

"Do you need something to drink? I'm not sure what I have," Audrey said. She opened her fridge and ducked her head in.

"Water would be great." Claire sat on one of the stools at the island in the kitchen.

They were hoping to visit Audrey's father today, but they had to call first. Claire had no experience with people with Alzheimer's disease, so she had no idea what to expect.

Audrey handed her a glass of water and went to leave the room to call her father. She came back into the kitchen frowning.

"I can tell by the tone of his voice that he's not having a good morning," she said. "We can't visit yet." Her eyes were glassy.

Claire's chest tightened at the pain in Audrey's expression. When was everything going to stop being painful? It seemed like each moment in her life lately elicited physical pain. "It's okay. Do you need to go see him?"

"His nurse is there right now. She told me he's a little agitated and could use some time to rest. This afternoon might be a better time to visit," Audrey said. After a pause, she looked around the room and then back at Claire. "Why don't we go get some breakfast? I have nothing here."

They chose a local restaurant with the best eggs and bacon in town according to Audrey. It was a tiny spot, with only a straight, narrow rectangle of a room with booths on one side and high-top tables on the other. It was loud and buzzing with the chatter of people and music overhead, despite it being early morning. Probably a good choice, considering neither one of them quite knew how to fill the silence between them.

After they were seated and had ordered, Audrey motioned at her purse. "Do you mind if I take another look?" She meant the photo. At the house, Audrey had tried to give it to Claire, but Claire didn't want to touch it again. She couldn't bring herself to hold onto it, even if it was her only clue as to who she was. Audrey had taken it and a few other photos and put them in her purse to discuss later.

"It's fine," Claire said.

Audrey placed it on the table in front of them and studied it.

"Do you have any memory of this house?" she asked.

"None," Claire replied.

"I wonder where it was. I don't remember anything either. It could have been anywhere," Audrey said. She stared at the photo a while longer. "Have you thought about what this photo might mean? Or what answers it might lead to?"

"I'm afraid to think too much about it." Claire couldn't think of anything else though, and they both knew it. Her imagination had run wild from the moment she saw it. The only thing that was certain was that she needed an answer soon. The unknown was killing her.

The waitress placed two coffees and two orders of scrambled eggs and bacon with rye toast in front of them. It didn't escape Claire that she and Audrey both liked their eggs the same way and the same kind of toast. The food smelled delicious. Claire's stomach lurched with hunger.

"Do you remember her from back then?" Claire asked tentatively. "Like, being with them?"

Audrey shook her head. "I have flashes of memories of me and Dad, but I don't remember any time with her, or with you. I was so young."

That was true. They were both so young, and it was so hard to remember anything before a certain age.

"Do you think he'll be able to tell us anything?" Claire asked.

Audrey sighed and her eyes looked sad. "I'm not sure. He's changing more and more all the time. In little ways, but he's not quite the same. He's never going to go back to the way he was, so I have no idea what he'll remember."

Claire's head tilted a tiny bit to one side in sympathy. It must be awful. Cancer was terrible, but it hadn't made Veronica suffer for years and years.

After breakfast, they went back to Audrey's and tried calling her father's house again. This time, Audrey said he sounded much better after a mid-morning nap. They should go.

"You'll do the talking, right?" Claire asked. "I don't want to stress him out or upset him."

"Yes, I'll talk to him, but don't worry about upsetting him. Even though he's not himself, his emotions are still there. I can see a flash of it in his face every now and again. He loves me. He'll be happy to see me in his own way."

Claire smiled at the warmth in Audrey's voice when she spoke of her father. It struck her that Audrey wasn't upset with him for not telling her about the truth, whatever that was. She supposed everyone handled stress differently, but if Veronica was alive right now, how would Claire react to her? How could you look at someone who was supposed to love and protect you but had lied to you your whole life and not be angry?

They arrived at another modest house. Audrey let herself in and motioned for Claire to follow. This one was darker than Audrey's, with dark cupboards and countertop in the kitchen. The walls were a light beige, but the windows were smaller here and didn't let much light in.

There was a woman with a kind face moving around the kitchen, who stopped and smiled at Audrey. "Hey, you," she said. "He's in there." She gestured to the living room.

"Thanks, Sue," Audrey replied. She turned to Claire and said quietly, "Dad's personal support worker. She's amazing."

In the living room, Audrey's father was on the couch. His hands were folded across his stomach and his head was reclined back. He looked peaceful, like any older man resting in the early afternoon. Despite this, and despite the fact that Claire knew he was suffering with a disease she was certain he wished he didn't have, the sight of him upset her. He must have known her when she was little. He had some part to play in whatever happened.

"Hey, Dad," Audrey said. "I brought someone to meet you. This is Claire."

Robert opened his eyes and smiled at both of them. "Nice to meet you."

Claire nodded back and smiled tentatively.

Audrey sat near him and touched his hand. She spoke to him softly for a while. She had told Claire she wanted to ease into this. She brought up Veronica's name and he seemed to respond. She had said he could remember pieces of the past here and there. He wasn't too far into the late stages yet. Audrey pulled out the photo and showed it to him. He smiled at it.

"Here's me." Audrey pointed at each of them, one by one. "With you and with Veronica."

"Yes," Robert said. He looked up at Claire. "And who are you?"

"This is Claire. Veronica's daughter."

"Claire? I don't know any Claires."

"She's right here. This is her in the photo," Audrey explained. She pointed to Claire in the background.

Robert's face changed. Almost like it lit up, something flashed across it.

"Dad?" Audrey said.

He looked directly at Claire. "You never lived with us," he said. "You weren't ours. She shouldn't have taken you."

Claire caught Audrey's eye.

"Who?" Audrey asked.

"Veronica," he answered. "She took you."

Claire gasped. She choked on the air she was trying to take in. Her vision narrowed.

Robert looked down and his face changed again. It fell.

"It's okay, Dad." Audrey's tone was soft as she took his hands and comforted him. "It's okay."

Claire looked to her. "What's going on?"

"He's done."

FOURTEEN

Claire walked. She didn't know where she was going, but it didn't matter. As long as she was moving, she might not completely fall apart. She had left Audrey behind to talk to Robert and his caregiver. Audrey seemed torn between the two of them.

"I want to be there for you," she had said. Her voice was filled with pain, and her forehead creased. But she also held onto her father's hand, attached to him like she couldn't let go. After his reaction to the photograph, he'd seemed to disappear back into his disease, and be confused by Claire and how visibly upset she was. Audrey said this happened. He grew frustrated and wanted to be alone, and Claire didn't want to make it worse for him—he was already unwell. Besides, she couldn't process what she had been told, so she had left.

"Will you come back?" Audrey had called after her. Claire had waved a hand, but didn't answer.

She walked and walked for what could have been hours or could have only been fifteen minutes. It was hard to tell. She came to a bench at the side of the road with the intention of sitting on it, but she didn't make it. Instead, her body told her it needed to crouch. She hung onto the top bar of the bench back and curved her body in on itself. She knew she must look so strange, crouched down next to a bench, as if she was in pain. She was. It was an intense, white-hot pain she didn't know how to manage, and it came with finding out your entire life up until that point wasn't what you thought it was. Learning that Veronica wasn't her mother had been unbearable enough, but this...

Claire took a few deep breaths to try to steady the shaking.

What had Audrey's father meant, Veronica should never have taken her? Her mother wasn't a kidnapper.

He had to be confused, that was the only rational explanation.

Her phone rang. She wanted to ignore it, but something compelled her to look at it.

Hockey Opportunity Camp flashed across the screen.

Shoot. Something had to have happened with Lilah, otherwise they didn't call.

"Hello?" Claire croaked.

"Is this Claire?"

"Yes, it is. What's going on?" Claire asked.

"Hi, my name is Emma and I'm calling from HOC," she started.

"What is it? Is Lilah okay?"

"Everything's fine. Lilah's okay. She had a bit of a reaction to something she ate, and she said it had never happened before so we wanted to give you a call. Just a courtesy call. Lilah wanted to speak to you and we thought we could allow it this time."

"Put her on," Claire said. "Please."

"Mom?"

Lilah's voice was like cool lake water. It calmed Claire, brought her body temperature down.

"Lilah," Claire said. She tried to make her voice sound normal.

"Are you okay? You sound weird."

Claire closed her eyes. Thank goodness for Lilah. "I'm okay."

"You don't sound it. Do you miss me too much? I can come home if you're too lonely."

Claire paused. She couldn't trust herself to speak yet.

After a moment, she took another breath in. "I'm doing okay. You don't need to come home. How's camp? What happened?"

"I don't know. My stomach started cramping up even though I was only eating fries."

"Did you check to see if it was—" Claire started to say.

Lilah cut her off. "It's not. I checked. I'm fine." She didn't want to discuss the potential of getting her first period while away at camp. Claire couldn't blame her. "I'm going to drink a lot of water. I mostly wanted to call to check on you."

That wasn't like Lilah. Claire frowned. She unclenched from the ball she was in and stood. A passerby gave her an odd look but kept walking.

"Is she still there?" Lilah asked.

"Who?" Although Claire knew who Lilah meant.

"Audrey. Is she with you?"

"Yes," Claire said. She couldn't lie.

"Why?"

"I don't know. It's complicated."

"Do you want her around?" Lilah asked.

What a good question. Claire hadn't thought of it as so simple before. Did she want Audrey in her life? That seemed to have been pushed back in her mind. She was instead consumed by learning her mother wasn't her mother, and now she was meant to believe she was also a kidnapper? No. It didn't make any sense. She gave her head a tiny shake. Even though

Audrey's father had said it, Claire wanted to push it out of her mind.

"I think so."

"She seems nice," Lilah said.

"Yeah," Claire agreed. That much was true. Audrey was nice. She had been so thoughtful during all of this, and Claire hadn't really let her in. Shame rippled through her. She needed to be a better person to Audrey. "Anyway, how's camp?" Claire asked. "Are you having fun?"

"It's good." The typical Lilah answer. Claire had to ask more probing questions if she wanted anything other than *good* as a response.

"Are you eating some healthy foods? Veggies? Some protein maybe?"

"Yes, I'm eating healthy." Lilah's voice was back to its usual tone when Claire asked too many questions: slightly exasperated. That was a positive sign. "I should probably go. They told me I can't talk too long."

"Okay, Li. Thank you for calling."

"You sure you're okay?"

"I promise," Claire said. She tried her hardest to sound upbeat.

"Okay, tell Dad I say hi. And Mom?" Lilah's tone was airy and light. She was happy. "I love you."

Claire closed her eyes. Those words were like a balm to her sore heart. "Love you, too. See you soon."

They hung up. Claire looked around her and realized she was completely lost. Both in this town and in the world. It was a terrible feeling to think you knew who you were and your place, only to be completely overwhelmed by doubt and uncertainty. She had spent most of her life being safe and careful. Now she didn't even know how to properly grieve, not to mention understand who she was supposed to be and how much she was supposed to hide from Lilah. Claire felt like she knew very little for sure.

All she knew in this moment was that she was on a street called Regal. She sat on the bench and gave herself some time. After a while, she glanced back down at her phone and called Audrey's number.

"Can you come get me?" She told Audrey the name of the street and what was nearby.

Audrey's voice was low, as if she understood everything and Claire didn't need to say another word. "I'll be right there."

Audrey showed up on Regal only a few minutes later. Her face was pale. She looked at Claire but didn't say anything when she got in the car.

"Is your dad alright?" Claire asked. "Do you think we could go back to Summerville now?" She didn't have to explain that she couldn't stand to be here any longer.

Audrey nodded. "He's good." And then she drove.

They took the highway ahead and went straight, leaving the suburbs behind. After a few hours, Claire took some comfort in the familiar sights of Summerville. Up ahead was the pie and coffee shop on the corner of one of the main intersections next to an independent grocery store. They drove past the abandoned steepled church nestled into a bend in the narrow road. It wouldn't be long before she arrived back home.

"Are you ready to talk?" Audrey asked suddenly. They hadn't spoken more than two words during the car ride. Now they were somehow already back at Claire's house, in her driveway.

"Why don't you come in? I can make us coffee," Claire said numbly. Keeping herself busy was how she operated in crisis. Even though her hands were still shaking, she could go through the motions of brewing them coffee.

Once it was ready, she poured them two big mugs full. She splashed almond milk into hers and handed Audrey her mug to fill it the way she liked. It was as if she were on autopilot.

They went out to the covered porch and took seats on one of the couches. The sound of kids playing in the lake floated up to them. It was late afternoon in July, the perfect time to be out in the water as a kid. Claire longed for that feeling again, of being a kid in summer.

"How was your father after I left?" Claire asked. It pained her to speak, but she wanted to show Audrey she appreciated her. Audrey had done so much for her.

Audrey shrugged. "It's hard. He has good moments and bad moments. He's not always lucid and he struggles to remember, but when he does, he's usually able to think clearly, and what he says is true." Audrey looked at her carefully, as if she knew what she said was difficult to hear.

"I'm sorry," Claire said. She didn't really know what for. For all of it, she supposed.

"After you left... he did say a little more." Audrey rubbed at her lips while her eyebrows drew together.

Claire stiffened. What more could there be? The words *she took you* moved through her mind again. Her mother took her away from someone or something? It was incomprehensible. She had instantly wanted to get home to go through her mother's files again, but even now she realized it was probably futile. What could she find that would explain any of this?

"He said that Veronica took you from the neighbors. He also said at the time, he never knew if she'd really done it; she'd talked about it, seemed obsessed with getting you out of that house, to the point that she seemed to have stopped caring about me. He said she barely reacted when he told her he was leaving and taking me with him." Audrey's face was pale and drawn. Her jaw flexed and she pressed her lips together.

"She kidnapped me?" Claire asked. She hadn't yet said the word out loud.

Audrey nodded.

Claire's throat thickened. Her body was cold, even though it was summer. She was taken from the neighbors? A kidnapped child. How could that be possible? Whoever had lived in that rundown house next to Veronica and Audrey might have been her biological parents. Claire tried to picture what her birth mother might have looked like. Was her hair the same color? Did she have a similar face shape? The details were impossible to work out, and she couldn't think straight; how could a regular, everyday person like Veronica kidnap a child and get away with it? It just wasn't possible.

"Wait. She stopped caring about you?" Claire asked. That wasn't possible either. Not for someone as loving as Veronica.

Audrey nodded and then pressed a palm to her mouth. Her eyes filled with tears.

"Oh, God. I'm so sorry." Claire moved to Audrey's side and put an arm around her shoulders. After a moment of silence, she spoke again. "What else did your father say?"

"He said something about telling Veronica he was taking me away from her. He didn't want me around her when she seemed so unstable, so obsessed. He never wanted to see her again."

"Is that how we ended up here?" Claire said quietly, looking around her. The lake was flat and smooth. The trees were so green right now, so gorgeous in the way they moved slowly in the summer breeze. It all felt so surreal. Like she couldn't possibly imagine what was truth and what wasn't. "Did he tell you where we used to live?"

"No. He couldn't remember. And I know this all sounds bizarre, but I believe he's telling the truth about everything. What he remembers is vivid. He took me away from her to protect me. And she let me go."

They were silent for a long time. Eventually, Claire found it within her to speak again.

"I can't understand why she would do that. How could she do that to you? How could she be okay with your father taking you away?" Claire remembered all the crying her mother used to do back then, but was it enough? Did it match the gravity of the situation? Claire couldn't imagine the intense pain she would feel if anyone took Lilah from her. She wouldn't be able to live.

"She chose you," Audrey said. She pointed her face down and looked at the ground. "I don't know what was wrong with me." Her voice broke.

Claire's head pounded. Even though she had been hit with this, and it was ridiculously hard to understand, she could see how upset Audrey was. They had both been blasted with bombs. Audrey's mother had left her behind. That had to be an awful realization.

Claire found herself wondering about her real parents, but then shook her head. She couldn't think of them as her real parents; it felt unkind to Veronica. Veronica was her mother, even with this new knowledge. That hadn't changed for Claire. It couldn't. She was a grown woman, a mother herself, not a child in need of her parents. She didn't want her idea of Veronica to be altered, and she couldn't welcome this tidal wave of change because it was too complicated. It didn't fit into her life.

"I wonder why the police didn't find me," Claire said. She tried, but couldn't piece it all together. Her mother had kidnapped her from her neighbor. Veronica was separated from her own biological daughter. And then she was never found out? It didn't make any sense. "Did he tell you why she didn't try to get you back?"

Audrey shook her head. "I only got bits of it. Everything is so hard for him now." Her shoulders drooped low.

Claire looked back out at the water. What on earth could she do now? She had a strong urge to call Greg.

"I have nobody," Audrey said. Her voice was so small, it caused Claire's chest to hitch. "Do you think... I mean, is there any chance I could stay here with you? Just for a little bit? We could try to figure this out together. I think we might need each other."

Claire's immediate reaction was to say no. There was a part of her that knew there was no way she could handle having Audrey here. She still didn't know her all that well, and she didn't want someone around her while she tried to process all of this. A larger part of her, however, knew that they were tied together. When she looked at Audrey, at the pain etched on her face now as she stared out at the lake, she couldn't help but feel for this woman, who was almost her sister. They were connected by their pasts and by Veronica. They both needed answers, and this had been so hard on Audrey, too. She had been nothing but warm and kind to Claire. Besides, Claire's house would feel empty for another week and a half while Lilah was at camp. Nothing was normal or ordinary right now, so why not?

Claire touched her forehead. "Okay," she said.

Audrey's head shot up and her eyes locked onto Claire's. "Really?"

"Yeah," Claire said. She found herself once again hoping she wouldn't regret this. Something inside her sensed she wouldn't.

"Thank you," Audrey said quietly. After a while, she spoke again. "What do you think we should do first? Where do we even begin?"

Claire sat back and put her mug of coffee to her lips. Her hands still had a slight shake to them, but it was quieting. It was so odd to be here, surrounded by the beauty of Summerville, to feel so at home in a place she was raised by her mother, where she had felt safe all her life, knowing now that it was mostly a lie. There was no way she could ever be the same, but she also knew that the only thing that would help now was finding some truth. Some reason why.

It came to her then, right after she took a sip of her coffee and put her mug down on the table in front of her. Maybe it was the scent, rich and nutty, and the way it reminded her of her mother and early mornings by the lake together. Maybe it was because her mother used to sit out by the water with her friend, the way Audrey and Claire were sitting now. From afar, they likely looked like friends, relaxed and unshaken.

"I'm going to call her best friend Fatima," Claire said.

Audrey nodded and took a sip of her coffee, too. "Maybe she knew me."

There were so many maybes to uncover.

FIFTEEN

When Claire was a kid, there weren't many grownups in her mother's circle. It never struck Claire as odd at the time. Her mother was a self-proclaimed homebody. She went to work, they went on small outings together, but Veronica rarely went on dates or had nights out with coworkers or dinner with friends. There was only Fatima.

Claire's mother loved telling her the story of how she and Fatima first met. It was one afternoon at the grocery store, when Fatima had tried to pay for her groceries and realized only at the checkout, a cart full of food in front of her, that she had forgotten her wallet. She had no way to pay. Veronica, who was standing next in line to Fatima, felt for her. What a pain, and the man at the checkout counter was being unreasonably rude. Veronica wasn't sure why; it was an honest mistake.

Fatima tried to explain to the checkout man that she had the money, she just needed to get her wallet, but he rolled his eyes and sighed rudely. Something about the dismissiveness of the man bothered Veronica. Everyone should be treated with basic human decency, even when they made mistakes. Veronica pulled out her wallet to pay for Fatima's groceries. She had enough cash to pay for them and her own because she had just gone to the bank that morning.

Fatima tried to stop her, to tell her she didn't need to. "You don't have to save me," she said, a sharpness to her tone.

Veronica was surprised. "I'm not trying to." She eyed the checkout man and then spoke quietly so only Fatima could hear. "I want to get out of this one's presence. He's a ray of sunshine, isn't he?"

Fatima looked from Veronica to the checkout man and back at Veronica again. Then she laughed, a deep, hearty laugh. The man gave them both a dirty look.

Veronica ended up paying and Fatima thanked her. Veronica nodded and then left the store quickly. Shortly after that, a bouquet of flowers and a basket of treats from the bakery in town arrived at Veronica's front door. So did Fatima. Claire remembered that part. She was thrilled, she loved the cookies and fresh cinnamon buns from the bakery, but she also remembered how, at the time, Veronica had frowned at seeing Fatima on her front step.

"You were hard to find, but I have my ways," Fatima had said.

"I don't usually have many guests." Veronica had spoken in a stilted manner. It was true, they didn't have many unexpected visitors. But despite her initial cool response, Veronica soon moved to one side of the doorway, making room for Fatima to come in.

There was something about Fatima that Claire couldn't put her finger on. She was drawn to her. So was Veronica, Claire could tell. That was just Fatima's innate charm. Veronica and Claire both soon came to find out that Fatima was full of light and energy. She laughed loudly and told great stories and almost always seemed to be in a good mood. She brought food or wine with her whenever she came over, and she always spoke to Claire like she was the most interesting person in the world.

Veronica and Fatima were instant friends. They could often be found sitting outside on Veronica's porch and playing cards or just watching the water and talking. On Sundays, Fatima joined Claire and Veronica for dinners. Fatima's partner at the time worked long hours, and she hated being alone. She was the extrovert to Veronica's introvert. Claire thought it was funny how different they were, but somehow their friendship worked. It not only worked, they were as close as Claire imagined sisters to be.

That was why now, on the back porch with her mug of coffee in hand and Audrey across from her, Claire was certain Fatima must know something. After she took the last sip, she pulled out her phone and called her mother's only friend. She hadn't seen Fatima since the funeral. They both had a lot going on in their lives.

"Hey, you," Fatima said when she answered. Her voice was low, like she was tired. "How are you holding up?"

"I've had a lot going on," Claire said. "Can I come see you? I want to ask you some things about my mom."

"Sure," Fatima replied. "But I'll come to you. I've got a bottle of red I've been meaning to share with you."

"Someone else is here," Claire said. She didn't want to blindside Fatima with Audrey, especially if she knew who Audrey was.

"Oh, yeah? That's fine. The more, the merrier. I'll bring two bottles of wine then." She chuckled a little.

They made arrangements for Fatima to come over within the next hour, and then Claire waited. This would be interesting.

· · ·

When Fatima arrived, she kissed Claire on the cheek and squeezed her into a tight hug. After she pulled away, Fatima whisked through the house to the kitchen and opened up cupboards. She located three wineglasses and pulled them down.

"Where do you keep your bottle opener again?" she asked, pulling open drawers one right after the other.

"Right here." Claire handed her the opener and watched as Fatima went straight to work opening the bottle and pouring three glasses.

"I hope your friend likes Cabernet from California. I didn't even think to ask," Fatima said.

"It's fine. That's nice of you."

"If we're going to have a chat about our favorite person, it might as well be over a good bottle of wine." Fatima smiled and touched the side of Claire's face, the way Claire liked to touch Lilah's soft cheek. "Out back on the porch?" Fatima asked.

Claire nodded. She picked up one of the glasses of wine and followed Fatima outside to where Audrey was sitting.

"This is Audrey," Claire said carefully. She watched Fatima for a reaction, but there wasn't one. If she knew anything, Fatima didn't show it.

"Nice to meet you," Fatima said. She took a seat and motioned for Claire to sit. "How have you been doing? Are you holding up okay?"

Claire took in a breath. "There's been a lot going on."

She explained as much as she could, about how Audrey had found out about Veronica and about Claire. How they thought Audrey was her sister, but it turned out she wasn't. Everything Claire could choke out, she did.

"My mom. She's Audrey's mother, but she isn't... she's not my mother," Claire said. She slumped back into her chair, weary from so much truth.

Fatima's face was unreadable at first. She remained very still, frozen in place. Then her eyes filled with tears. "Claire. My God."

"What did you know?" Claire asked. She tried not to sound too accusatory, but it would be almost impossible to believe Fatima wouldn't know anything. She was too close to Veronica.

"I—I didn't know any of it." Her voice was shaky.

"Nothing? Did she tell you about Audrey? Or that I wasn't her child?"

Fatima stared over Claire's shoulder, out toward the lake, her mouth hanging partially open. Her gaze was distant and glassy. "Nothing like that, no," Fatima said. "I suppose some of the little things make sense now."

"Like what?" Claire asked. She glanced over at Audrey, who was shifting in her seat, straightening her back and leaning forward at the waist, as if she was waiting for more. Fatima looked back at Claire.

"Well, she never took you anywhere outside the country, for one. You never had a passport. For a while, I thought it was due to money, but she had enough."

"Mom was a homebody," Claire said. How long would she keep referring to her as mom? "She didn't like to go far."

"She never went out of her comfort zone," Fatima agreed. "I thought that was just Veronica. But maybe she was afraid of being found out."

"Did she tell you where she lived before here?"

Fatima shook her head.

Claire studied Fatima for a moment. This woman was her mother's best friend. She had been around for as long as Claire could remember. It was hard to believe she knew nothing about this.

"I really can't believe it. Could it be true?" Fatima shook her head slowly. Then she touched the bridge of her nose with her finger and thumb, like she had a headache.

"What about Audrey?" Claire asked. Audrey looked up, hopeful.

Fatima's eyebrows pushed together, and her head tilted. "I'm so sorry, but I don't have any information. I thought you were... gone, just like she always said."

An anger roiled through Claire, hot and fierce. It struck her that she hadn't been angry at Veronica yet, but now it was all coming to a head. How could a mother do something like this? To Audrey and to Claire. To take someone else's child and leave your own. Claire didn't want to admit it, but that was the sign of someone who had something very wrong with them. It was so messed up and there was nothing she could clear up, no answers she could get, because Veronica was gone.

"Are you okay?" Fatima asked. Now her eyebrows were high up on her forehead. Claire's face must be giving her away. She couldn't hide an intense feeling like this.

"No, I'm not. I'm not okay at all," Claire replied. She sat upright in her seat, placing her hands on the arms of the chair like she was going to stand up. "My entire life is in question. I don't know anything about who I am, or who she was. She destroyed my life and Audrey's. I don't know where my real parents are or even who they are." Claire's voice was rising, getting louder and louder. She couldn't stop it. The anger took over. "Who am I?"

"Hey," Fatima said, her voice shaking. "Hey, I know. I can't believe this either. And none of this is okay, but even though there isn't much I know, I'm certain she was a good mother to you."

Claire let out a harsh bark of a laugh. Audrey's face had a pained expression.

"No, she was," Fatima said. "She loved you so much." She turned to Audrey. "And even though she didn't speak about you often, when she did, there was so much love in her words, too.

She may have made some terrible choices that we don't understand yet, but I know she loved you both. Try to hold onto that."

Claire wasn't sure that was possible, but she didn't say it.

Fatima pushed her wineglass away from her before she
stood up. "I should get going."

"Already?" Claire's muscles tensed up in surprise. Fatima
always stayed for longer than one quick drink. She usually liked
to linger and chat about anything and everything for hours.

"I just remembered... there's something I need to check on."
She fumbled over her words. Then she leaned in to kiss Claire
on the cheek and reached out to touch Audrey's arm. "Nice to
meet you, Audrey."

Claire stood to walk her to the door, but Fatima waved her
away.

"Stay here. I'm good. I can find my way."

After she left, Claire sat back in her chair and tried not to
overthink. It was almost impossible.

"Was it weird how quickly Fatima left?" Audrey asked.

"Yeah, it was," Claire answered. Everything was weird and
uncomfortable.

"So, now what?"

Claire thought about it. They had nothing further to go on
from Audrey's father, nothing from Fatima. She felt helpless,
which also made her feel like things were beyond her control.
Her heart rate sped up, so she took in a deep breath and let it
out slowly.

"I have no idea what to do next," Claire said out loud,
although on the inside, she was thinking about calling the
police. She could ask if there was any information from forty
years ago. It felt like a stretch, but at least she would be doing
something. Then her mind flashed to Lilah at camp. When she
eventually came home, would any of this be resolved? "Please
don't say anything about this to Lilah when she gets home. I
have to sort it all out in my head and get some more information

first. I need to find out what really happened before her view of her grandmother is shattered."

"Of course," Audrey said.

They sat on the dock for a while longer, mostly in silence, and Claire wondered how she was going to keep something so monumental and huge from her daughter.

SIXTEEN

Audrey and Claire ended up finishing the bottle of wine, then they went inside and washed the glasses. Claire showed Audrey Lilah's room and told her she could sleep there. Audrey tried to refuse, she didn't want to impose, but Claire insisted it would be fine.

"Do you think she'll mind?" Audrey asked.

"No," Claire said, and she meant it. Even though Lilah could be so much like a teenager at times, with unpredictable mood swings, she could also be gracious. Besides, she might not even know Audrey had been staying here. Lilah wasn't due back home for another week and a half. The only thing Claire had to figure out in that time was how to keep the weight of this secret from Lilah. It was too much to put on a twelve-year-old.

"I have a spare toothbrush somewhere in the bathroom," Claire said. They stood in Lilah's room after Claire had found a pair of pajamas for Audrey to borrow.

"Thank you. I'll go home tomorrow to pick up some things. I'm sorry about this—I just don't want to be alone while we're going through all of it."

"It's fine, really," Claire assured her again.

"Are you going to go to bed now?" Audrey asked.

Claire held her phone up. "Actually, I was thinking I would try to do some more research. There has to be something I can find." She knew she had to try to get some facts to confirm that what she'd learnt was true. Fatima hadn't been able to help, but maybe there would be some document online or report about a missing child that would prove it—or disprove it. For a brief, fleeting moment, after seeing Audrey there in Lilah's room holding onto her pajamas, Claire wished there was some way she and Audrey could be in one another's lives without learning about any of this.

"Do you want to find them?" Audrey asked. She meant Claire's biological parents, Claire could tell.

She shrugged. Maybe she did. She wasn't sure. She was forty-three years old. What did she expect to find at this stage? She hadn't spent her life knowing she wasn't Veronica's biological daughter, so she didn't have a deep desire to connect with a mother figure. She had a mother. There was no real need for justice either. Now that Veronica was gone, there was nobody to arrest, and Claire wouldn't want that for her mother anyway. She couldn't deny that she was curious, however. What if her name or her photo was posted somewhere? What if she had other family out there? She supposed it was natural to feel curious about what might have happened to you as a child, or what your full life story might be.

"I can't believe I never knew," Claire said, shaking her head.

"How could you? You were too young to remember anything, and you had no reason to think it. Who would ever dream up that their mother wasn't their mother?" Audrey moved an inch closer to Claire, but stopped short of trying to comfort her with a touch. "I thought I might do some digging, too. Do you want to do it together?"

At her deepest core, Claire wanted answers. In this case, she wasn't sure what she would do if she found out who these two people were who were biologically related to her, but at least she would have the knowledge.

Claire nodded. "I'll get my laptop."

They went downstairs to the living room and Claire settled herself on the couch, her laptop propped up in front of her. There were several websites dedicated to finding missing children, but nothing as far back as Claire needed. She tried searching her name, but found nothing unusual. She even used her library account to look through archives of old newspapers. There seemed to have been nothing in the press about parents looking for their lost child forty years ago. It was a stretch to think her birth parents would have lived nearby in this area, but Claire didn't have anything else to go on.

"I wish we knew something more than what we've got," Claire said.

"I know." Audrey scrolled through her phone. "I've found nothing."

"Do you think we should call the police?" Claire asked. She worried that calling them might uncover more problems—what if there was paperwork she would have to fill out or medical records she would have to get hold of?

"I think so," Audrey said. "Only, what would we tell them? We don't know where that house was or if your name was the same as it is now."

It felt helpless.

Claire nodded and went back to scrolling through page after page online. After searching for at least an hour, she came across a statistic that said the majority of missing persons cases were resolved within a week, but that approximately five hundred cases were left unresolved every year. Claire's lips pinched together. Her head pounded and her eyes were tired and sore. Five hundred. What were her chances of finding anything about herself? Or maybe none of this was true, maybe there was some rational explanation for everything that her brain could understand if she wasn't so tired.

She closed her laptop. It was all so tense and confusing. She needed a release.

"Do you want to go somewhere with me tomorrow morning?" Claire surprised herself with the invitation, but she could use a break from all the heaviness.

"Sure. Where?"

"Skeleton Lake," Claire said. "It's one of my favorite places. We used to go there all the time when I was a kid. Veronica didn't take me on trips out of the country, but she took me to Skeleton Lake and I loved it."

Audrey smiled. "I'd love a little break and a trip to the beach."

"Okay, I'll pack us a lunch." Claire could try to delay the grief and the confusion over everything for one more day.

"Sounds great. Are you off to bed?" Audrey asked.

"Yeah. I'm wiped."

"Me, too," Audrey said. "Goodnight. Have a good sleep." She smiled at Claire, a tired smile. Audrey's face was drawn. She must have been exhausted, too.

Claire touched Audrey's arm and it didn't feel odd or unwelcome. She allowed herself to like this moment; having someone to sit next to and talk to, to share thoughts with, someone to look out for and someone to look out for her in return. It felt natural and comfortable. Claire smiled back, maybe for the first time in what felt like a very long time.

The next morning, the drive to Skeleton Lake took just over an hour. When they arrived, Claire pulled over at the edge of the road right under a canopy of trees to park.

Audrey craned her neck to look around. "What? Here? You're just going to stop your car here?"

"There's no parking lot."

"There's no beach either. I thought we were going to the lake?" Audrey said.

Claire smiled. "Follow me."

She got out of the car and grabbed her bag and the beach chairs from the back seat. Then she crossed the gravel road and took the path that didn't look like it was public access. She glanced over her shoulder to make sure Audrey wasn't far behind and caught sight of Audrey's face. Her brow was furrowed, and her mouth was turned down. She was speed walking to keep up, like she might get lost if she didn't. It did seem like you were lost, but this was part of the charm of the place. Claire used to love following her mother through a short path of trees and grass that quickly led to the opening and the very small beach that gave way to the lake. It had a magical air to it, the kind that could impress upon a child.

"This is it," Claire said when they came out of the clearing. She could almost taste the lake water on her lips, cold and fresh. How long had it been since she had come here? It had to be at least a year. She didn't visit it as often once summer was over, but she should. She could feel her stress levels instantly going down at the nostalgia of her surroundings.

"It's beautiful," Audrey breathed. She came up to Claire and stood beside her. "The beach is smaller than I expected."

It was a tiny patch of land, a rectangle made up of dark sand with bushes and trees on either side of it. But in front of the beach was the lake that stretched as far out as you could see. It was relatively quiet, with only a few boats way out on the horizon. It didn't look like anything extremely magical when you saw it with adult eyes, but there was something undeniable about it. It was peaceful and almost always quiet. They were in luck today; nobody else was there.

Claire placed her towel on the sand and unfolded her beach chair. It was low to the ground, so when she sat in it, she could stretch her legs right out in front of her. Audrey did the same. Claire placed her bag in between them and propped it open before searching for her bottle of water.

"Help yourself. I brought loads of snacks," Claire said.

Audrey had already reclined back into her seat and placed her hands over her stomach. Her eyes, partially hidden behind a pair of sunglasses, were focused on the horizon.

"It's so calming," she said. "What is it about this place in particular that makes it seem like a little oasis?"

"I don't know. I thought it was because my mom always brought me. We spent so many summer days here—swimming, eating picnic lunches, talking. It was our place." It had been perfect. Claire found it still was, despite everything. It was soothing to be there again.

"Thank you for bringing me." Audrey turned her head to look at Claire.

Claire nodded.

"Now that I'm an adult, I can see that the magical quality to it can't be explained." Claire shifted in her seat and stretched her arms over her head to pull her shirt off. She adjusted the strap of her black one-piece bathing suit that was underneath. "Wait until you get in the water. Want to join me?"

Audrey stood and pushed her shorts down and then kicked them off with one foot. "Lead the way."

Claire searched through her bag until she found two pairs of snorkel masks and then went toward the shallow water. When they waded in, Audrey recoiled for only a second.

"It's so cold!" she gasped.

"It warms up partway out there."

"How far are we going?"

Claire pointed way out at the horizon. "See where the water goes dark blue?"

"Yeah."

"That's where the drop-off is. You can walk out until there and the water will only come up to about shoulder height."

"That far?"

It was another part of the charm of Skeleton Lake. It had a sandbar which meant it was shallow. As a kid, she used to follow her mother in the water and not worry about being unable to touch the bottom. She did somersaults and handstands and her mother watched, smiling and laughing at her enthusiasm.

Claire kept walking forward, enjoying the feel of the cool water on her legs, swirling around her calves. Audrey followed, bending over every once in a while to run her fingertips through the lake. It was such a quiet moment, nothing special, but Claire felt close to Audrey. They were two women who had met only recently and, for a brief moment, thought they were sisters. Now they were here together trying to forge ahead through the shallows and determine what their futures should look like together. Everything that had happened to Claire had also happened to Audrey.

Claire stopped. "Here." She handed Audrey one of the snorkel masks. "This is my favorite part."

"What is?" Audrey asked. She had a slight, confused smile as she strapped the mask to her face. She turned her head toward Claire just as Claire finished putting her mask on. Both of them looked ridiculous, with the way the masks pressed on their skin and made their lips stick out. They laughed at each other, Audrey pointing at Claire and Claire pointing back.

"Come on," Claire said. She dove forward, momentarily shocked by the cold. Her body adjusted quickly, and she pushed ahead a few strokes and then felt herself float up to the surface of the shallow water. The sun was shining and it warmed her back while creating beams of yellow through the water that illuminated the ground underneath her.

It was quiet, the way it is underwater. Claire floated,

pushing herself forward every now and again, scanning the ground for little rocks and shells, pieces of plants and grass. Tiny fish swam by her in a school. This was part of the magic. This was where she felt most relaxed, in her own watery world, a pool of silence; no talking, only floating and observing. Weightless.

Audrey swam up beside her and smiled at Claire. Her hair floated wildly around her face. She pointed at a tiny crab below them and looked back at Claire again with a bigger smile. Claire loved the way the water made you childlike. She smiled, too.

They kicked their feet gently, side by side, with their arms at their sides and heads moving from left to right as they observed everything below them. When they came up to the surface, Claire sat on the bottom of the lake with her shoulders and head above the water. She pulled her mask off at the same time that Audrey did.

"It's so beautiful here!" Audrey exclaimed. She looked up toward the sun and pushed her hair off her face. "No wonder you love it."

They stayed there for a while and then swam some more, gliding through the coolness. They didn't say more than a few words to each other, but Claire felt another surge of fondness for Audrey. It was as if she understood what Claire needed and knew how to be a participant in it. She was gracious.

"Thank you," Claire said afterwards when they were back on the beach.

Audrey nodded but said nothing.

Being here at Skeleton Lake gave Claire a new sense of calm. She felt ready to face everything again, so eventually, she brought up the topic of the photo. "We need to find out where we were in that photo. Where we used to live."

Audrey turned to face her. She didn't speak.

"If we knew that, we'd be able to find some answers," Claire said. "Like who lived there, if there was a search conducted in the area."

"I wasn't sure how you felt about continuing on with all of that after not finding much last night," Audrey said quietly.

Claire brushed some sand off her leg. It was hard for her to know, too. She did know she needed some kind of answer so she could stop wondering. Though she wasn't sure yet if she wanted to find her parents. She could only handle so much pain at once. On the other hand, she felt the need for some closure. Something she could put away in a box and not need to think about again.

"How do you feel about all of it?" Claire asked.

"I don't know." Audrey frowned. "I'd like to know more about who I am."

That was the real question. Who was Claire? Who was Audrey? More importantly, who could they be for one another?

Claire realized now that she hoped they would have a chance to find out.

SEVENTEEN

Over the next week, Claire and Audrey learned how to live with one another. It was a little like having a roommate, Claire supposed, although she had never had one before. She had gone from living with her mother to her first home with Greg. This was different. Neither one of them spoke about the moment when Audrey would leave and go back home. Claire decided that if Audrey wasn't going to talk about it, she wouldn't either. She only admitted this to herself, but she didn't want to break the spell that floated around them. Despite the trauma of the last few days, it was a peaceful kind of feeling as they spent the time getting to know one another, sitting out on the dock chatting, making dinner together. Claire had called Greg to tell him everything she had learned, and he wanted to come over immediately, but Claire told him it would be better if it were just her and Audrey for the time. They were figuring it out together. They were also doing more research into the past, although they hadn't found anything yet. Nevertheless, Claire had a glowing inside her stomach. It was like they both belonged here, and Claire felt settled. She wondered if this was what it felt like to have a sister in your life as an adult.

One morning, Claire found Audrey standing in the kitchen by the cupboard, pulling a mug down from the shelf.

"Oh," Audrey said. "Is it okay if I grab some?" She held up her mug with one hand and gestured to the coffee maker with the other.

"Of course." Claire set down the laundry basket she had been carrying. "You don't have to keep asking me if it's okay to do things." She meant it, and again was surprised at how easily she found Audrey fit here. They were comfortable when they moved past one another in the hallway or sat together in the living room reading.

"Thanks," Audrey said. "Can I get you some?"

"That would be great. I was going to go down to the dock. Want to come?"

"Sure," Audrey answered.

Sitting on the dock with coffee was one of Claire's favorite things to do. If she wasn't out there with her mother, she used to go with Greg when they were married. She had adjusted quickly to the silence of being alone after Greg, but having Audrey join her reminded her of how nice it was to share a moment like this. A lot of what she did was solitary after Greg moved out. You tended to forget how alone you were when the person you spent all your time with was no longer there. She didn't want someone else romantically, that thought hadn't crossed her mind, but she did like company. She did like moments like this.

"What are your plans for the rest of the summer?" Claire asked.

"I don't really have any." Audrey glanced sideways at Claire.

Claire folded her legs under her. She took her sweater off and placed it on the arm of her chair. It was warm now early in the mornings, but it wouldn't be long before the air chilled. It was a sign of summer starting to change. It didn't escape Claire that it was already the end of July and time was moving quickly. School would start in just over a month. Life would resume, and Claire would need to go back to it—and to work. What would it be like when Audrey left? Claire felt a swooping sensation inside her, like her stomach was dropping. It wasn't just the company she liked. It was Audrey.

"I've been thinking more and more about our past. There has to be something somewhere that would help us narrow down our search," Claire said. They had spent so many hours researching these last few days with no luck. She wasn't ready to give up, though. Claire cast a sideways look at Audrey. She took a breath in. "I think we need more time. Do you want to stay here a little longer?"

Audrey shifted in her seat, but kept her gaze out on the water. "I'd love to." She smiled to herself.

They sat on the dock in silence. Even though Claire's mind was whirring with questions, and it felt almost impossible to decide where to start, let alone how she would find what she needed, Claire noticed her body felt calm. Her chest didn't hitch when she breathed, the way it did when she felt anxious or nervous. It was the realization that she wouldn't have to shoulder the burden or carry all the weight of this herself. She wasn't alone.

"What about Lilah?" Audrey asked. Claire was picking her up from camp tomorrow. She could hardly wait to see her again. "Will she mind me being here?"

Claire shook her head. "It'll be fine."

It would. Claire could feel it in her bones.

After going back home to pick up some more of her things and visit with her father that evening, Audrey found something. She'd been rummaging through the old filing cabinet at his home when she came across it.

"My birth certificate," Audrey said over the phone.

"What about it?"

"Until I looked at it again, I hadn't had a reason to think about it. It didn't click for me."

"What didn't click?" Claire asked.

"The town I was born in is only an hour and a half away from where I live now."

Claire's pulse sped up. "You think that might be where we lived?"

"It could be," Audrey said. "It's a place to start anyway."

Claire had thought this would set off a feeling of relief in her, but it didn't. She had spent so much time searching, but now that they had something, Claire didn't want to do anything with it. The realization shocked her. She had never had a panic attack before, but her body was now doing things she didn't understand. Her mouth had gone dry, her hands were shaking, and she was so dizzy and hot. What else could it mean that her body had reacted this way so swiftly and suddenly to the news that they might have a lead they could follow? It was too real, too fast.

"Want to call the local police there tomorrow?" Audrey asked.

Claire shook her head even though she was on the phone. "No," she choked. "I can't."

"Do you want to go visit them in person instead?"

"No," she repeated. "I don't want to. I'm not ready." Her voice was strangled, uncertain. A shudder ran through her body. She knew that she couldn't do this. Not yet. Once you opened that box up, you couldn't close it again. She might find out who her parents really were, and she might not like them. Or she'd learn things about Veronica she didn't want to know. The fact that Veronica was her mother and Lilah's grandmother didn't change for Claire.

"Okay," Audrey replied. Her voice was quiet. There was

something she wasn't saying, Claire was certain, but she wasn't sure she wanted to know. She changed the subject instead.

"Were you planning on coming back today?"

"Probably tomorrow now, once I've sorted a few things here. Is that okay with you?" Audrey asked.

"Of course," Claire said.

There was a silence over the phone and Claire wondered if Audrey had heard her.

Eventually, Audrey's voice came through the phone line. "Great, I'll see you then."

Claire's body felt light again, and she closed her eyes. Lilah would be home tomorrow. Audrey was going to stay for a while. She was safe here.

Late afternoon the next day, at the bus stop, Claire waited impatiently. She had promised Lilah she wouldn't run at her as soon as she saw her, like she had done the year before, but would let Lilah walk over to her. She was almost a teenager, Claire had to try to play it a little cooler than she was used to. Audrey had stayed back at the house, even though Claire had said it was okay if she came, too. Audrey didn't want to impose, so Claire had left for the bus stop alone, and also a tiny bit relieved. She wanted all of her focus to be on Lilah.

When Lilah walked off the bus, Claire's heart almost stopped. There she was. In the flesh. Her hair was wild, and her clothes wrinkled. Her body moved somewhat slower than usual, like she was tired, but her face was bright. She was happy. Claire's pulse sped up and she swallowed rather than calling out to Lilah, mostly because she knew her voice would break if she tried to speak.

My goodness, she'd missed Lilah. It was funny how seeing her daughter after a couple of weeks could create such a visceral response in her in a way that wouldn't happen in Lilah. This was the thing about mothers and daughters; when you were the mother, you loved your child more than she would ever love you, but it wasn't upsetting. It was the way it was supposed to be. It had taken Claire a long time to realize that.

Claire raised her arm in the air and waved. She could do that at least without later being accused of acting over the top or embarrassing.

Lilah spotted her and sauntered over casually, like it hadn't been weeks since she had been home.

"Lilah!" Claire shouted. "I missed you!"

Lilah's pace sped up a fraction as she neared Claire. Then she melted into Claire's open arms and allowed Claire to hold onto her without trying to break the embrace. This was her gift to Claire. The long, uninterrupted embrace said everything, so Lilah didn't need to.

"How are you?" Claire asked, her voice muffled by Lilah's hair.

"I'm good."

They eventually pulled apart and Claire grasped onto Lilah's elbows. She horrified herself by breaking down into ugly sobs.

"Mom?" Lilah's voice went up at the end and was filled with confusion.

Claire tried to speak, but she couldn't stop crying. She was completely overcome, by seeing and holding her daughter again, by what she would have to keep from her, by the thought of her own mother and the way they used to hug, just like Claire had hugged Lilah. Everything would be brought into question now, every little moment between Lilah and Claire would cause Claire to wonder if her mother had truly loved her and how she could take a daughter away from a mother.

"I'm okay," Claire said eventually. She wiped at her eyes with the edge of her hand.

A camp counsellor from the bus walked by Claire and

Lilah. "You're not supposed to cry *now*," she said. "You've got your kid back. She's home."

Claire sniffled and nodded. She tried to ignore Lilah's red cheeks, flushed with embarrassment, and picked up one of Lilah's bags.

"Let's go home," she said.

In the car, Claire asked every question she could think to ask about camp. She wanted to know everything. Then, when they were almost home, she told Lilah about Audrey.

"She's come to stay with us for a while."

"Why?" Lilah asked. Her head snapped to the side and her eyes focused on Claire's face. Claire could sense the intensity of her stare. "What's been going on?"

"Well, we haven't figured out much, but we feel like we could use one another's support," Claire said. She had to be careful.

Lilah turned back to look ahead, her sun-kissed and freckled brow slightly furrowed. Claire could tell she was thinking seriously about something.

"I don't get it. If Grandma wasn't your mom, and she's not my real grandma, but she's Audrey's mom, why is Audrey still here?" She meant it in a logical way. Claire knew Lilah well enough to know that even when she asked questions or made observations that sounded rude, she was simply looking for clarification. It just happened to be blunt.

"Well, first of all, Grandma may not have been my biological mother, but she raised me, and she's my mother." It was the first time Claire had said it out loud. "And she's your grandmother," she added. She wasn't about to tell her the part where her grandmother was a kidnapper.

"I know," Lilah said, "Still, I don't get why Audrey is staying."

"I think she wants to see if she can find out more about Grandma. And maybe find out what happened."

"Do you want to know what happened or where your real mom is?" Lilah asked.

Claire shrugged one shoulder. "I don't know." She did want answers, she had established that much, but she wasn't sure how she felt about her biological mother, a person she didn't know, who hadn't raised her. She must not have looked for Claire very hard. There hadn't been a trace of her all of Claire's life.

"What about your dad?" Lilah asked.

Claire sighed. "I honestly don't know what I want. What do you think about all of this?"

"I don't know either," Lilah said. She pointed her face to the right to look out her side window. The conversation was done. Claire almost felt relieved; there was so much more to say but it would probably take time for them both to feel ready.

When they arrived home, Audrey pushed herself up off the couch and came to meet them as Claire and Lilah walked through the door.

"Hi. I hope it's okay that I'm staying here with you and your mom," Audrey said.

Lilah didn't answer. Her eyes went to Claire's instead.

"We talked about it on the way over and it's completely fine," Claire said. "Right?" She looked at Lilah.

"Yep." Lilah dropped her bag and went into the kitchen.

"It's all good," Claire said to Audrey. She felt the need to apologize for her daughter. Twelve-year-old girls were hard to understand if you didn't have one.

"Okay." Audrey didn't look very sure of herself, but she lifted her chin and kept talking anyway. "I made all of us a snack." Her voice rose so Lilah would hear from the kitchen.

"You did?" Claire said.

"I hope that's okay." Audrey gestured toward the back deck. "I set it out."

Lilah had already started to head that way, toward the screen door, with Audrey and Claire following behind. Lilah pushed the door aside and stepped out onto the covered back deck.

"Chips? We never have chips around the house," Lilah exclaimed, her voice light.

"I ran to the store," Audrey said to Claire. "I thought I would get this ready in time for when you got back. I'm sure you don't want to do anything but spend time chatting."

On the table that sat in the middle of the deck was a spread of every kind of food that could delight a twelve-year-old—two bowls of chips and several small dishes of candies, chocolate-covered almonds and vanilla cupcakes—but there was also sliced raw vegetables and cubes of cheese, a platter of meats and fresh fruit as well.

"Wow." Claire's mouth hung open.

A smile flashed across Lilah's face. She pushed her curly hair off her forehead and then went straight for the bowl of chips. "This is awesome," she said. She turned to Audrey and grinned. "Thank you."

"No problem at all," Audrey replied. Then she smiled to herself. Claire thought she could detect a touch of pink in her cheeks.

EIGHTEEN

Claire got up early the next day. It would likely be hours before Lilah woke up. That first sleep at home in her own bed after a couple of weeks at camp was a heavy one. Last night, after sitting at the table and lingering over snacks, Lilah had filled Claire and Audrey in on everything she had done at camp. Then she went for a long, hot shower, put on clean pajamas and headed to bed early. When Claire went in to say goodnight, Lilah had looked up at her from the bed and Claire could see on her daughter's face how glorious her own comfortable bed covered with clean sheets felt. A simple pleasure, but one she wouldn't take for granted.

Claire went to the laundry room now and pulled Lilah's first load of laundry out of the dryer. She was happy to be able to bring Lilah other small joys, like fresh clothes. Later, she would make Lilah a big breakfast of pancakes and fruit salad. This part of summer was so nice, the time when Lilah came home from camp and was thrilled to be there. It surprised Claire to realize that she didn't mind sharing this time at all with Audrey. In fact, it was nice to have another person around to enjoy Lilah's company. For so long, it had been either just

Claire and her mother or just Claire and Lilah, but it had always been enjoyable when more people were around. Claire only wished Greg was there, too. He would get his time with Lilah soon enough.

After getting Lilah's laundry from the dryer, Claire intended to start mixing up the pancake batter and chopping up fruit. In the kitchen, Audrey's back was turned to her while she stood at the counter. Her upper body shook slightly, like she was doing something in front of her. She turned around when Claire said hello.

"Hi." Audrey smiled. On the counter was Claire's big stainless-steel mixing bowl, filled with pancake batter. "I thought I would start breakfast for Lilah. Do you want some?"

Claire's body deflated. "Oh."

"Is this okay?" Audrey's smile faltered. She glanced down at the counter.

Claire couldn't very well tell Audrey it wasn't okay that she did something kind for Lilah. It was nice, of course it was. Only, Claire had wanted to make breakfast for her daughter the morning she was back from camp. It was what she always did. She took care of Lilah, treating her to fresh sheets and clean clothes and a big breakfast made just the way she liked it—all the comforts of home.

Lilah came into the kitchen then, her face creased with lines from her pillow. "Are you making pancakes?" she asked sleepily.

Audrey hesitated, so Claire answered for her. "Yes. Audrey is. With fruit. You hungry?"

Lilah nodded and smiled. Audrey resumed whisking the pancakes. Claire pressed down the disappointment and went to get the maple syrup.

· · ·

Later that afternoon, when Lilah was busy in her room, Audrey and Claire were sitting out back reading. Claire put her book down and turned to Audrey. "I've been thinking more about calling the police in that town from your birth certificate."

Audrey's lips pressed together. She took a piece of her hair and fiddled with it.

"What?" Claire asked.

"I gave them a call already, when I was back home. I know you said you weren't ready, and I didn't want to upset you or push you into hearing about it because you seemed so uncertain after I first told you about finding it, but I just had to know if they could tell us anything."

Claire's mouth went dry. She was still uncertain, but the curiosity kept coming back to her, kept spreading within her, whether she wanted it to or not. "What did they say? Is that where we lived?"

"Nothing, unfortunately. No leads there. It's a dead end," Audrey said. She let go of her hair and her hands dropped to her lap. "But I found something else."

"What?"

Audrey paused. "You're sure?"

"Yes. Tell me."

"Okay. When I was at my father's house, after coming across my birth certificate, I wondered if there would be anything else I might find with a bit more digging."

"And?" Claire asked. She shifted in her seat, feeling stiff.

"I found a bunch of old mail in a filing cabinet. Envelopes and letters addressed to my father, but there was an address on it that wasn't familiar."

"Another city where that house from the picture might have been located?" Claire asked.

Audrey nodded.

Claire's head spun. Another lead. "Where was it? Did you call the police there, too?"

"It was Goderich. And no, I wanted to wait until you were ready for that one, at least until we'd had a chance to talk about it."

Claire's body relaxed. It was kind of Audrey to be so cautious. Yet, she knew the curiosity would likely never go away if they didn't follow the lead. She just wasn't quite ready yet.

"Think we could call later? Maybe tomorrow?" Claire asked.

Audrey nodded. "Of course. Only when you're ready."

It was hard to know if she would ever be.

A little while later, Claire took a nap. One of the best times to nap in Summerville was in July or August, in the middle of the afternoon with the bedroom window open so you could hear the wind whispering through treetops. It lulled Claire to sleep. She must have only been dozing, not quite fully asleep but not awake either, when she started to dream. She was somewhere unknown, and alone. She was okay at first, calm. It wasn't until she had been walking that a panic gripped her. She had no idea where she was. She didn't recognize her surroundings and didn't know where she was going. She tried to walk faster, but her legs were like lead. Claire was certain this was going to end up bad, she felt it in her bones. When she tried to call out, only a strangled yelp came from her throat.

That was when she felt it. A tender, soft kiss on her temple.

"Hey," a voice said.

Claire was back in her bedroom. Her eyes opened. Greg was standing over her.

"Hey," he said again. "You were upset. You cried out. I tried waking you, but it didn't work."

"Did you kiss me?" Claire asked. She was still in a muddled, hazy state after waking.

"Yes. It looks like that worked." Greg smiled, embarrassed.

"It did work. Thank you," Claire said. The kiss was soft and comforting, just like Greg. She rolled over and pushed herself up to sitting. Greg sat on the edge of the bed. "What are you doing here?"

"I wanted to see you and Lilah," he said. "Bad dream?"

"Just an anxious one. I felt lost," Claire replied.

Greg paused and looked at her intently. "Are you going to be okay?"

"I think—I mean, I hope so." Claire shivered.

Greg's forehead creased, but he didn't say anything.

"I'm still waking up," Claire said, as if that would explain the shiver. She wasn't cold though. She was unsettled. Greg could likely see it. "Can you lay with me for a minute?" It was a ridiculous question to ask your ex, but Claire knew Greg was the best at making her feel better just by being him, and it felt so nice when he was next to her.

"Sure." He stretched out beside her and Claire turned onto one side, so he could get closer.

"Thank you," she said in the quiet of the room.

Greg wrapped an arm around her tighter.

NINETEEN

The next several days were spent the way the last month of summer should be spent. Claire, Lilah and Audrey went for swims in the lake and then sat out on the dock to dry under the sun. The mornings usually started with Claire and Audrey drinking coffee in the same spot and the evenings ended back there with a glass of wine for them and a hot chocolate for Lilah. During the day, they sometimes went into town to shop and get ice cream. Lilah spent more time with them than Claire expected, but she didn't dare bring it up and break the spell.

For the most part, Audrey and Claire didn't discuss all the questions still swirling around them. It was like they'd both made a silent agreement to enjoy this time with Lilah, back from camp and eager to soak up the comforts of home. But within a few days, Claire told Audrey she was ready to call the local police in Goderich. The way her limbs tingled and her breath caught in her throat when she thought about it made Claire not so sure, but she couldn't sit on it forever either.

Claire did the talking while Audrey sat next to her, her forearms resting on her thighs, body bent forward. She watched Claire intently.

"I don't know any names of anyone involved. Unless there's a Claire Brown?" Claire said into the phone after the officer had answered her. She frowned at Audrey while she listened to the officer explain that they couldn't find anything under that name.

"There's a missing persons database available to the public," the officer suggested.

"I've tried that. No luck."

"Sorry," the officer said. She sounded busy, so Claire thanked her and clicked off her phone.

Audrey hung her head and sighed. "Back to the drawing board."

It felt like yet another dead end and was discouraging, so, instead of dredging up more questions, she focused on Lilah. Soon school would start, and Lilah would be preoccupied with her friends, hockey would start up, and Claire would feel like time was slipping by too fast. But for now, the days were slow and the nights lingered and because Claire didn't want to face any more disappointments, she tried her best to just be here, in the moment, with her daughter. Finding out who she was would have to wait.

One day, after they had already been swimming and draped their bathing suits over the backs of the chairs on the dock to dry, Claire made them lunch. She invited Greg to join them, too. It had been a while since he had spent time with Lilah, and Claire didn't want him to miss out.

In the kitchen, she chopped up crisp lettuce and rinsed it under the tap. Bacon was frying that she would turn into bacon bits later and the blender was filled with all the ingredients needed to make her own Caesar salad dressing. She had the luxury of time to make everything from scratch now. It didn't happen often when she was working, and she would have to return soon. Claire had told her coworkers she could come back when Lilah went to school. She hoped her coworkers weren't too put out. She knew how much it was to ask, so she made a mental note to thank them properly when she returned. She'd start by bringing them a box of butter tarts from the town bakery. Everyone loved those.

Claire looked up from the colander full of lettuce and out the large windows at the back of her house overlooking the lake. Audrey and Lilah were both outside, setting the table. Audrey said something Claire couldn't hear and Lilah's face lit up with laughter. She doubled over at the waist, her shoulders shaking. When she stood, her mouth was still open. She wrapped an arm around her stomach, like it hurt from laughing so hard, and then looked directly at Audrey. She smiled the most genuine smile Claire could recall seeing.

Tears sprang to Claire's eyes. Was it because it was a beautiful, touching moment of connection between her daughter and another person? Or was it jealousy? Claire didn't want to admit it to herself, or anyone else, but it might have been the latter. These little moments had been happening more and more between Audrey and Lilah over the past few days, and it bothered Claire that she couldn't remember the last time her preteen had looked at her that way. Audrey wasn't younger and cooler. She was like Claire; a woman in her forties who looked and spoke like Claire. Yet there was a clear difference according to Lilah.

"Hello." Greg entered the kitchen and came over to Claire's side, peeking over her shoulder at the salad in front of her. "This looks good, thanks for inviting me over."

Claire wiped at the edge of her eye, hoping Greg wouldn't notice the tears, but he did. Of course he did.

"What's going on?" He put a hand on the side of her arm.

"Nothing," Claire said. "I'm fine." Whenever she was asked if she was okay, it made her feel like she was about to cry more, so Claire turned in the other direction to grab a mixing spoon.

"You can tell me," Greg said.

The muscles in Claire's body softened. She didn't have to lie when she was around Greg. He made it clear, over and over, that he would be there for her. She was lucky.

"Oh, my goodness, I love the smell of bacon cooking." Audrey came in from outside, pushing the screen door to one side, her nose pointed up in the air and her eyelids closed slightly. She stopped when she saw Greg and smiled. "Hi. I'm Audrey."

It struck Claire that they hadn't been properly introduced yet. Then again, both Greg and Audrey must have felt like they knew the other, Claire talked about them so much. And even though she kept telling Greg she was fine, she had also let him in on everything she learned. He knew the whole story. "This is Greg," Claire said.

Greg reached his hand out to shake Audrey's but was interrupted by Lilah bursting through the screen door.

"Dad!"

"Hey, Li." Greg wrapped his arms around Lilah's shoulders and touched his cheek to the side of her head. Lilah looked so grown-up in moments like this, standing next to Greg and almost as tall as him now.

After they let go of one another, Claire watched as Lilah remained close to Greg, her shoulder touching the side of his arm. The relationship they had was special; they were so alike in so many ways. Claire thought tears might spring to her eyes again, so she turned in the other direction. It was happening at the drop of a hat lately.

"Is it almost ready?" Lilah asked. "I'm starving."

"Almost done. Your salad is over there." Claire pointed to the one she had set aside, the plain version, without croutons or shaved parmesan on top. Even at twelve, Lilah still liked her food as simple as possible.

"I don't need a separate one, it's okay," Lilah said.

"Since when?"

"Audrey was telling me how fresh the parmesan is and how much flavor it adds." Lilah glanced sideways at Audrey who smiled back at her.

"I've been telling you that for years," Claire said. She tried not to let any of the annoyance she felt creep into her voice.

Lilah just shrugged.

"Take this." Claire handed Lilah a pile of napkins with a sharp nod toward the back deck. "Put them on the table."

"I could have done that," Audrey said.

"I know, but I asked Lilah."

Audrey pursed her lips. She tilted her head slightly to one side, but didn't say anything.

Greg watched Lilah and Audrey leave the kitchen to go back out to the table. His gaze lingered on them for a while before it turned to Claire.

"How long is she staying here for?" he asked. His jaw flexed as he waited.

"Why? Do you think it's a bad idea?"

Greg hesitated and then shook his head slowly. "No. But I can see all of this is a bit hard on you. It's a lot to take in."

"We haven't talked about all the details yet." Claire moved around the kitchen, attempting to avoid Greg's stare. He knew when she was agitated, she could tell by the way he watched her with a probing gaze, like he was doing now.

"Hey," Greg said. He reached out for her. "Claire. Stop for a second."

She paused and put the spoon in her hand down. "What?"

"It's okay."

"It's *not* okay," Claire said. Why did it feel like control was out of her grasp? Just as soon as she thought she knew what direction and path she wanted to take, her mind changed. And although she thought at first it would be nice to have Audrey here, now she was oddly bothered by her presence and the attention Lilah was showering onto her.

"It will be. I promise. I won't let you struggle with this." Greg put a hand on Claire's shoulder. He was being so kind. Claire almost felt like she didn't deserve it. She hadn't made much time for him lately.

"Thank you," she said.

He moved a step closer. "So, is it actually necessary that she stay here with you and Lilah?"

Claire opened her mouth to say something, but Greg continued, "If you're not able to find answers about your past or your parents, does she need to be here?"

Claire sensed his questions were because he was wary of Audrey and the situation in general, but he didn't understand. He didn't carry the weight of not knowing who you were. And he didn't know Audrey, or the kind of closeness Claire had developed with her already.

"She's welcome here," Claire answered. She wouldn't explain further. Instead, she changed the subject. "Anyway, how are you?" She genuinely wanted to know. He had been so good to her lately. He always was, now that she thought about it. Claire had nothing else to compare to, but this amicable separation was confusing. They hadn't worked out together as a married couple, but it felt like they should have. Especially in moments like this. Especially in moments like the other day, after her nap.

"I'm good. Same old," he said. He shifted his weight, placing both hands on the counter in front of him. Maybe that was what Claire found most reassuring. Greg was the same steady, reliable man she always knew him to be. He was comfort, and right now, that was exactly what she needed.

.   .   .

When they were seated around the table and almost done with lunch, Audrey said, "We should go on a trip together. The three of us." She gave Greg an apologetic look. "Like a girls' trip."

Greg held up a hand and shook it. "No need to explain. I understand. I'm used to this dynamic." He gestured toward Claire and Lilah.

Lilah's face lit up. "That would be amazing!" She straightened in her seat and looked from Audrey to Claire and then back to Audrey again. "Like where? New York?"

Claire immediately felt her muscles tighten. "I don't like going too far," she said. Both Lilah and Audrey knew that, and Lilah, especially. Claire kept close to home because it was where she felt safest.

"But we can go somewhere, can't we? I mean, there's nothing really stopping us." Audrey raised her brow in a hopeful kind of way. Cutie eyes. Lilah used to joke that when she wanted something from Greg, all she had to do was give him "cutie eyes" and he was putty.

"I don't know—" Claire tried to shoot a warning look at Audrey. She didn't like this idea. She didn't have a passport, and Audrey knew she couldn't get one without revealing everything.

"Why not?" Lilah asked. She turned to Audrey. "If not New York, where were you thinking?"

"Oh, I'm not sure. Maybe a weekend away mid-month, before school starts and you have to go back to work again," Audrey said to Claire.

"I don't want to go far," Claire repeated, her voice firm.

Lilah's face fell. She scowled the way she did when she didn't get what she wanted. It only cemented in Claire's mind that her decision was firm. She would not go somewhere far, and Lilah would have to learn to deal with it.

"What if it was a road trip?" Audrey asked.

She wasn't going to let this go.

Lilah lifted her head. "We could do that, couldn't we, Mom?"

Darn. Claire didn't want to go anywhere. What was wrong with here? They'd had a great lunch, sitting by the water, relaxing in a beautiful cottage town. People came *here* for vacations, and Audrey and Lilah were desperate to leave?

Claire glanced at Greg. He gave a small shrug, like he didn't know what else to do or say.

Lilah's eyes were wide, and her mouth hung partially open in anticipation as she watched Claire, waiting for her answer.

An answer Claire didn't want to give.

TWENTY

They eventually talked Claire into the capital. Ottawa was a perfect road trip, Audrey said. It would take them four hours to get there—not too long or too short—and it was bigger than Summerville, but not so big a city that Claire would feel overwhelmed.

"There are lots of good restaurants," Audrey remarked. "We can sightsee, and I can book us into a spa for some pampering."

A week later, with some planning from Audrey—Claire stayed out of it for the most part because she was still reluctant to go—they were in the car. Lilah had begged to sit in the front with Audrey because Audrey had offered to drive. Claire had protested at first, but she quickly gave in. Lilah was so thrilled about all of it: the idea of going on a road trip, getting out of Summerville, shopping and dining in a city. Claire was excited for her, yet at the same time, felt an immense amount of guilt, too. She had never given this to Lilah before now because she had never wanted to step outside her comfort zone. She should have known it would mean so much to her daughter.

"Where are we staying again?" Claire asked.

Audrey had arranged the hotel, the reservations for the

restaurants. She had been to Ottawa several times, so she knew what to do and where to go.

"It's a great place, right downtown. We can walk to just about everything," Audrey called over her shoulder to the back seat.

When they arrived, they checked into their hotel and brought their things to their room. Like in Toronto, the room was clean and cool, the bedsheets crisp and white. Claire had to remind herself this wasn't Toronto, however.

Even though she wanted to stay in the room for a while to relax, Lilah immediately asked to go out and explore.

"Come on, Mom," Lilah begged. "There's so much to see."

Claire begrudgingly went. She could do this. Ottawa was a bigger city than she was used to, yes, but it wasn't as big as Toronto, and she wasn't alone here.

They walked through the streets and Claire found it wasn't as jam-packed or as claustrophobic as it had felt in Toronto. There was space to look around, take in the shops and restaurants. It buzzed with people, but in a comfortable way. Eventually, they ended up in a place called the Byward Market. A buzzy little center of the city, teeming with people sitting outside restaurants and pubs on patios, enjoying a drink in the summer sun. There was so much shopping, too. Kiosks filled with flowers in every color, fresh vegetables, a deli. It looked like it went on for blocks.

"I heard there are fantastic food stalls," Audrey said. "And maybe you could do some shopping for back to school."

Lilah smiled. "I'd love that."

Claire wasn't sure what Lilah thought she would find here that she could use for school. This place was more whimsical and exciting than it was practical for back-to-school needs.

Anyway, Audrey wouldn't know what Lilah needed. That specific knowledge came with years of mothering.

"If that's okay with you, of course," Audrey said. She was looking at Claire and smiling, her head bowed forward a touch. She was being careful. Claire appreciated that.

"Sure," Claire said.

They made their way inside the big brick warehouse-type building that held the market and were met with rows and rows of food stands. Claire's stomach grumbled. She was suddenly hungry and could admit to herself that she was glad they chose to come here. There was a stand with so many kinds of cheeses, and almost as many samples. Claire popped a cube into her mouth. Then another. She wanted to buy several blocks of it, but had no way of taking cheese back home and keeping it fresh. After the cheese, they wound their way over to a cupcake stand with the most vibrant-looking colors of cupcakes. Lilah, Audrey and Claire each bought one; Claire's was lemon, a flavor she wouldn't normally choose, but it was incredible.

"I'm going to pop over there for a second," Claire said. She had noticed a coffee stand and wanted to grab herself a cup. Its nutty and rich scent wafted over to her, pulling her closer. Claire took a sip and was pleased to find it tasted as good as it smelled. Maybe all of this—the road trip, being in a city and wandering around in crowds—wasn't such a bad thing after all. It had taken Claire most of her life to want to leave her comfortable bubble, but how much had she potentially missed out on?

When she turned around to join Audrey and Lilah again, they weren't there. Claire fanned her head back and forth to find which stand they had moved on to, but couldn't spot them. She started down one aisle, glancing at the kiosks as she went. There were rows and rows of fresh fruits. Lilah had likely dragged Audrey over to a chocolate kiosk somewhere, or maybe to that fresh donut stand they had passed when they first came in.

Claire craned her neck to look over the crowd. Audrey and Lilah were nowhere.

She pulled out her phone and clicked on Lilah's number. No answer.

Next, Claire texted.

> Where are you guys? I've lost you.

She waited for the dots to indicate Lilah was typing back, but saw nothing. Her jaw clenched. Lilah was terrible at texting and returning calls in a timely manner. What was the point of a phone if you weren't going to respond when someone (Claire) was trying to get hold of you? She was about to click on Audrey's number to call when there was a hand on her shoulder.

"Hey. Here you are," Audrey said. "I wandered off and couldn't find you two for a bit."

Claire's pulse sped up.

"What do you mean 'you two'?"

Audrey's eyebrows formed a knot. She laughed. "You and Lilah."

"Lilah's not with me. I thought she was with you. She *was* with you." Claire's head whipped around. Her eyes searched the crowd around her, but there were so many people. Her mouth went dry. She started walking, as quick as she could without jogging, down the aisle in front of her.

"I don't know where she is. But she couldn't be far." Audrey followed behind Claire. Her voice didn't sound anywhere near as worried as she should be.

"She was supposed to be with you," Claire spat. "Why weren't you with her?"

Audrey stopped. "You didn't tell me she needs to be watched. She's twelve years old."

Claire spun around. "So? You think a twelve-year-old is safe in a busy crowd? This is the most ideal place for someone awful to do something terrible like take her."

"How would I know what a twelve-year-old can and can't do?" Audrey's tone edged on concerned and her face had a pained expression to it.

Claire glanced down at her phone: 1:12 p.m. She clicked on Lilah's number again and waited. No answer. She turned and continued walking. This was awful. She touched the tips of her fingers to her lips and picked at a piece of skin as she remembered how, once, when Lilah was only two years old, Greg and Claire had lost track of her at their local Santa Claus parade. There were so many people lining the streets, much more than Claire had expected to see in Summerville. Everyone was in bulky winter coats, standing shoulder to shoulder, clumped together. One second, Lilah was there, and the next, she was gone. The terror Claire had felt, from the bottom of her feet rushing up to the top of her head and out through her limbs, the sheer and utter terror of losing your baby, was unbearable. Thankfully, it had only been a few minutes later that they'd found Lilah by a lamppost, petting a puppy. She was oblivious, even though Claire had just experienced the single most terrifying moment of her life.

Her eyes searched the crowds and she only hoped Lilah was just as oblivious now, here in an unknown city at a busy market, and they would find her as quickly as they did then.

Claire pulled her phone out and looked at the time again: 1:16 p.m. It hadn't even been five minutes. The thought didn't help ease any of Claire's anxiety. She called Lilah and waited, but still no answer, so she picked up her pace as she went down one aisle.

Audrey trailed behind her, irritating Claire—it would be better if they split up. "Why don't you go down that next aisle? I'll take this one. We can meet at the end of it."

Audrey nodded and left, her mouth turned down at the edges.

Claire walked fast down the row and then began to jog, looking left and right, trying to remember what Lilah was wearing and searching the crowd desperately hoping to spot her. Lilah was nowhere. There were rows of fruits and flowers and people everywhere, but no Lilah. Claire's legs felt wobbly. Her chest hurt, like she couldn't catch her breath. Where was she?

At the end of the aisle, Audrey stood with one arm crossed over her chest, her hand up on her shoulder. Her forehead was wrinkled, and her eyes narrowed. She was still looking.

"You haven't seen her yet?" Claire said.

Audrey only shook her head.

No. This wasn't happening. Lilah was here somewhere. She had to be.

She typed out a quick text.

> Call me. Now.

"How could you do this?" Claire snapped.

Audrey flinched. "I didn't know."

"You didn't know that you had to keep a child close to you in a busy location? Or at least communicate where to meet up?"

"Claire. She has a phone. She'll call you. We'll find her." Audrey's jaw was set, and her gaze was zeroed in on Claire's face.

"She doesn't use her phone like a typical teen. It's often on silent. I've told her over and over again to answer it when I call, but she never hears it." Claire's voice sped up. She wasn't in control of it. The worry was taking over. "I knew coming here was a bad idea. We should have stayed in Summerville until school started. I didn't even want to come. And now this has happened."

Audrey moved closer. "I think we need to calm down. It will be okay. She has a phone and hasn't gone far."

"You don't know that!" Claire shouted. "You don't know anything about her. Or me."

Audrey's eyes widened. It only annoyed Claire more.

"We should have stuck to finding answers about Veronica and then moving on with our lives. We're not related, it's not like we have to have this relationship. What the heck are we doing going on a road trip together?" The idea of it all seemed so ridiculous to Claire suddenly. She should be back home, clearing out Veronica's house, looking into her will to find out how to move forward. She had to get back to work and get her life back on track. She didn't need to know who her real parents were; she was forty-three years old and had no memory of them. Her life should carry on like it had before, like nothing had changed. Lilah didn't need to know about any of this.

"But I thought you and I could be like—" Audrey reached up and pulled at her ear.

"Like what? Sisters? We're not sisters though. We're nothing to one another." Claire knew how awful and mean she was being, but it was like an out-of-body experience. She could hear the words coming out of her mouth, but she couldn't stop them. She was too stressed.

Audrey's head jerked back like she had been slapped. Her hand dropped.

Claire closed her eyes and pinched the bridge of her nose. "I need to find Lilah," she said.

"Okay."

Audrey was silent as they continued walking. She followed Claire, her head also fanning back and forth, not saying a word. Claire regretted it. She did. But she was also so focused on Lilah, she couldn't worry about Audrey's feelings right at this exact moment.

Claire's phone said 1:54. Too much time was going by. She

was hot and clammy. Then, as if the heavens above were taking pity on her, Lilah appeared in Claire's sight line. She was halfway down the aisle Claire and Audrey were standing in, bent at the waist and looking closely at a kiosk filled with hand-stitched purses and wallets.

"Lilah!" Claire shouted. Her voice was hoarse and came out scratchy.

Lilah turned her head and then stood upright. She waved and smiled like her mother's world hadn't just about imploded. She was oblivious, just as she had been all those years ago.

"Hey," Lilah said as Claire and Audrey got closer. "Where have you been?"

"Where have I been? Where were you? We've been looking for you. You didn't answer your phone," Claire snapped.

"Sorry. Sheesh. It's on silent." Lilah's expression went from relaxed and happy to irritated, which annoyed Claire, but she was too relieved to start an argument. Lilah turned to Audrey. "Are you okay?" she asked.

Audrey only nodded silently. Her face was pale, almost green.

Lilah held her gaze for a moment, then looked at Claire. "What's going on?"

"Nothing," Claire said. "Let's go. It's time to leave."

TWENTY-ONE

On the way back to the hotel, Audrey barely spoke, and Lilah kept asking what was going on. Claire didn't trust herself to say a word until they got back into the room. Even by then, she hadn't cooled down much at all.

"Grab your things, we have to go," she instructed Lilah.

"What? No," Lilah said. "No way. We just got here."

"Don't tell me no. Get your things. Pack up."

Audrey drew back a step from Claire and Lilah. Claire appreciated the way Audrey could seem to read the room and knew to give them space. This was not the time or place for Audrey to provide her opinion. Only, Lilah didn't realize this.

"We haven't even stayed one night," Lilah shouted. She looked to Audrey. "I want to stay. Don't you want to stay?"

Audrey's head tilted to one side when she looked at Lilah and her mouth was pursed. After a pause, she turned back to Claire. "The room is paid for. We booked two nights."

Claire's arms tingled. She could sense her face flushing with color. She needed Audrey to agree with her, not side with a child. She took a steadying breath in

"I don't care. This whole thing was a mistake, and I knew it from the beginning." She turned to Lilah and looked at her directly. "We are going home. Immediately."

Lilah glared at Claire, as if she were the most terrible thing that had ever happened to her. Claire frowned. There was something about Lilah that could both anger her and make her doubt every parenting decision she had ever made. She wanted to go home, but Lilah clearly wanted this so much, and she was going through a lot right now. Her grandmother had died, then she'd learned Veronica wasn't her grandmother at all. It frightened Claire when Lilah had to handle something big and confusing like this. It had the potential to make Lilah stronger or cause a lot of upset. Every time her daughter was sad or struggling, Claire wanted to take it away, but she knew that wasn't the right thing to do. All the parenting advice was to let your children struggle because it built resilience and made them stronger. To Claire, it felt like all it did was create a divide between them.

"I have to get back and get ready for work, and you need to get ready for school," Claire said, as if a final word on the subject was needed.

"There's still a week left of summer," Lilah mumbled.

Claire didn't answer. Lilah would get the hint: there was no room for negotiation.

Lilah looked over at Audrey once more, and Audrey nodded back at her as she spoke in a low, heavy voice. "I have to get going, too. I'm heading back to my home. I'll need to start work soon."

After a tense drive, back at home, Audrey came inside just long enough to gather her things and give Lilah a hug.

"You're leaving already?" Lilah asked.

Claire stood close by, looking around at anything but Audrey. Her neck was tense and there was a headache brewing at the base of her skull. Her brain had worked overtime during the drive home. Had she made the right decision? She wanted to believe she had, but she could swim in her self-doubt.

"Yes." Audrey didn't offer any explanation. She hoisted a bag up onto her shoulder and frowned.

"When will you be back?" Lilah asked.

Claire sighed. Since when was Lilah so attached? She'd only recently met Audrey, and she knew just part of the backstory.

"I'm not sure. But you have my number. We'll talk," Audrey said. Claire wished she would speak in a brighter tone, not one that sounded like she was about to cry any minute. It was only making things seem much worse. Audrey turned to Claire. "Bye."

The air around them felt thick, like mud. Claire didn't know what else to say or do, so she only nodded. Then she and Lilah stood and watched as Audrey reversed out of the driveway. They stayed until Audrey's car disappeared down the gravel-filled road in front of their house, leaving a trail of smoke-like dust behind.

"What do you want for dinner?" Claire asked.

"Nothing," Lilah snapped. She stormed back into the house and slammed the door behind her.

Claire took a breath in and slowly released it. Lilah was only twelve. She was twelve.

The next night, after a mostly quiet dinner, Claire took a glass of red wine out back to the covered deck, alone. There were tiny white lights strung up so that when you sat outside, it felt magical. Claire needed some kind of magic to get through the next few days with Lilah.

She put her feet up onto the chair opposite her and watched the lake shimmering as the sun went down. When her phone buzzed, she glanced at the screen warily. It couldn't be Audrey, could it? Claire wasn't ready.

Greg's name flashed, and Claire felt her body release all its tension. She picked up the phone and pressed the button.

"Hey. How are you?" Greg asked immediately.

"I'm okay. Why?"

Greg let out a small laugh. "I haven't heard from you in a while. There's been so much going on and you haven't called."

"Did Lilah call you?" Claire had a feeling she must have.

"Yes," Greg said. "She told me you made them leave the trip early."

Claire shook her head, annoyed with the statement, even though it wasn't coming from Greg. "That's not the full story."

"I know." Greg let out a breath. "She also said Audrey left?"

"Yes. I think it's for the best. I'm trying to leave it all behind. I can't change the past," Claire replied, hoping she sounded more definitive than she felt.

"Claire." Greg's voice was flat.

"What?"

"You learned your mother isn't your mother, but you still have to clean out her house and sell it and move on with your life while getting to know her biological daughter. That's a lot."

Claire closed her eyes. She waited for the lump in her throat to subside before she spoke again.

"I know, but what can I do? My mother is gone. Audrey's father can't give us answers. Fatima knows nothing. We searched, but couldn't find a thing. I don't know what else to do but move on."

"And not find out who your parents are? Who you are?" Greg asked.

He didn't get it. What if her parents were terrible people? Or, even worse, what if they were wonderful, incredible people and she had missed out on a lifetime of getting to know them? It was a betrayal to Veronica to even think like that.

Veronica was a wonderful mother. She was kind a lot of the time, and strict and in control when she needed to be. She was the type of mother who would listen to all your stories about the things you did that day, and what you were learning at school, and never rush you or cut you off because she had to do something. She listened when Claire worried endlessly about every stage Lilah was in as a baby, and then a toddler, and a little kid. She was silly and funny, but also a fierce protector. She was everything. She was love. But now there was a worm of doubt within Claire that had unsettled her more than she wanted to admit.

She wanted desperately to go back to a time before she knew. When her mother was still a saint, when Claire didn't think of her as a kidnapper. She couldn't reconcile the woman she knew as Mother with the woman she was learning Veronica was.

"I'm not ready," Claire said to Greg.

He was silent for a moment. "How's Lilah handling it all?"

"Well, she only knows that my mother isn't my mother. She doesn't know all the other stuff."

"What other stuff?" Lilah's voice came from behind her.

Claire went still. A wave of cold washed over her, causing her skin to tingle. She whipped her head around. "Oh. I didn't see you there."

"What other stuff?" Lilah repeated.

"Greg, I'll give you a ring back later." Claire hung up and looked up at Lilah. She didn't want to get into this. It would be hard to process, and she didn't want to mess with Lilah's head. But Lilah stood with her hands on her hips, her mouth a straight line across her face. She was waiting. "I learned some things while you were away at camp."

"Like what?"

"Well. This is kind of hard to talk about. I'm not sure I want to get into it right now."

"I want to know. Tell me," Lilah said sharply. "Please," she added, her tone softened.

A bead of sweat trickled down the spot in between Claire's breasts. It was hot tonight, plus the wine and now this.

"I found out that Grandma—well. Grandma, she, uh..." She couldn't do it. Claire couldn't say it.

"I can call Audrey and she'll tell me," Lilah said.

Damn it, she was so smart.

"We think that Grandma took me. From her neighbors. And then she disappeared." It sounded so awful. It couldn't be her mother, Lilah's grandmother.

Lilah's eyes widened. Her mouth dropped open. "She kidnapped you?" She stood motionless.

Claire nodded. Hearing that word again, especially coming from Lilah, brought Claire up short. She couldn't speak for a moment.

"From who? Where did she go? Why didn't the police find out?"

"I think she came here and raised me. I don't know who she took me from or what happened with the police. Sometimes cases go unsolved, though."

She stood up and went to Lilah, opening her arms. There was a fraction of a second when Claire was unsure if Lilah would let her in; a split decision when Lilah could go either way and push Claire away or let her be a mother. It was the latter, thank God. Claire could tell by the way Lilah's head dipped forward, the way she didn't turn away. Claire wrapped her arms around Lilah.

"This is very confusing," Claire said.

"How could she do that to you?" Lilah's voice was muffled by Claire's shoulder where her face was buried, but Claire could still hear the crack in it.

"I don't know. I don't know much."

"I wish we never knew any of this. It's all so awful." Lilah buried her head again and sobbed quietly. When her shoulders stopped shaking, she pulled away from Claire. "How could you not tell me? Were you ever going to?" Her eyes, now red and watery, were narrowed. Lilah was suddenly angry, in that way she could be. The moment of mothering was over.

Claire sighed. "You were at camp and then I needed time to figure out how to tell you. I wanted to have some answers. And I didn't want to upset you."

"Well, you did!" Lilah shouted.

"I'm sorry," Claire said, though none of this was her fault, really. It was Veronica's. But how could you be mad at a woman who was dead and couldn't defend herself? How could you be mad at someone you were still grieving?

Lilah glanced down and then her eyes flicked back up to Claire. Her mouth was a small bow on her face. It was the face she got when she was thinking, deciding what to do next. "I'm going to my room," she said. Then she turned on her heel and left.

Claire sat back down and reached for her wine. She wanted to keep Audrey at a distance and now Lilah wanted to do the same with her. Everything was a mess.

TWENTY-TWO

The next morning, Claire rose earlier than usual. Her head was foggy, and her eyes hurt. One too many glasses of wine on the back porch. She rarely stayed up late having wine anymore, especially by herself, but last night had called for it. She had sat listening to the sounds of nature, wondering how the hell this had become her life. Up until that point, she'd led a careful, controlled life. She went to work and delivered babies, took care of new mothers. She took care of Lilah, too. She made them meals and kept the house clean, took her to hockey and went to her school events. She rarely went out. She had a few friends, but when was the last time she had seen any of them for a night out? Everyone led busy lives. It struck Claire that the older she got, the less she would deviate from her routine. And then suddenly, everything had changed. Veronica had died, she'd met Audrey, she'd learned about her mother, and Lilah had slipped away even further. The loss of control unnerved her.

Claire went straight for the coffee machine that morning. She made herself a pot and then took a cup and went out back in her pajamas and bare feet. The air outside was already warm. Claire took her sweater off and went all the way down to the dock at the water's edge. This was the best place to spend the early part of each morning. It was so peaceful. Still water, and quiet surroundings.

She sat in her chair and watched the sky turn from a gray-blue into yellow and pink. She sipped her coffee and thought about what was next. The idea of sorting through her mother's house was exhausting, but it had to be done. Things had to be finalized, and she was the executor. Right after Veronica had died, Claire had reviewed the will and found nothing out of the ordinary. Next, she had cancelled and closed her mother's accounts and subscriptions, went to the bank to manage all of those details, as awful as it had been. The only thing left was the house, but Claire had trouble bringing herself to do it. Not to mention, trying to figure out how Audrey fit in to all of it.

Audrey. Claire's stomach dropped at the thought of how complicated everything was. It was times like these that she could use someone to talk to. Well, not someone. Her mother. Grief came over her in a wave. She hadn't taken time lately to try to understand her grief. It was a confusing kind. She missed her mother and wished she could talk to her, but she was also mad at her. For not telling Claire anything, for doing something so unspeakable and hard to understand.

Claire tipped her head back and finished the last of her coffee. She stayed in her seat, watching Shadow Lake for a while longer before eventually getting up and heading back to the house. She poured herself another cup and picked up her phone. The screen was covered in notifications. A text from Greg asking her how she was, the weather app reporting the forecast for the day—Claire didn't remember putting that notification on, but couldn't be bothered to try to figure out how to turn it off. The last notification was a missed call from Audrey.

After texting Greg back to say things were fine and maybe they could catch up over lunch or something else in-person, she clicked on Audrey's name to call her back.

"Hello?" Audrey said.

"Hi. I saw you called." Claire stepped back outside so Lilah wouldn't overhear. She had selective hearing, but was excellent at zeroing in on adult conversations when she wanted to.

"I know you're upset with me, but I was hoping we could talk again." Audrey's voice was gentle, and Claire appreciated it.

"I'm not upset with you," Claire said. "I was, but I'm not anymore." It was true. Audrey had made a mistake, but it had ended up okay. Claire could see now that she might have over-reacted. It was part of who she was to be so protective.

"Okay," Audrey replied. "But I wanted you to know I'm so sorry for everything. I don't have a daughter, so I don't know how to react to situations. I shouldn't have pushed for going away when I could see you didn't want to. I guess I've just been so caught up in getting to know you and Lilah and I've wanted to keep you both close. It's been so nice. I never had much family growing up."

"I know. It has been nice," Claire agreed. Audrey meant well, Claire knew this. "We're both figuring things out as we go."

"Yeah," Audrey said. After a pause, she continued, "Do you think it would be okay if I dropped by again? Summer is almost over, and then who knows how often I'll get to see you or Lilah."

Despite the fact they weren't related, Claire knew that Audrey was going to be in their lives; she was going nowhere. She wasn't even sure she wanted Audrey to go anywhere. Besides, it was exhausting trying to push her away. Maybe it was unkind as well. Claire was adult enough to admit that to herself.

"Okay," Claire said.

"Really? Great, okay. I can be flexible anytime during the rest of the week. I'm just taking care of a few things with my dad today."

"How is he?" Claire asked.

"He's not doing great."

Claire didn't push. "I'm sorry."

"Thanks. It'll be okay." Audrey's voice was sad, and Claire felt a stab of sympathy for her.

"Tomorrow is good," Claire said. "How about early afternoon?"

"Perfect."

Claire and Audrey said goodbye and then hung up. She went back down to the water to finish her second cup of coffee, thinking of how this would all work out when Greg popped into her mind. She had been thinking of him often lately. She clicked on his number.

"Hey," he said when he answered. "What's up?"

"Did you see my text?" Claire asked. "I thought maybe we could grab lunch or a coffee or something."

"Sure. Is everything okay with Lilah?"

"She's doing fine," Claire answered. "I thought this could be more about us."

"Oh." Greg's tone was filled with surprise. "Yes. I'd like that."

"Are you free today? Maybe we could go to Grazie?" It was Claire's favorite pizzeria in town.

"You love that place," Greg said warmly. "Yes. See you there at noon?"

"Perfect." Claire hung up and smiled to herself.

At Grazie, Claire took a seat at a corner table. It was right beside the patio, so she could feel the warm summer air, but was seated in the shade. Greg arrived shortly after her and leaned over to kiss her cheek. Claire wondered what they must look like to others. They appeared to be a happily married couple, she supposed.

"How are you?" Greg asked.

"That's a loaded question."

Greg raised an eyebrow. "I know."

Claire took a sip of her water. "I think I'm okay. I just have to sort out what I want."

"That's tough." There was a tenderness to his voice, and the look in his eyes—it was like an eagerness to help. It warmed Claire and made her grateful she had him.

The restaurant was hot today, which is why Claire blamed what she said next on the fact that she was a bit light-headed.

"Why do you think our marriage didn't work?" The truth was, she wanted to know, no matter what the answer was. She was feeling nostalgic for their past and was also certain whatever the reason Greg gave, it could probably be fixed.

As suspected, Greg looked taken aback. "Why didn't we work?"

"Yes. We clearly care very much about one another. You've been so wonderful. I like having you around."

"Claire." Greg's voice was soft now.

"What?" Her back stiffened. She wondered why he'd said her name like that. Was he going to tell her this was something he didn't want to talk about?

"It's just—"

"Don't you love me?" Claire immediately regretted asking. But how could this man, someone she had known for so long, who knew everything about her in the most intimate of ways, the father of her child, not love her? He was her family. He couldn't possibly not love her, could he? Claire needed his answer to be that he did. He did love her. She needed someone to tell her this, right now, to affirm that she was a loveable person, that she was valued.

"Of course I love you," Greg said.

Claire breathed out. A calmness came over her. Thank goodness he'd said that.

"I think you're feeling very stressed out and tired these days," he continued. "Understandably so."

Claire stiffened again. She could sense he was going to say something she wouldn't like.

"I love you, but the truth was our marriage didn't work, and you and I both know why," Greg said.

Claire frowned and looked away. "No. I don't. I thought I did, but I don't anymore. You've been so kind lately." Her voice broke. "I need you."

Greg leaned forward in his seat and reached for her hand. "You need some answers. You need to know more about your mother." His voice was so gentle and full of warmth, but Claire didn't want it to be. She knew that meant he was placating her.

She pulled back. "Okay. Fine," Claire said. "Maybe we should order."

Greg's eyebrows shot up. "Claire..."

"No, it's okay. We don't need to talk about this. Let's order. I'm hungry."

Greg frowned, but eventually picked up his menu.

Claire decided she would focus on talking about Lilah, and not the embarrassment she felt at being rejected in her most vulnerable state by someone she thought she could count on.

If she was being honest with herself, Claire still knew she could count on Greg. He was a good person and a good friend. But maybe she didn't want him as a friend any longer. If things could only go back to how they used to be—and not just with Greg, but with every part of her life.

Audrey's car appeared on the gravel road outside Claire and Lilah's house early afternoon the next day. She pulled into the driveway and was out of the front seat before the dust from the road had settled.

"Hello!" Audrey raised a hand and called out cheerfully when she saw Lilah.

"Audrey! Hi!" Lilah waved back with enthusiasm.

Claire greeted her by holding up a bag with snacks and towels in it. "I thought we could go back to Skeleton Lake."

"Oh. Sure," Audrey said. She turned around again and followed Claire to the car.

Claire drove. Audrey sat in the front, but most of the time her body was twisted and her neck craning so that she could talk to Lilah in the back seat. They had developed a bond so quickly, one that Claire wasn't sure about. Not because there was anything wrong with it, but because Claire didn't know how all of this was going to work. She wasn't sure if Audrey was going to be in their lives forever. She had said it before; they weren't sisters. So what were they? Then again, Claire didn't want to have to think about this today. She wanted to have a relaxed day at the lake.

When they got to the beach, it was windy. Not the best conditions for a beach day, so they found only one other family there. A little boy was playing in the shallow water right by the edge of the beach, splashing and squealing while his parents sat next to him, laughing, applying more sunscreen to his nose, pushing his hair out of his face.

Despite the wind, it was warm out. The breeze felt nice on Claire's bare arms.

"I'm going for a swim," Lilah said. She stood and pushed her shorts down and pulled her T-shirt off.

"Love your bathing suit," Audrey said. "So stylish."

Claire would have called it cute, and that would have been all wrong. Lilah didn't want to be cute, but stylish was the perfect word.

"Thank you." Lilah beamed. She ran toward the lake and shrieked when the water splashed up on her. Claire loved the way those childlike flashes came through every now and again.

When Lilah ran into the water, she ran with the excitement of a little kid, not an almost-teenager.

Audrey and Claire sat side by side, but Claire felt a distance between them.

"I took a road trip." Audrey looked down and ran her hand over the ground while she said it.

"Oh?" Claire asked. She watched Audrey's fingers make designs in the soft sand.

"Yes. Yesterday. It was just a short one," Audrey said. "I went to Goderich. The town that was on the old mail I found."

Claire froze. "Why? We already called the police."

Audrey looked up and squinted into the distance. "Does she need a life jacket or something?"

Lilah was relatively far out, alternating between swimming and floating.

"No, she's fine. Remember how shallow it is?" Claire said, only a little annoyed that Audrey was questioning her parenting. She watched Lilah moving through the water for a minute and then pushed on. "Why did you go to that town?"

"I wanted to see if it would jog any memories for me."

"Did it?" Claire asked.

Audrey shook her head. She looked back down at the sand. "I would have asked you if you wanted to come, but it seemed like you needed space." She looked up and met Claire's eyes. Claire said nothing, so Audrey kept talking. "I really needed to go. I need answers, too."

"I know," Claire said. "Did you get any?"

"Yes. I found the house from the picture. It wasn't hard. The town is small. I only needed to show the photo to a few people and they directed me to where I needed to go. It was on a street called Raspberry Court. Funny, isn't it?" Audrey's favorite fruit. Her smile was sad, despite her words.

Claire's skin prickled up and down the backs of her arms. "How did you know you would find our old houses there?"

Audrey shrugged. "It was a hunch. And it was the only lead we had. I also found someone. A neighbor. She still lived there after all this time."

"And? Did she remember you or Veronica or your father?"

"Not really," Audrey said. She turned her head and looked into Claire's eyes. "She remembered you."

Claire didn't think it was possible to feel more tension in her body than she already had in the past few days, but her shoulders went tight again. Her forehead began to throb, almost instinctively, like her body knew she couldn't take much more.

"Who was she? What did she remember?" Claire croaked.

"She used to live a couple of houses down from the one we saw in the picture. I showed it to her. She said she didn't know your parents much because they kept to themselves. She didn't even know their names. They never said more than a quick hello to anyone. She said when they were out, they would come home, drive directly into the garage, close the door and enter the house through the door in the garage. That way they never had to interact with anyone outside or around them."

"That's so weird." A chill went through Claire. Something about it felt off. And how could she remember none of this? No flashes of memories at all. It didn't seem right, even though she was so young. "What did she say about me?"

Audrey smiled with half of her mouth. "She said you were really sweet. A cute kid. She remembered you being around, always outside playing by yourself. She didn't think much of it, but then you were gone and she wished she had paid more attention."

"Did she say anything about my parents after I was gone?"

"Like what?" Audrey asked. Her voice was gentle.

"Like, how they reacted. Or, if they tried to find me."

"Not much about your parents." Audrey shook her head. "She didn't know them well enough. I'm sorry."

Claire waved her off. "It's okay." It wasn't a big deal. It wasn't.

"She did say that the cops were involved. All the neighbors were questioned, but then the case went cold. They had no leads."

"The police must have gone looking for Veronica and your father?"

"My father took me away first—before this all happened. After he left, the neighbors thought Veronica had moved at the same time. So, my dad wasn't questioned, and Veronica wasn't found."

Claire frowned and tried to process what she was hearing. Did she want Veronica to have been found back then? No way. Her life wouldn't have been the good life she had in Summerville all these years.

"She said something else about your parents." Audrey shifted in her seat. Her mouth had turned down and a deep line had formed between her eyebrows.

"What?" Claire asked.

"They're gone. They passed away."

Claire closed her eyes and let it sink in. She didn't know if she had ever planned to try to find them, so this wasn't the horrible shock it might have been for someone searching for their parents. Still. It was hard to process. Another dead end.

Audrey reached for Claire and put a hand on the side of her arm. "I'm sorry."

When Claire opened her eyes again, she looked out at Skeleton Lake. Lilah was still way out there, wading through the water and then submerging herself under. She was swimming, stopping to look at things, swimming again. Claire could watch her forever.

"Do you know what happened to them?" Claire asked. Lilah might have questions one day.

"The neighbor had a few details," Audrey said and then paused.

Claire swivelled her head in Audrey's direction. "What did she say?"

The frown on Audrey's face deepened. "They were alcoholics. They drank themselves to death. They both died a long time ago."

Claire's jaw clenched. Her neck was instantly tight. How much worse could the news get? Everyone involved in bringing her into this world and raising her had serious problems.

"I wonder if they drank because you were taken from them," Audrey said quickly, as if she was trying to soften the news. She put her hand on top of the sand again and watched as she moved it back and forth.

Or maybe Veronica knew they weren't fit parents and had tried to save Claire, in her own twisted way. It was what Claire preferred to believe.

"I guess we'll never know," Claire said. It was true. It felt like there was so much she wouldn't know. They had run out of sources and now summer was ending, Claire had a life to focus on. The past would have to remain in the past.

Still. A deep, painful feeling had hollowed its way into her stomach. Maybe it was grief. A grief because she didn't know who she was, why her mother took her, who her real parents were. All she knew was that she was left with this surreal feeling that came with finding out someone you thought you knew better than anyone wasn't who you thought they were at all.

Then a wave of anger came over her. She wasn't going to wallow in grief. Forget that. They didn't deserve her grief. Not her parents, not Veronica. None of them.

"I feel no responsibility to anyone other than Lilah. Just because they were my biological parents doesn't mean I need to know them," Claire said.

"No, of course not."

"And just because Veronica was my family doesn't mean I need to keep her memory alive."

"Claire." Audrey's voice was soft once more. She reached out and placed her warm hand on Claire's forearm again.

"I mean it. I need to get on with my life. I don't have to come undone over them because they were technically my family. I want to move on."

Lilah came splashing out of the water and up to the beach. "The water feels so refreshing. Are you going to come in?" She was looking at Claire when she asked.

A tiny thrill went through Claire's limbs. These moments were rare, Claire was not about to pass up on it.

"Definitely," Claire said. She patted Audrey's hand as if to say thanks and stood and peeled her sundress off, revealing her soft body in her black one-piece. She adjusted the straps and then smiled at Lilah. Thank goodness for Lilah. Being responsible for her was going to keep Claire's head above water for the next while.

"Are you coming?" Lilah asked Audrey.

Audrey was still seated in the sand, her knees both bent and her arms wrapped around them. She looked up at them and squinted one eye from the brightness of the summer afternoon sky. "No, you go ahead. I'm going to relax here a bit."

"Okay," Lilah said, turning around and already making her way back to the water's edge.

Claire caught Audrey's eye and Audrey smiled up at her. Claire nodded and then went to join her daughter in the lake.

Later that night, Claire did something she instantly regretted. She let her curiosity and her need for order and facts get the better of her. Even though she told herself she was done with it all, she searched for news of missing children in Goderich. Only this time she added "Raspberry Court". After clicking through page after page of search results, she eventually came across a story in a local paper.

She read the headline *Local girl goes missing over 30 years ago—case never solved*, then her eyes landed on names she didn't know.

Her body went cold. She read the article, her eyes moving quickly over each sentence. A rehashing of something that had happened when Claire would have been three years old.

Sadie Green's mother, Denise Green, was doing laundry in their home on Raspberry Court when her daughter went out to play and then disappeared. There were no eyewitnesses and no description of a car. According to Green, the police did little, perhaps partly owing to their focus on the bushfires that attacked the area for months during that time.

The article then shared an excerpt of the original story. There was a quote.

"They've searched my house twice already, and given me a polygraph test," Green says. "I'm not the one they should be looking for."

Claire couldn't feel her fingers, they had gone so cold. Sadie Green. Denise Green. Those names were so odd to her. She had no way of knowing if the story was about her. It didn't have photos to go with it, but she had been pulled in.

Claire clicked open a new tab and typed the name Denise Green into the search bar. So many names and photos came up, as Claire had suspected it might. It was a common name. She browsed through them briefly before giving her head a shake. This was ridiculous. What was she hoping to find? Although, there was something that stirred in her stomach that she couldn't ignore, as much as she wanted to, when she read the name.

She scanned the list of names and stories and profiles, looking for one that might be her mother, but it was impossible. She bookmarked the news article so she could look back at it again later if she wanted to and then shut the laptop down.

This was too much. Even if Denise Green was her mother, it didn't matter. She was dead.

Claire let the name Sadie Green roll through her mind. It was a pretty name, but it wasn't hers. She was Claire Brown. A very common name, now that she thought of it.

A name that could be hidden well.

TWENTY-THREE

When Monday rolled around two weeks later, Claire got ready for work for the first time in what felt like a very long time. She put on her most comfortable cropped leggings and a loose T-shirt. After pulling her hair up into a ponytail, she made coffee and brought it up to her office where she logged into her email to get caught up. She wasn't on call, but would need to be in the clinic soon and wanted to get a jump on the backlog of emails first.

She clicked on a tab and was reminded of when she was searching through the news. Ever since she had learned about the name Sadie Green, she had made a conscious decision to ignore it. She had the story saved if she felt the need to look at it again. For now, it didn't fit the way she wanted her life to go, so she pushed it away.

Lilah was going to stay home alone and relax today. She claimed she needed "chill days" before school started up again in a week. She would spend most of the day on her phone, but Claire didn't care. Summer was meant for chill days, and once she was back at school, there would be much less time for staring at screens, watching ridiculous videos and scrolling through apps.

Downstairs, after she was done with the admin and emails from work, Claire poured another coffee into her travel mug and grabbed her keys.

"Don't answer the door unless it's Dad," Claire cautioned Lilah. Nobody showed up around here unexpected anyway. Nobody ever had until Audrey came into their lives.

"What if it's Audrey?" Lilah asked, as if she knew what Claire was thinking.

"Yes, you can open it for her," Claire said. How odd this all was now. Audrey had an automatic in with Lilah and Claire. She was on the same level as Greg.

Claire leaned into Lilah and kissed her cheek. Lilah returned it with a one-armed hug.

"Can you make me my cereal before you go?" Lilah asked.

Claire straightened up and stared down at her daughter. "You're almost a teenager." The thought that Lilah was still asking for Claire to "make" her cereal was ridiculous. She meant pour it into a bowl with some milk on top. Claire had definitely babied Lilah too much over the years, but it was hard not to when you had an only child. She drew the line at making cereal for a twelve-year-old. "Seriously? Come on, Lilah."

Lilah looked up and grinned. "Okay, okay."

At the clinic, Claire found comfort in the normalcy of the busy day. There was a full client list. She checked vitals, made notes, listened to clients talk. She was surrounded by happy, excited women who were looking forward to meeting their babies one day soon. These were women who were thrilled to be mothers. They would raise their children and take care of them their entire lives, the way it should be.

Claire wouldn't allow any of this to make her feel bad. It shouldn't. This was what children should have: a loving, stable parent who would teach them right from wrong and raise them with all the care in the world. It was what Claire had—or how it had seemed at least. Even though she knew differently now, it didn't take away from how she was raised. That was part of what made all of this so confusing.

"Hey, welcome back." It was Jen, one of Claire's coworkers, and Claire smiled when she saw her. Jen was warm and genuine, always with a broad smile on her face. She stopped moving about in the kitchen of the office and turned to face Claire. "How are you?"

"I'm good, thanks," Claire said. "It's nice to be here again."

"Right back into it, I suppose. It's a busy one today," Jen remarked. She pulled a glass down from the cupboard and filled it with water. "You're not on call already, are you?"

"No, just clinic today."

"That's good. There's something about the end of summer. Everyone is ready to have those babies." Jen laughed. "Hey, since you're not on call, do you think you might be able to do me a big favor?"

"What's that?" Claire asked.

"I have a client who needs a home visit later today. Very standard, her baby is healthy and growing. It's all good, I'm just swamped here."

Claire could do that on her way home. "Sure."

"Great, thank you. I'll call her and let her know you're coming instead."

"She'll be fine with that?" Sometimes new parents could be uncomfortable with change.

"It's her fourth baby." Jen gave Claire a knowing look.

"Ah. Say no more." Women who had been there and done this before tended to be more flexible. They had to be. Claire had a soft spot in her heart for first-time moms, however. It was so hard when it was all new.

Jen touched the edge of Claire's shoulder as she left the kitchen. "Thank you so much. And again, welcome back."

It was good to be here. This would give Claire purpose and normalcy. She loved delivering babies and didn't realize until this moment how much she had missed her job.

After a full, busy day, Claire pulled together a bag of things and went to her car. One last stop to see Jen's client about thirty minutes away near Curve Lake, and she would be done.

Claire pulled open the car door and got inside. She put the key in the ignition but didn't turn it. Instead, she sat staring at her hand, thinking about the route she would take to get there. That's when it hit her.

I can't do this.

She couldn't leave Summerville. The stop wasn't far by any stretch, but it was to a place she hadn't been before. She had already done that very thing—gone to places she'd never been before—twice this summer, and both times hadn't been good. She had almost lost her daughter on one of them, for God's sake. She couldn't go somewhere new again. She couldn't leave her comforts of home and have something bad happen. Ever since she had opened the door to Audrey, she had invited in one terrible thing after the other. Leaving wasn't the answer. No. She needed to get back home, that's what she needed to do. The desire to stay safe, to make sure Lilah was okay suddenly came over her like a wave, and she couldn't think of anything else.

The back of Claire's neck was damp with sweat. Her heart fluttered in her chest. She had to get home. She had to make sure Lilah was there and she was okay. How could she have told Lilah it was alright to open the door to Audrey? What if Audrey took Lilah out somewhere and they didn't come back home? It wouldn't surprise her, with all the terrible things that had been happening to Claire lately. Even with

the best of intentions, Audrey could take Lilah somewhere
where Lilah could be hurt. Or, and Claire could barely
handle the thought, someone could take Lilah away, the way
she had been taken.

Claire searched her phone for Jen's number with shaking
hands. When she got through to her, her voice came out rushed
and wobbly at the same time. "I can't see your client. I'm sorry."

"Claire? What do you mean?" Jen's voice was filled with
confusion.

"I can't do it. I have to get home. I have to check on my
daughter."

"Is something wrong?" Jen asked.

"No, it's just... I have to go. I'm sorry," Claire said again. She
clicked the button to hang up and tossed her phone onto the
empty seat next to her. She turned the key and pulled out of her
parking spot in a rush, the car roaring as she sped back home on
the twisted, narrow roads of Summerville.

When she got to her house, she flung the door open and
rushed inside. The living room was empty.

"Lilah?"

The kitchen was quiet, too.

She went to the back, to Lilah's favorite spot to lounge
around, but it was empty, too.

"Lilah!" Claire projected louder, trying not to let the panic
overtake her, but she was hot and clammy at the same time. Her
legs felt weak. Where was Lilah?

Claire went up the stairs and pushed open Lilah's door with
a bang.

Lilah's head snapped to the doorway. "Mom? What the
heck?" She was lying on her bed, her phone in hand, staring at
something on the tiny screen.

"Why didn't you answer me? I was shouting your name,"
Claire snapped. She was angry and she wasn't. The tension in
her body put her on edge, but she also went to Lilah's side, sat

on the bed next to her and touched her face to feel that she was real and okay.

"I didn't hear you. I don't see what the big deal is," Lilah said.

"I was worried about you. I thought something had happened to you." It was irrational and she knew it, but she couldn't help it.

"I haven't gone anywhere. How could anything happen to me?" Lilah sat up in bed. She narrowed her eyes and examined Claire. "Are you okay? You look sweaty."

"I'm fine," Claire said. She stood and went to leave the room. "I'll make dinner soon."

Downstairs, Claire tried to still her shaky arms and legs by sitting outside. She needed air and a moment to be quiet, but her phone rang, interrupting her thoughts.

"Hello?"

"Claire. It's Jen." Her voice was cool. This wasn't good.

"I'm so sorry," Claire said.

"You can't do that kind of thing. You know that, right? This is a pregnant woman's health we're talking about."

"I know. I had to get home. I'm really sorry."

"You said sorry already, but that doesn't cut it. When you say you're going to see one of my clients, you can't flake out," Jen said.

Claire had no idea how to respond. She had never in her life been unreliable.

"It wasn't a flake out. I was genuinely worried about my daughter," she replied.

"Why? Did something happen to her?" Jen's voice softened.

"Well, no. But I thought something might have."

There was a silence over the phone. Jen was mad, Claire knew it. Her reason for not seeing a client was ridiculous, even Claire could hear it.

"Why would you think that?" Jen asked.

Why was she falling apart? Would Jen accept it if Claire told her she was in the middle of a crisis? She would sound like one of those women who wakes up in their thirties or forties and wants to travel to India to pray, or Italy to eat. That's not what this was. She was afraid. Her entire, safe, careful life had crumbled, and she couldn't take any more uncertainty or questions or bad news. She needed everything to stay as calm as it had been.

She didn't know how to articulate that, though, so instead, she said nothing, and when Claire had no answer, Jen eventually said goodbye and hung up on her.

TWENTY-FOUR

By the next morning, Claire regretted everything. She felt so awful about not seeing Jen's client, about being so unlike herself and unreliable, she had barely slept the night before. She was tired today, a bone-deep kind of tired that not even her giant mug of coffee would fix.

After her first cup of coffee, she called the clinic to speak to the most senior partner in the practice, Sarah.

"Your actions could have resulted in a bad outcome for mom and baby yesterday. You know that," Sarah said. Claire was used to all her coworkers speaking gently, but there was no warmth in Sarah's voice.

"I do. I know. And I'm so sorry." This was awful. Claire was sick with guilt. "Is there anything I can do?"

"Not right now. We're writing up a disciplinary letter to keep on file," Sarah explained. "Are you sure you're ready to come back?"

Claire couldn't take leave forever. Yes, she had been through a lot, but at some point, she had to try to get back to normal, whatever that new normal was. She couldn't help but long for that moment in time before any of this happened. Before Audrey.

She didn't wish that she had never gotten to know Audrey—it was more about what Audrey represented. Claire wished she hadn't gone looking for answers or learned that her real parents were alcoholics. She wished she had never read the name Sadie Green. She wished her mother was simply her mother—the woman who used to run her fingers through her hair at night when Claire was a little girl and couldn't sleep. The person Claire still turned to for answers and advice about even the simplest of things as an adult.

The truth was, Claire was unsettled, and she didn't know how to function. That was the problem. Her quiet life in beautiful Summerville felt uneasy and uncomfortable. It wasn't how she wanted it to be. She couldn't handle the discomfort that came with new and unknown things, that's why she had stayed here her entire life—it was familiar. When most of the kids from her high school got out of town as soon as they could, moving away to bigger cities for bigger lives, Claire had been content to stay home and get a house just across town from where she grew up. She bristled when people implied there was something wrong with that. You didn't have to leave to experience life. Claire was proof of that. Although now even this view of life was questionable. Did she only feel this way because of her mother, a mother who wouldn't let her out of her sight for good reason? Claire ran a hand over her eyes. She was so tired.

Down on the dock, she placed her large mug with the big letter C painted across the front of it on the flat, wide arm of the chair she was sitting on. She stood in her nightgown and went to the end of the dock, where she curled her toes over the edge and looked into the water. It was early enough that it was crystal clear. So clear, she could see down to the bottom of the lake. It would likely be chilly right now since it was early morning, but something about the thought of jumping into cold water, refreshing her body, cleansing it from the bottom of her feet to the top of her head, was appealing. It was exactly what she needed. Getting into the water was what she yearned for in that moment. It was the way she had spent so many mornings when she was a kid.

Claire was too impatient to go back up to the house and get her bathing suit, so she backed up several steps and then ran toward the water. When she reached the end of the dock, she plugged her nose and jumped feet first into the lake, making her body into a C-shape so she wouldn't hit her legs on the bottom. After all these years, all this swimming, Claire had never learned to dive properly and preferred to jump in. Lilah teased her endlessly, but Claire didn't care.

When she broke the surface, Claire gasped. The water was cold. So cold it tightened her chest. It would take a little while to get used to. Her nightgown billowed around her body, but it was light, so it didn't weigh her down. She went forward through the water, ducking her head under the surface to push herself forward and then bobbing back up every now and again to breathe in. She was freezing, but also fresh. Alive. There was nothing like it. There was nothing like Shadow Lake, or Summerville, or her perfect house.

Claire swam to the middle of the lake and then back again. When she heaved her body up onto the dock, she rolled over onto her back to catch her breath for a moment. Her arms and legs were worn out. It was the good kind of exhausted, though, the kind you get from much-needed physical activity.

She stood and shook her legs and arms, trying to rid her body of some of the droplets. Then she picked up her mug and made her way up to the house to have a hot shower. Somewhere between the shampoo and the bodywash, Claire made a decision. She was done with all of this. With looking for answers about Veronica, finding out who she was, trying to learn what had happened all those years ago. It was time to empty out her mother's house, sell it, and then get back to work and give it all her focus. It was time to be the person she used to be: a good midwife, a good mother. It was time to move on.

After a relatively uneventful week of work at the clinic, where Claire was careful not to step out of line to avoid any further disciplinary warnings, she came home and set her keys on the counter. She wondered briefly how long everyone at work would be upset with her and would be watching her closely. It was uncomfortable, but Claire could only try to do her best now and wait it out.

Lilah's backpack was leaning up against the island in the kitchen, the way it always did after school, her lunch bag emptied and her containers sitting by the sink.

"Lilah?" Claire called. She opened the fridge and stared inside, wondering what she wanted. Nothing, really. "Lilah!"

"I'm up here!" Lilah called back.

Claire followed the sound of her voice and found Lilah in her bedroom, writing in an agenda.

"How was the first day back at school?" Claire asked.

"Fine." She continued writing, her head bent forward.

"Anything interesting happen?"

"No."

Claire sighed at how impossible conversation could be. "Do you like your teacher?"

Lilah had a newer teacher this year, an outsider, which didn't happen often in Summerville. He was on the younger side, full of energy and enthusiasm, Claire had heard.

"Mr. Fitz? Yeah, he's good. I like him," Lilah said. She looked up from her agenda. "He makes us fill in our homework tasks every day. I'm just writing down what I need to do for math."

Claire liked him already.

"How come you're home?" Lilah's forehead creased when she looked at Claire. "Aren't you on call? Or shouldn't one of your clients be having a baby?"

Sarah had told her at the clinic today that they didn't think she was ready to be on call. Claire agreed. She was still embarrassed about not seeing a pregnant woman and not being there to assure her that her baby was fine. She wasn't going to let it happen again, but for now would have to do her time.

"I'm just doing clinic for a while. Easing back into it."

Lilah nodded and then went back to her agenda.

"I'll be out back if you need me," Claire said. She planned to do what she usually did after work. Sit outside while the sun was still bright, enjoy the warm air and the sounds of the water for a while before making dinner and cleaning up afterwards, throwing laundry in and getting to bed early so she was ready for another day.

She went straight for the covered deck and sat in one of the most comfortable chairs. She had only been there for five minutes when a voice came from behind her.

"I'm back with the gardening tools." It was Greg. She hadn't seen him for a while, not since the uncomfortable lunch at Grazie, but she was over that now. In fact, she was struck by how happy she was that he was here again. His familiarity was comforting; the way he stood with one hand in the front pocket of his old jeans, his face relaxed with a hint of a smile.

"Hey. Come sit," Claire said. "I don't have any beer. There's coffee though?" She posed it as a question, even though she knew him well enough to guess what his answer would be. He rarely drank coffee in the afternoons. Made it too hard for him to sleep.

"I'm good. Anyway, how are things?" he asked.

"Fine."

Greg studied her, probably waiting for her to expand on

that. No wonder Lilah was the way she was with the one-word answers. She learned from the best.

"What's going on?" he asked.

Claire sighed again. Her shoulders dropped. She might as well be honest with him, he could read her anyway. "I missed seeing a client, so they've suggested I be on clinic only for a while."

"You missed seeing a client? Like, you forgot?" Greg's eyebrows shot upwards on his forehead. "That's never happened to you before, has it?"

"I didn't forget. I was worried about Lilah, so I skipped the client and came home. I feel awful about it. It was a dumb decision."

"Why were you worried about Lilah? Is she okay?" Greg asked, his expression tight.

"She's fine. There was nothing wrong with her." Claire pulled her feet up onto the chair and placed one arm around her bent legs. Her chin rested on the top of her knees. It was harder for Greg to see her face this way.

"I'm worried about you," Greg said. "If you keep avoiding everything you're dealing with and not trying to get answers, you're not going to feel settled or comfortable. I know you."

"You don't know everything about me anymore," Claire said, even though it wasn't kind. It was true that they hadn't been together for a while, but Greg still knew her. She was defensive, though.

"I realize that, but I know that you need closure here. I can see it."

"Closure doesn't matter. Not when she's gone."

"There has to be some way to find out the truth about what happened back then." Greg took the seat opposite Claire. He watched her, but she didn't make eye contact. She didn't want him convincing her that she needed to take a different path. She had made up her mind. Forget everything about the past and move on. It was the only way forward.

"I don't want to. I want to forget it all happened. I don't need to know who my birth parents were, I don't need answers about Veronica or why she took me. It was probably because they were alcoholics."

"Or maybe they became alcoholics because you were taken away."

"Greg!" Claire snapped. It annoyed her that Greg had the same thought as Audrey, like all of her family was more like Audrey than they were like her. Anyway, even if it were true, he didn't need to put it that way. Was he trying to make her hate Veronica? She didn't, and she didn't want to.

"What? I'm surprised by you. You usually wouldn't just do... nothing," he said.

"Well, this time I am." Claire didn't feel the need to explain her reasoning any further. This was what she wanted to do. Greg should accept that.

"Okay." He sat back in his seat and looked out at the lake. He was quiet for a while, but Claire didn't try to coax any conversation out of him. They remained that way, silent and still. It wasn't the comfortable silence they used to have, and Greg must have noticed it, too. He eventually got up from his seat. "I'm going to go say hi to Lilah and then I have to run." His voice was quiet. He was awkward, Claire could tell.

"Okay."

After he left, Claire remained in her seat, simmering. It wasn't anyone else's business what she did with her life. Greg couldn't even begin to understand how difficult it was to make sense of any of the news she had learned over the summer. She didn't have to handle it the way he would, and she didn't have to handle it the way Audrey would want to handle it either.

The thundering sound of Lilah jogging down the stairs came from inside. She was never quiet with her movement, which struck Claire as odd. How could a relatively small human make so much noise when just moving through a house?

"Hey," Lilah said as she came outside to join Claire. "I'm on the phone with Audrey. She wanted to know if I'm free this weekend."

An immediate wash of mixed emotions came over Claire. The back of her neck prickled with jealousy and her muscles tensed with defensiveness. Lilah was her kid. She had put in the years of work raising her, ensuring she had everything she needed and was happy, and Audrey acted like she could waltz into their life and reap all the benefits of having a twelve-year-old in her life. She acted like Lilah was her niece and Audrey was the fun aunt, but she wasn't. It wasn't fair.

"Let me speak to her." Claire held out her hand to take Lilah's phone.

Lilah paused, a slight hesitation, as if she didn't want Claire to talk to Audrey. That angered Claire even further.

"Hand it to me. Now."

"Okay. Sheesh." Lilah passed her phone to Claire, who held it up to her ear.

"Audrey? Hi. Listen, I need some time with Lilah. Alone."

Lilah's eyes widened and her head jutted forward. She opened her mouth to speak, but Claire held a finger up at her to silence her so she could hear Audrey.

"Alone? What do you mean?" Audrey asked.

"I mean, I want to get back to how our life used to be. When it was Lilah and I, the two of us."

"Oh. I thought it was getting back to normal now that school and work have started up again." Audrey's voice had a confused lilt to it. She wasn't getting the hint.

"I don't want to keep pursuing whatever it is that we have going on here," Claire said. Lilah was bouncing in front of her, eyes bulging.

"What do you mean?"

"You're not my sister and you're not Lilah's aunt. If Veronica were alive, it would be one thing, but she's gone. I'd like to go back to my old life. I think we need to move on."

"No!" Lilah shouted it. Her mouth hung open.

Claire tried raising a hand again to silence her.

"What are you doing?" Lilah asked. She moved toward Claire, reaching for the phone. Claire jerked her body away.

"I don't understand." Audrey's voice sounded far away.

Claire put a finger in her other ear to try to hear better.

"I don't want you around right now. Lilah isn't free this weekend. This is all too confusing, so I think you should leave us alone," Claire said.

"Mom!" Lilah yelled. Her face had gone red, flushed from her neck up to her hairline. She grabbed the phone out of Claire's hand this time, but Claire managed to hang up before Lilah got it back.

"It's for the best," Claire said. "She's not family."

It was true, technically. Yet, Claire was unable to control herself. She knew she was being slightly irrational and even quite mean. All Lilah wanted was to get to know Audrey, but who was Audrey? She could be anyone. Claire wasn't about to let some stranger who seemed okay hurt her or Lilah. It wasn't worth it.

"I can't believe you! You can't stop me from talking to her," Lilah shouted. Her arms were stiff and straight by her side. She was threatening Claire, but there wasn't anything behind her words. Claire knew it by the look in Lilah's eyes. There was a flash of uncertainty. The kind that comes from a kid who hasn't rebelled against her parents before. She was a good kid. She would understand and forgive Claire eventually.

"Give me your phone," Claire said.

"No." Lilah folded her arms across her chest.

"Give it to me now, Lilah. Or you will regret it, I promise you."

Lilah hesitated. She stared at Claire for a beat and then, when it seemed like her face couldn't get any redder, she slammed her phone into Claire's outstretched hand.

"We have barely any family and this is how you handle the first person that comes into our lives and wants to be with us?"

It was such a grown-up thing for Lilah to say. Claire's chest tightened at the honesty of it, but she said nothing.

Lilah stormed away, up the stairs and into her bedroom, where she slammed the door. She somehow managed to be even louder than she was before.

Claire sat back and tried not to cry.

TWENTY-FIVE

That night, after Lilah had stormed upstairs, she refused to come down for the rest of the evening. Claire made dinner, but ended up eating it alone. She didn't have the energy to force Lilah to come out of her room and sit with her. Instead, she sat in front of the television and ate in silence, cleaned up the dishes, packed away Lilah's portion into a container and placed it on the shelf right around her daughter's line of sight so she would spot it if and when she came down to the kitchen to admit she was hungry.

It didn't happen, though. After Claire went upstairs to wash her face and change into her pajamas, she was sure she would hear the telltale sign of Lilah's feet walking through the hallway, storming down the stairs. She didn't. Only the silence that comes with late night in cottage country.

The next morning, Claire rose earlier than usual, when the sky was still dim and the entire world was sleeping. She went to the kitchen to make a cup of coffee. After clinic, Claire planned to go to her mother's house to finally finish emptying out what she could. She had been doing bits here and there, but now it was time to get it all done. She made a mental note to contact a real estate agent and double-check with the lawyer again, even though she had asked several times already about Audrey and how this complicated things. Thankfully, it wasn't complicated because of the will.

It wasn't that Claire didn't want Audrey to have anything, she even offered her some photos and other small mementos, it was that Claire didn't want any further roadblocks. She wanted this done and dusted. It had been almost impossible lately to keep her life organized and safe. At least she could control this part.

After coffee, Claire went upstairs and showered. She then stepped into a pair of loose-fitting joggers and a T-shirt with Summerville written across the front of it. She didn't usually give in and purchase any of the touristy-type clothing around here, but she had been in need of a T-shirt one day and had bought the first casual, loose-fitting one she could find in town. It quickly became her most comfortable and, therefore, most-loved shirt.

She made herself a smoothie to take in the car to work and was about to leave. Lilah still hadn't made an appearance. Claire paused at the foot of the stairs and waited, listening. Normally, Lilah was up for school by now, but there was nothing but silence. Claire put her bag and smoothie down. She would have to deal with Lilah's anger once more before leaving. There was no way she was going to be late for school simply because she was mad at Claire.

"Lilah?" Claire knocked gently on the door. "You have to get up."

Silence.

Claire supposed she should get used to this. Lilah was still only twelve. Imagine her at sixteen years old.

"Lilah?" Claire opened the door slowly, giving Lilah privacy and time to prepare for her mother entering her room. Claire had only started doing that recently. Up until Lilah had turned eleven, she had no issue with her mother coming in unannounced. In fact, she rarely closed her bedroom door all the way.

Claire stepped inside and found that the room was empty. Lilah's bed was a mess, tangled up from sleep. Her pajamas were on the floor next to the foot of her bed and her fan was on, oscillating slowly, but no Lilah. Claire left the room and went to the bathroom a few steps away. It was dark, and also empty.

Claire's heart sped up a fraction. She didn't feel the need to panic, not yet anyway, but it was jarring when you expected to find someone somewhere and they weren't there.

Claire quickly went through the rest of the hallway, checking from room to room. Lilah wasn't in any of them.

"Lilah?" Claire yelled. "I have to go to work!" She went down the stairs and out back, thinking that maybe Lilah had slipped outside while Claire was showering. The only thing she found was an empty back porch and a silent dock. There was noise coming from across the lake; a motorboat roaring to life, the distant sounds of voices calling to one another carrying over the water.

Claire went back inside and grabbed her phone. She dialed Lilah and waited. The familiar trill of Lilah's ringtone came from the kitchen. Claire's head snapped to the side in search of the noise.

Shoot. She had taken Lilah's phone away from her last night and put it in the cupboard. Lilah didn't have her phone on her and Claire had no idea where she was. Claire's fingers were suddenly cold. A sour taste formed in her mouth. This had never happened before; Claire always knew where her daughter was at all times. She took care of Lilah, protected her.

Until now.

Claire closed her eyes, remembering the fight last night. It was stupid of her, she should have been gentler. Lilah wanted

Audrey in her life and Claire had ripped it away with no room for negotiation. That never worked.

Audrey's face flashed through Claire's mind. For a minute, she thought Lilah must be with Audrey, but she couldn't be. Lilah had no way of contacting Audrey. They had no landline. Any control she felt like she still had over her situation slipped out of her grasp.

She called Greg. "Is Lilah with you?" she asked in a rushed tone. Her head churned with possibilities and outcomes.

"What? No," Greg said, his voice laced with confusion. "She's not at home with you?"

"No. I got up this morning and got ready, thinking she was still sleeping. I just went to check before leaving for work and she isn't here. She's nowhere." Desperation seeped into her voice, she could hear it.

"Okay, calm down a second and we'll figure this out."

"How?" Claire shouted. Greg knew her. He knew this was one of her deepest fears. Being a parent was rewarding a lot of the time, but it was also cruel. It could whip you into the darkest moments of your life without warning. If Lilah was missing— Claire couldn't finish the thought. It was too horrible. "Want me to come over?" Greg asked, and then, without waiting for an answer, said, "I'll be there in five minutes."

Claire hung up the phone and placed it on the kitchen counter. The house was eerily quiet.

When Greg arrived, they got into his car and drove around Summerville, searching. Claire didn't know what else to do. They tried the coffee shop Lilah loved, the one with the big pots of flowers out front on Main Street. Then they went to the parks she sometimes hung out at. They drove by her friends' houses, but nobody was home at most of them. The kids were in school, parents working or out running errands. Claire called the school, but Lilah hadn't arrived. The last place they went to was Skeleton Lake. Claire knew it was a stretch. It would be hard for Lilah to get out there without a car.

The beach was empty. Claire stood at the edge of the water looking out at the lake because she didn't know what else to do. Then she started crying. Deep, gut-wrenching sobs that required her entire body's energy.

"Hey, it's okay," Greg said. He put one arm around her shoulder, and the other around her waist. They stood that way for a while. "She could be up to something. You know how she can be these days. So many hormones—didn't you say that was usually behind it all?"

Claire rubbed at her face. She sniffed and nodded.

They decided to head back home. Greg thought they should wait a couple of hours in case Lilah decided to come home, and then call the police, but Claire couldn't wait. As soon as she walked in the door, she called. They sent someone over to the house shortly after.

"This happens with kids from time to time unfortunately. They usually head back home," the officer said. He looked at Claire with kind eyes. He was trying to be gentle, but it wasn't what Claire wanted to hear.

"It's not like her. She's never done this." Claire wanted them to do something. Stop standing here talking and *do* something. Give her an answer. If they had something to tell her, she might not feel so helpless.

"Can you show us a recent photo?" the officer asked.

Claire pulled out her phone and clicked on her album. The most recent one she had was of Lilah and Audrey, from their weekend away.

"This is her," Claire said.

"And who is that?" The officer pointed at Audrey.

Claire hesitated. "She's a family friend," she said eventually,

The officer held Claire's eyes. He frowned. "Have you tried her?"

Claire shook her head and the officer frowned even deeper.

"She doesn't live in town. There's no way Lilah could have traveled that far. She doesn't even have Audrey's address," Claire said.

The officer nodded. "The best place to start is by calling her friends and any of your family friends. Check in with everyone first and see if they have any information you might not have. Then give us a call back and we'll go from there, okay? And keep your phone close by in case she calls you."

Claire wanted to explain that Lilah didn't have her phone on her, but she wasn't sure it would help. What the officer said was a rational way to approach all of this, but it wasn't enough in Claire's opinion. Someone had to search for her.

After he left, Greg started calling some of the families they had gotten to know over the years through Lilah's school and hockey teams. He was good in situations like this. Calm and steady. Claire couldn't make the calls. Her voice would shake too much.

When her phone rang, Claire jolted. That feeling she got when she was about to do something incredibly uncomfortable rocked her body, making it feel like she couldn't catch her breath.

"Hello?"

"Hey, it's me." It was Fatima's voice.

Claire immediately deflated. Her shoulders slumped.

"Is Lilah with you?" Claire asked.

"What? No. Isn't she at school?"

Claire filled her in, explaining the details in a rushed manner.

"Whoa. Okay, hang on. I'm sure she's just taken off some-where because she's angry at you. You know you did that to your own mother, don't you?"

The way Fatima used those words—*your own mother*—irked Claire at the moment. All of this was because of Veronica. Most of the time, Claire didn't want to be mad at her, but she was. Underneath, it had been simmering. She was angry and it was starting to surface.

"That was different," Claire said.

"Hey, so the reason I'm calling is because I found something I don't ever remember having in the first place. It's regarding you and your mother."

"Let's talk later," Claire said in her rushed manner again and told Fatima she had to go. She hung up the phone and rubbed at the back of her neck. How could Fatima change the subject of the conversation at a time like this?

While Greg continued with the phone calls to families, Claire called Audrey. She was the last person Claire felt like talking to, but it had to be done, she supposed. The officer suggested they call everyone.

"Claire, hi," Audrey said when she answered the phone.

"Hey. Is Lilah with you?" Claire cringed when she said it. She held her breath for a beat, waiting for the answer.

"Why would she be with me?"

"I don't know. Maybe it's because you're trying too hard with her, and she thinks you really care." It was the stress talking. Claire couldn't stop it.

"I'm trying too hard?" Audrey's voice was laced with hurt. "Of course I care about her. I care about both of you. Even if I'm not technically her aunt or your sister."

"You're nothing to us," Claire shouted. Before all of this had happened, she would never speak to someone that way. She was a nice person. She was empathetic. This wasn't her.

"Claire—"

"I just need my daughter back," Claire said. "She's missing." She hung up on Audrey and her entire body started to shake. She sat down to calm herself. Greg's eyes widened from where he sat, on his phone. He stood and came over to her, wrapping his warm arm around her shoulder. She felt herself sink against him. At least Greg was a constant in her life. Even though they weren't married anymore, he was always there for her.

"We'll get through this together. I won't leave your side until we've found her," Greg said quietly.

Claire would have cried then, but everything was numb.

Her biggest fear had come true. Lilah was gone.

TWENTY-SIX

After an hour, Greg had gone through all the calls with no answers. He tried to calm Claire by making her a tea, talking to her in his steady voice, but it agitated her. She didn't want to sit at the house doing nothing. They had to get out there and find Lilah.

When Claire was a child, she had disappeared once. She was in a shopping mall with her mother, and she was quite young at the time. She remembered this because she could recall how big everything and everyone had seemed around her. The two of them had been waiting by the elevator, surrounded by a crowd of people. Claire held onto Veronica's hand, but when the doors opened up to the elevator, the swarm of people jostling to get inside had caused her grip to loosen from her mother's. Claire had assumed her mother was still next to her when she got swept inside, but when she looked up and around her, she couldn't see her anywhere.

When the elevator doors opened again and Claire stepped out onto the upper floor, she had been confused at first. What was she supposed to do now? She didn't think to stay in place, although, afterwards, Veronica would tell her over and over again that if it ever happened again, that was what she should do. Instead, Claire had followed some of the other grown-ups through the mall, deciding who she should ask for help. She had tried her best not to cry, but it was hard. She had never been separated from her mother before. She could remember the feeling in her chest, like her heart was going to burst through it, she was so nervous.

Eventually, a stranger saw her standing alone, eyes wet, and asked her if she was okay.

"Are you lost?" the stranger had asked. "Is your mommy or daddy here somewhere?"

Claire had nodded her head, but wouldn't speak. She was too terrified of strangers. Her mother had instilled that in her by never allowing her out of her sight.

When her mother found her, it could have been five minutes later or it could have been an hour, it was hard for Claire to tell, but it was clear that Veronica was distraught. Her face was red and splotchy, and her makeup around her eyes was smudged, as if she had been crying, just like Claire.

"Claire!" her mother had shouted when she first saw her. She ran to Claire's side and picked her up into her arms, squeezing her tight to her body. "Oh, my goodness, I've been looking everywhere. I was so scared. I was so scared."

Claire was, too. Veronica must have noticed. She kept apologizing. "I'm so sorry, baby. I will never let anything happen to you," her mother had said. "You're safe with me. You're safe. I promise."

Now, Claire sat up straighter in her seat in the kitchen. There was a promise you made to your children when you were their parent. You would always keep them safe.

Claire couldn't sit here any longer.

"We should call the police back," she said.

"And tell them what?" Greg asked. "We haven't heard anything,"

"Greg," Claire snapped. "You're not helping." She was so on edge. This was the worst thing that could happen to her. Lilah may think she was an adult, but she was Claire's baby. There was still so much she didn't know.

Claire wouldn't let her mind go to the dark place. The one where you thought about the worst possible scenario. She couldn't. If she did, Claire wouldn't be able to move. She would be frozen in place, numb and empty. This was the thing about motherhood; the elation was indescribable in some ways, but so was the fear. Losing a child would be something Claire could never come back from. She was certain.

She shook her head, as if to ward off the dark thoughts.

"I'm going to get my keys and drive around," Claire said.

"Right. I'm coming with you." Greg stood and went to Claire's side. He touched her wrist and Claire reached for his hand. She wove her fingers in between his and held on tightly.

"I'm really scared," Claire said.

"I know. Me, too."

The sound of the front door opening caused Claire's body to jerk. She snapped her head to the right, to face the entrance-way. Walking through it was Lilah.

Claire stumbled backwards. Her mouth went dry. She ran to Lilah and wrapped her arms around her. "Lilah, oh my God. Lilah." She couldn't bring herself to scold her daughter in that moment. She was too weak with gratitude. Thank goodness she didn't have to go to the dark place. Thank goodness her daughter was standing in front of her again.

Greg was next to them, wrapping his arms around both of them. He rested his cheek on the top of Lilah's head and closed his eyes briefly.

Lilah didn't say anything. She stood and let them hug her, as if she knew she had done something bad, as if the weight of their emotions was holding her in place, keeping her silent.

When Claire pulled away, she put her hands on Lilah's

arms and moved her head back to get a better look at her daughter. Lilah's mouth made a straight line across her face. The freckles sprinkled across her nose made her look young. Her head was bowed, but her eyes pointed toward Claire.

"Where were you?" Claire asked. "I was terrified. You scared me so much."

Lilah rubbed at the back of her neck. "Sorry," she mumbled.

"You didn't answer me." Claire's voice wobbled.

"You can't do this kind of thing, Li," Greg said. "You can't just leave and not tell us where you'll be."

"I'm sorry," she said again. "I wanted to be alone."

"Where were you?" Claire demanded.

"I was with Audrey."

"Who?" Claire whispered, even though she heard it right the first time. A white-hot anger hissed through Claire's body. Her nostrils flared. All this time, all this worry, and she was with Audrey.

"Audrey."

"How?" Claire fumbled over the word. This didn't make sense. "You had no way of contacting her."

"I snuck your phone when you weren't looking and found a bus schedule. Then I grabbed my bank card and left. I needed her and she was there for me. It was really nice of her," Lilah said.

Greg's eyes darted to Claire. He gave her a look that said *Oh no. She didn't just say that.*

But she did and Claire couldn't contain herself.

"You think this was *nice* of her? I was worried sick about you. I can't even begin to tell you how upset I am with you, but Audrey is an adult, and she should have known better."

"You can't blame her!" Lilah shouted. "You don't know the whole story..."

Then it hit Claire. Audrey had lied when she spoke to her on the phone. She didn't tell Claire that she was with Lilah.

Audrey let her continue believing something awful had happened, let her have the worst day of her life. The back of Claire's throat ached.

"Get upstairs." Claire's voice was ice-cold and controlled. It was the kind of anger that was incredibly quiet.

"What? Why?" Lilah asked. She was being too brave for her own good.

"Get. Upstairs," Claire repeated. "I don't want to see you or speak to you right now."

"Claire," Greg said. His eyes had widened a little. She knew how she sounded. It didn't make any sense at all. She had spent the day worried sick and desperate to find her daughter; now she was here, and Claire wanted nothing to do with her.

Lilah's face flashed with hurt, but she went up the stairs, shoulders hunched and head bowed forward.

"Hey," Greg said, reaching for Claire again.

"Don't." Claire held up a hand. "Let me handle this."

Greg watched her, mouth closed, but eyes full of concern. "Okay," he said eventually. "I'm going to go talk to her." He motioned upstairs and then left the room.

Claire went to pick up her phone with a shaking hand to call Audrey, but stopped. She suddenly felt like this had to be done in person.

As she waited for Greg to come back down, she paced around the kitchen, looking for her keys and her purse. She pulled Lilah's phone down from where she had stored it in the kitchen and plugged it in to charge. Lilah didn't deserve to have it back, but Claire wanted a way to contact her daughter when she needed to.

Eventually, Greg came back down the stairs, moving slowly. His face looked tired.

"Can you stay here with her for a while?" Claire asked.

"Why? Where are you going?"

"I need to go out. I'll be gone for several hours."

Greg held her gaze. "Where? Lilah just got back. I know you're angry, but..."

"I need to go and speak with Audrey. In person."

Greg rubbed at his forehead. He closed his eyes briefly. "To Elora? That's a really long drive there and back."

"I know you think this is a bad idea," Claire said. "But I need to do it. I need to talk to her and determine some boundaries."

"Okay," Greg said. "But are you sure you need boundaries? I think what you might really need is family. Having family around could be a very good thing for you."

Having family around was important, yes. But how was family supposed to be defined? Who was Claire's real family? It was a murky, shadowy area that confused her, so Claire's instinct was to protect herself. And to do that, she had to get some space from Audrey.

Greg moved toward her. "Can I?" he asked, holding his arms out to her.

Claire nodded. It was sweet of him to ask, and she knew he probably did it because she had been so sharp with him lately. She realized that she should let him in. He was her comfort in moments like these, when she was uncertain and upset.

"Thank you," Claire said, allowing her head to rest on his broad chest for a moment. "But I still have to go and talk to Audrey. She has to know she crossed a line and I don't want her around anymore."

A sound came from the direction of the stairs. Lilah was standing on the bottom step, her hand on the railing. She stared at Claire, her face contorted with anger.

Claire looked from Lilah back to Greg and Greg's face flashed with sympathy. They were both so different, yet neither one of them understood her. This was for the best, even if they didn't understand Claire's decision. She didn't need sympathy right now. She needed to get her life back.

"Lilah..." Claire started, but her phone buzzed and interrupted her train of thought. She ran a hand over her throbbing forehead. There was too much going on at once. When she answered the call, Sarah's voice, her supervisor at work, came through the other end.

"Claire? Where are you? You didn't show up to clinic today."

Claire's stomach dropped. She had completely forgotten about it in all the commotion. She couldn't keep track of anything.

"I'm sorry, there was an emergency with my daughter," Claire said.

"Is everything okay?" Sarah asked.

"Yes. She's fine. Everything's fine."

"So, were you planning on letting us know? There were clients here we had to juggle." Sarah's tone turned stiff.

"I'm really sorry." Claire put her head into her hand. This was terrible. How could she have messed up this badly?

Sarah spoke again. "I'm going to have to look at your file, and I think we need to have a meeting."

"A meeting?"

"Yes. This is serious, Claire. Things clearly aren't working," Sarah said.

Claire's hands went clammy. She managed to work out a time to meet, the following morning, and then hung up. Back on the stairs where Lilah had been standing, it was now empty. She was gone once more.

Soon after, Claire was on the road. Once Greg agreed to stay at the house with Lilah for a while, he had gone up to her bedroom to speak to her. Claire felt it was best if she gave Lilah space, so she grabbed her purse and left the house without saying goodbye. She would have to deal with both Lilah and whatever was happening with work later. All that she could think about now was Audrey.

During the long drive to Elora, Claire sat in silence, thinking. She thought about how terrible things seemed to have gone for her lately and how she had managed to let her carefully curated life slip through the cracks. She was usually more cautious and responsible than she had been acting these past few weeks, and it bothered her.

It also bothered her that she was about to have an uncomfortable conversation with Audrey, but she knew it had to happen. There was no reason for Audrey to stay in their lives, that became crystal clear to Claire today. Even if she meant well, Audrey brought nothing but upheaval and uncertainty to Claire's life, and she couldn't have that any longer. It wasn't how Claire operated.

When she got to Elora, Claire searched for Audrey's street name in her phone. She found directions, thankfully, and navigated her way there. At Audrey's house, Claire sat in the driveway for a moment before getting out of the car. She could do this. She had come this far. She tried to ignore the thread of doubt winding its way through her mind. When Claire thought of Audrey's face, all she could envision was her kind expressions, the way she smiled broadly, the way she made Claire feel comfortable. No, this had to happen. Claire needed her life back and this was the only way to get it. Besides, all she had to do was think of how she felt when she thought Lilah was gone and her resolve came back.

Claire went to the front door and knocked. When Audrey opened it, her head jerked back slightly in surprise.

"Claire?" she said. "What are you doing here? Is Lilah here?" She stuck her head out of the doorway and looked around in the direction of Claire's car.

The mention of Lilah's name coming from Audrey angered Claire. It relit all the feelings she'd had back at home, sitting around helpless, thinking her daughter was gone forever—or dead.

"How dare you?" Claire said instead of hello.

Audrey flinched. She blinked at Claire. "What?"

"How dare you pick Lilah up and take her away and not say a word to me?" Claire's voice was low. It was the kind of low, calm tone you get when you know you're about to snap and blow up.

"Hang on, I didn't know—" Audrey started, but Claire cut her off.

"On the phone. You lied about Lilah not being with you. And not only that, you could have very easily let me know she was okay, but you didn't. You let me suffer."

"Wait! Wait a minute," Audrey shouted. "Lilah showed up on my doorstep and said she had a huge fight with you. This was *after* you called me. As soon as I realized you didn't know about her taking the bus here, we got into the car and I drove her straight back. I didn't have time to call you first, I just wanted to get her home. And I didn't come to the door because you've been clear you don't want me around." Audrey's tone was steady despite her voice being raised slightly.

Her story was rational, and it seemed she wasn't to blame, but Claire still shook with nerves and adrenaline. "It feels like everything in my life has been turned upside down since you've come into it." This was the truth. Although, it must have shocked Audrey. She sucked in a sharp intake of air. Claire felt a pang of remorse because she wasn't a mean person, she didn't like to hurt others. But the feeling was fleeting. She continued, "What do you want from us? Is it inheritance? That has to go through lawyers."

"I told you it wasn't about that," Audrey said. There was an iciness to her tone now.

"Then what?" Claire asked

"I thought we could be family," Audrey replied. "If you don't have family, what have you got?"

Family. Could they be one? Claire didn't think so. It was too hard, too much baggage. What made a family, anyway? Claire thought she had one with her mother. She thought she and Lilah were good and steady—heck, she thought that she could have it with Greg, too. Now she didn't know anything.

"No," Claire said. "I don't think we can be family. Stop talking to Lilah. She's my daughter and we're not related to you."

"I know that, but that doesn't matter, does it?"

"It does matter. Stay out of our lives. We want nothing to do with you."

TWENTY-SEVEN

After meeting with Sarah the next day, Claire left the midwife office with a numb feeling. She had never been fired before. She supposed this technically wasn't a firing. Sarah had said she was being put on leave. She'd said that Claire still wasn't herself and wasn't contributing in the way their clients needed her. She'd even said it wasn't safe for Claire to keep working with them. Claire sat in her car with her head in her hands. That hurt the most. Deep in her core, Claire felt wounded by that. She had lived her entire life in a cautious, planned-out manner. She was safe, if nothing else.

But she had done the problematic things listed in her disciplinary file. It wasn't untrue, so there wasn't much Claire could say in return. There was nothing to do but to head home. She put the key in the ignition, and followed the road home, the same road she had driven so many times she could get back to her house on autopilot.

When she got home, she stayed in the driveway in her car with the windows down. It was quiet outside now that it was September. There wasn't much splashing in the lake or sounds of kids swimming. Families had returned home to their regular lives and Summerville was left only with the people who lived there year-round.

The sound of the trees never disappeared, however. Claire could listen to them forever. They whispered as the treetops swayed back and forth. It was calming and it soothed Claire, if only for a moment.

Then it returned. The worry and panic about making ends meet, how she would pay for herself and Lilah if she wasn't welcome back after her leave and didn't have an income. In the short term, she would be fine. They had money from her mother to get by on. In the long term, however, Claire needed a plan. She supposed she would have to find a way to gently tell Lilah what had happened. Although, Lilah wasn't speaking to her, so maybe she would be saved from that special kind of torture.

After a few minutes, Claire pulled the key from the ignition and slowly opened her car door. She trudged to the front door of her house and pushed her way inside. Another quiet surrounding. Lilah was at school.

Claire went upstairs to the bathroom and turned on the tap to the bathtub. She needed a long, hot bath to soak in. Maybe a nap when she was done. After that, she could decide what the hell she was going to do with her life. She took her clothes off and stood over the tub, leaning forward to hold the tips of her fingers under the tap. Once the temperature was right and there was enough water, she slipped into the tub and slid her body downwards, until only her nose and eyes were above water. It wasn't quite the same as floating in Shadow Lake, but it would do. It gave her time to think.

How had she gotten here? Her life had imploded this summer. She had lost her mother, then the idea of her mother, her daughter was slipping away, her job was gone. What had she done to deserve this? There was no way to answer that, so Claire remained still, let her arms float next to her body and tried to clear her mind so she could think about nothing at all.

When her fingers and toes went wrinkly, Claire stepped out of the tub and threw on her housecoat. In her bedroom, she crawled under the covers. Her sheets were cool, which felt incredible after a hot bath. She was so tired. This was good. This was all she could focus on now. A nap. She would worry about everything later.

The sound of her phone woke her. Claire fumbled for it and clicked on the button before she focused on the name on the screen.

"Hello?"

"Claire? It's me. Fatima."

Claire rolled onto her back and closed her eyes. "Hi."

"Were you sleeping?" Fatima asked.

"Just resting my eyes."

"Can you meet me at Kawartha Coffee? Say in half an hour?"

Claire didn't want to get up. She also had no clue what Fatima wanted, although the urgency in her voice suggested this wasn't merely a leisurely coffee date.

"Is everything okay?" Claire asked.

"It's fine. It's been a while," Fatima replied.

"Alright then. I can be there."

"Great." Fatima's voice went low. "I have something you need to see."

After Claire got dressed and went out to the front of the house and locked her door, she turned just in time to see a familiar figure approaching. Greg walked up the driveway and lifted an arm to wave.

"You're early. Lilah won't be home for another hour and a half," Claire said. He was meeting up with her today.

"I'm going to pick her up from school. But I wanted to see you."

"Why?" Claire's forehead crinkled. She dropped her arms at her sides.

"Do I need a reason?" Greg smiled. He was teasing, but his words hit Claire like a ton of bricks. He didn't need a reason because he was Greg. He was the one thing that had been reliable in her life these past few months. He was welcome.

Once he approached and was standing next to her, Claire reached for him. "Can I?" she asked.

He paused and lifted an eyebrow but smiled at her, in a confused sort of manner. "Of course."

Claire wrapped her arms around him, rather than folding into his body. She put her head on his shoulder and breathed in his familiar scent. The terrible, sinking feeling that had been swirling inside her since speaking with Audrey and being let go from work lessened for a moment.

"Thank you." It came out of her mouth automatically, before she even knew what she was saying.

"For what?" Greg said.

"I don't know," Claire replied. "For all of it." She had to run to meet Fatima, but she didn't care if she was late. This felt too important.

Greg laughed. "All of it?"

Claire just nodded, staying in his embrace, not letting go when she felt him pull away a touch. She wasn't ready to let go.

Eventually, they pulled apart.

"I'm meeting Fatima in town. I have to run."

"Mind if I pop in and leave this for Lilah?" Greg held up one of Lilah's favorite hoodies. "She left it at my place."

Claire gestured to the door and smiled. Then she went to her car and opened the driver's side door.

"I think I might know why we didn't work," Claire said before she got inside.

Greg stopped on his way to the front door. His back was turned to her, but she could see him stiffen even from where she was. He turned. "Claire..."

"No, it's okay," Claire said. "I'm not mad or upset. I don't want to start an argument."

"Okay..."

Claire brushed away a piece of hair. She wanted to tell him more, to explain how she felt, but she was still in a fog from the past few days. She wasn't sure she even knew what she was feeling, but there was something there. She knew it as soon as she saw him.

Her phone buzzed with a message. She looked at her screen and saw it was Fatima.

I'm here early.

"I better run," Claire said, holding her phone up. She thought she noticed Greg frown, but he was a little too far away for her to see his expression clearly.

He nodded and lifted a hand again to wave. "See you later?"

"Sure." Claire realized she wanted to. Very much.

TWENTY-EIGHT

Claire arrived at the coffee shop and found Fatima at a table on the patio. She had on a white golf shirt and a pair of white capri pants. She looked tailored and put together, like she always did. The only sign that something was wrong was the frown on her face. Fatima almost never looked upset if she could help it. She was a positive person on all accounts.

Claire approached the table and leaned in to kiss Fatima on the cheek. "How are you?"

"Okay, I suppose. How about you?"

Claire thought about Lilah and how they hadn't spoken more than a few words to each other in the last couple of days. Lilah mostly grunted her answers when Claire asked a question or kept her earbuds in while listening to music on her tablet so she could claim she couldn't hear Claire. Claire supposed she deserved it after the way she spoke to Audrey. Yet, she just wanted Audrey out of their lives so they could try to go back to the way things used to be. Claire hoped they would get there one day soon. Life was pretty good pre-Audrey. Lilah would remember that eventually, wouldn't she?

"Not so great, I guess," Claire said.

"I can tell." Fatima eyed her. A flash of concern crossed her expression.

Claire hadn't really put herself back together after the bath. Her hair was still in a messy ponytail, and she hadn't bothered with makeup. There were circles under her eyes when she looked at herself in the rearview mirror of the car, and she was slightly embarrassed that Greg had seen her that way, but it was too late by then to do anything about it. Besides, he had seen her at her worst. This look would startle Fatima, though. She was used to the put-together version of Claire.

"What's up?" Claire asked, not offering up an explanation for her appearance. Fatima wouldn't push. She was respectful of boundaries.

"I was in my office cleaning up this morning, and I decided to do a thorough job, the kind where you move furniture to actually get all the dust and dirt," Fatima said.

"Okay." Claire nodded as if she understood why Fatima was telling her this.

"Anyway, when I was down on my hands and knees by my desk, I noticed something had fallen behind it." Her eyes went wet, rimmed with red for some reason. She looked beside her and picked something up out of her purse.

"What?" Claire asked. Her mind started swimming with what this meant, but she couldn't understand.

"I found this." Fatima handed Claire an envelope. "After you told me about what happened with your mother, I thought I remembered seeing it somewhere in the house. That's why I left so abruptly that night. But I couldn't find it when I got back home, so I figured my mind was playing tricks on me."

There was something written across the front. It took Claire a moment, but as she reached her hand out, and then held the envelope in front of her, she saw it. A recognition came over her.

"It's your mother's handwriting," Fatima said.

Claire's name was on the front. Nothing else.

A dizziness came over her. She managed to croak out a question. "What is this?"

"I didn't open it," Fatima said. "But on the front of it was a sticky note addressed to me." She held up a small piece of yellow paper and showed it to Claire.

Fatima,

Please give this to her when I'm gone. She'll need it. You'll know when.

Veronica

"I don't understand," Claire said, frowning.

Fatima watched her expression carefully. "I have no idea when she put it there or how long it had been hidden behind my desk. It must have fallen back there at some point, but I don't know much else. I'm glad I found it when I did." Fatima reached out and touched the back of Claire's hand.

"Thank you," Claire managed. She put the envelope down with a shaking hand.

Fatima continued to watch her for a moment and then looked away.

"Right. You should read that when you're feeling ready. I'm sure there's no rush."

Claire nodded. Her mind whirred with thoughts of what it could possibly say, but she had to be alone for that. She wasn't about to open it up and start reading here.

They drank the coffees that had been delivered to their table, making small talk mostly to fill the time. Fatima kept watching Claire with wet, concerned eyes. She meant well, and Claire loved her like an aunt, but she needed space and time to think. She needed to get home.

When they were done, Claire stood and so did Fatima.

"Thank you for this," Claire said.

Fatima leaned in to kiss her on the cheek again. "Call me if you need me, okay? I'm here."

Claire squeezed Fatima's hand and then left, the weight of the envelope heavy in her hands.

Back at home, Claire checked her watch on the way in the door. It was two o'clock, which meant she had about forty-five minutes until Lilah finished school. She wasn't sure if Lilah was coming by to drop off her bag before heading out with Greg, but Claire thought she might have enough time to read and process whatever was in the envelope from her mother either way.

She sat on the couch and dropped her bag next to her. She pulled out the envelope again. Seeing the handwriting made her chest tighten. As much turmoil as her mother had put her through after her death, she would give anything—anything at all—to be able to be close to her again. To see her face. To hear her voice. Reading her words would have to do.

Inside the envelope were several pieces of paper, folded. She opened them up and found a handwritten letter.

Dear Claire,

I asked Fatima to give this to you after I'm gone. I hope you're not upset about that, but I thought it would be of more help to you later, after some of the dust had settled.

I'm not sure I even know where to start. Maybe by saying this: I'm sorry. I'm sorry for everything. I hope there's some part of you that can forgive me one day.

The reason I decided to sit down and write this letter was not only because I knew I was dying and I wanted to try to help you. It was also because I called Robert—Audrey's father. My

husband. When I knew I was terminal, I felt like he would have
to listen to me finally. I told him I was dying and I wanted
Audrey to know the truth. And yes, I suspect you will have met
Audrey by the time you're reading this. I'm sorry. Please let me
explain.
It was very, very hard living with myself these past thirty-odd
years. What kind of mother leaves her child behind? I did. I don't
know what kind of mother I am. All I know is that I wanted to
save you.

Claire's heart sped up. She tried to calm her nerves by
taking a deep breath so she could keep reading, but her hands
were shaking and the words were blurring into one. The information was all so dizzying.

She took another deep breath in, releasing it slowly before
she looked down at the paper again.

Anyway, I will try to recap the truth as clearly as I can. Here
goes.
When I called, Robert said he refused to tell Audrey anything.
He said I'd made my bed all those years ago and had to live with
it. I could tell he was suffering from something. He kept losing
track, forgetting what I said. I called several times and he almost
never remembered what we had spoken about last. So I knew he
wouldn't be able to tell you everything one day. I knew I would
need to write this all down. For both you and for Audrey.
Please don't be mad at her. It was so long ago, and she had
nothing to do with it. But my heart broke for her every day—every
single day. My only saving grace was that I knew she was with
Robert. He was a good man and an even better father. I knew she
would be loved.
You, on the other hand, were living in the house next to us
with people who didn't love you. I would often see you by your-
self, with your hair a tangled mess, dirty clothes, looking like

nobody took care of you. It was when I started seeing bruises on your arms that I couldn't sit by and watch any longer.

My heart broke for you. You were only a child. You were way too young to be left alone. I tried calling child protective services, but nothing happened. You always ended up back in that house, with that man and woman because they were your parents. I overheard them talking to the police one time. They said they had no family members you could stay with—no relatives at all who could take you in. They were functioning adults, technically. The house you lived in was fine, you had clothes, there was some food, but your parents should never have had a child. They didn't seem to have the capacity to love and care for you the way you deserved. They weren't loving parents.

Robert worried about how "obsessive" I was becoming with you. That was his word. But how could I not help? How could I sit by and watch and do nothing? It broke my heart to see you day in and day out, looking alone and uncared for. He threatened me with taking Audrey away. He said the way I was acting was getting unhealthy and he didn't want her around me. Then, one day, he took her and left. It nearly killed me. I tried my best to find them, tried to get her back, but I couldn't. I don't know why I didn't immediately call the police. Maybe it was because in the back of my mind, I knew what I was going to do.

When I couldn't stand seeing what was happening to you any longer, I took you. I didn't have time to think about what it all actually meant or what I was doing. I just took you. I don't know what overcame me, but all I knew was that I wanted to save you. I didn't want to send you to foster care, or even try fostering you myself, only to have you taken away. The system is heavy with processes and red tape. I couldn't risk you ending up back with your parents—or with someone worse.

Because I had no idea where Robert and Audrey were, and because he didn't know what I had done, I ended up running away, to a new town. I was going to protect you, an innocent kid,

*and I thought eventually I could talk Robert and Audrey into
joining us, but I couldn't get hold of him. He changed his
number and eventually I had to stop looking for him for fear of
being found out.*

*He called me a few times, many years later, but his mind never
changed. The last time I spoke to him, he said he didn't want
Audrey to know me at all, or what I had done. It was my fault.
Everything was my fault.*

*When I got to Summerville with you, I changed our names and
got you a fake birth certificate so you could get a Social Insurance
Number. The police searched for us, but the case went cold eventually. Your parents never really pushed it. They gave up
searching and went on with their lives.*

*I'm sorry. I'm sorry to tell you that about them. But they were
awful people—*

The front door swung open and made a thud as it bounced
off the wall. Claire jerked in surprise. She crammed the papers
under her thigh and looked up to see Lilah with her backpack
slung over her shoulder.

"Hey." Lilah's tone was low and cool. Things were still very
uncomfortable between them.

"Hey. Where's Dad?" Claire asked.

"I have too much homework tonight. We're going to meet
up another night." Lilah must have noticed the expression on
Claire's face, or the redness in her eyes, because she came to
Claire's side immediately. "What's going on?"

Where could Claire begin? Lilah was still a kid, even if she
seemed mature. It was hard to know how much of the truth she
could handle. Claire didn't have it in her to keep fighting,
though. She didn't have much left in her at all.

"I have a letter from Grandma."

Lilah inched closer to where Claire was on the couch and

stood over her. She looked down at Claire with a frown on her face. "What? How? What does it say?"

"It says... a lot."

"Can I see it?" Lilah asked.

"I don't know if you should read it. It's adult stuff."

"Please? I just want to be told the truth."

Claire's shoulders softened. Lilah's beautiful face was twisted with concern. She looked both innocent and so grown-up at the same time. The truth wasn't what Claire had always wanted. She would have preferred to remain in the dark, unaware and okay with it, but something about Lilah's words struck Claire. The truth was important. No matter how old you were.

"Come sit," Claire said. She patted the seat next to her on the couch. She let Lilah read up until where she had stopped, watching her face, ready to pull the paper away the instant it seemed like too much for her to handle.

Lilah's expression was calm while she read. When she stopped, she looked at Claire, her greenish eyes now glassy. "Why would your parents do that to you?"

Claire shook her head, unable to speak. She hadn't had time to process her mother's letter yet, let alone explain it all to her daughter.

Lilah reached one arm out and wrapped it around the small of Claire's back and waist. She tilted her head and rested it on Claire's shoulder. They stayed there, silent, unmoving.

TWENTY-NINE

Later, Claire sat at the edge of the dock, her legs dangling and her toes skimming the water. Lilah was behind her on one of the chairs.

"Come in with me."

"It's September," Lilah said.

"Barely. Anyway, since when did that stop us?" Claire asked.

They were being careful around one another. Or, Claire was, at least. After reading the letter up to the part where Claire had stopped, they had decided to take a break. It was enough heavy stuff for the day. Instead, they had ordered in pizza and sat on the back deck. They had talked about Lilah's day at school, what Claire was going to do about work (she still didn't know). They had skirted around Audrey for a while, but eventually, Claire was ready to go there.

"I'm sorry about how I've been handling things," Claire had said. "I've never gone through something even remotely like this before. I don't know how to deal with it or what to say or do. All I want is to make sure you're okay."

"You have to make sure you're okay, too, Mom." Lilah had picked a piece of pepperoni off her slice and eaten it.

A lump had formed in Claire's throat at her daughter's thoughtfulness.

"I know. I'll try. And I realize I've been pushing Audrey away when, really, she hasn't deserved it. At all. I'll try harder with her, too, if she'll speak to me again," Claire had said. Since reading Veronica's letter, something was softening within Claire. When her mother wrote that Claire shouldn't blame Audrey, a ripple of shame went through her. Audrey had been only a kid when all of this happened. She was merely looking for the truth—like Lilah was. They were so similar.

Lilah didn't speak. She only twisted her mouth and then shrugged before taking a bite of pizza.

After they were done and had cleared away the leftovers and dishes, they had gone down to the dock. Now, Claire felt the urge to jump into the water. The coolness of the lake, the sensation of floating, it always served as a salve to whatever was bothering her, even if it was only temporary.

"Come on," Claire pleaded. She turned to face Lilah.

"In our underwear?" Lilah's tone was skeptical. She raised an eyebrow.

"Sure, why not? We've done it before," Claire said. She stood at the edge of the dock. The water was glassy this evening. It would be cold, that was for sure.

"No, thanks," Lilah said, crossing her arms.

Claire pulled her shorts off and backed up a few steps and then moved forward again, launching herself into the water. When she went under, her breath caught in her chest at the cold. She broke the surface and shouted a garbled noise. Then she whipped around to see if Lilah was still on the dock.

"It's great," Claire said.

"It is not! I can tell," Lilah called back. Half of her mouth turned up in a smile.

Claire laughed. "Okay, it's not *great*, but it's refreshing." She started treading water to keep herself moving, to warm up her limbs. She wouldn't last long out here, but it made her feel like she was suddenly awake. "I'm going to swim out a bit and then come back."

Claire turned her back to the dock and moved forward, stretching her arms out in front of her and then pulling them back. Her legs kicked in time with her arms. There was something undeniable about the water for Claire. Like you could forget everything and just enjoy the way your body felt when you were floating.

The familiar sound of a splash came from behind her. Claire didn't need to turn around to look. Lilah couldn't resist the water either. When she caught up to Claire, Lilah fell in line next to her, and they swam out to the middle of the lake silently.

"Let's go back," Claire said when her limbs were starting to get tired.

Once they reached the dock and were out of the water, the tiniest bit of a chill in the wind forced them to hurry back to the house and change into dry clothes. They both put on their pajamas and went to the living room. Claire didn't want to say or do anything that might break the mood. She wasn't sure when or why Lilah had decided to possibly forgive her, but she was happy she had.

"Do you think we could read the rest of the letter?" Lilah asked.

Claire was stretched out on the couch, suddenly overcome with exhaustion. She was too tired to think about the letter, but she could see Lilah wanted to know.

"Okay," Claire said. "But if there are any parts I feel aren't appropriate for you, I'm pulling the plug. No more reading and no questions asked."

"Fine." Lilah shifted her seat on the couch. When Claire

came back from getting the letter, Lilah shimmied herself over until she was right up next to her.

Claire opened it up and started reading to herself. She angled the paper so Lilah could see it, too.

I'm sure you're wondering what your name used to be. I will tell you, but I also want you to prepare yourself for what you might find if you go searching for family. Your parents were horrible people, and they were estranged from most of their families. All I know is that their parents are dead and, I'm sorry to tell you this, but they've also passed away. I know that doesn't leave you with much, but I don't want the questions to bog you down for the rest of your life.

Your name was Sadie Green. After I took you, I followed the news closely about you. That's how I learned that you didn't have much family.

I'm so sorry about everything, Claire. One split-second decision by me and it changed all our lives forever. I don't regret anything about you, though. I hope you know that. I grieved my entire life over Audrey, even though I did my best to hide it from you. My grief was so heavy, it was unbearable at times, but I want you to know this: I didn't regret you once. Not for a second.

Please know that Audrey knew nothing about this, and also please know that she's a wonderful person. I got updates once in a blue moon from Robert. He showed me that small kindness. I hope you get a chance to get to know her. It must be incredibly confusing, but I'm hopeful you two will find a way to one another. You might need each other now with me gone and Robert so sick.

Over the years, I've learned that family can be where you find it, not just what ties you together by genes. I always considered you and Lilah mine, Claire. Both of you are everything to me. I am your mother, and Lilah's grandmother. Learning what happened

all those years ago doesn't change that. I wish I had made better
decisions, but I will always love you.
I'm sorry.

Love,
Mom

Claire closed the letter and sat on the couch, not moving.
She wasn't sure her body could function yet. Her senses were
overloaded. Somehow, flashes of memories from that time came
to her. How had she forgotten everything? It must have been
pushed down. Now, reading these words and seeing her old
name, it was like a dam had been opened, and she could recall
some of the small things. The scratchy feel of dead grass
beneath her bare feet. The way her hands would get caught in
her hair at the nape of her neck, it was so tangled and matted.
The hollowness of her stomach. She was hungry so often then.

Other things came to her, too. Memories of Veronica. The
scent of her shampoo, like fresh air and lemons, when Claire
would bury her face in her hair. The weekend mornings spent
cuddling in her bed and watching a movie. The way Veronica
hugged with her entire body. The sadness in her eyes sometimes, especially when Claire asked about Veronica's life before
her. It was an innocent question that most kids ask their parents,
but Claire could see it caused her mother pain, so she had
stopped asking, just as she had stopped asking about Audrey.

Lilah let a long, slow breath out. She didn't ask Claire how
she was or what she was thinking. She only reached for her
hand. That was enough for Claire. It was everything, in fact.

THIRTY

The next day, as Claire was cleaning the dishes from the night before, Lilah came down to the kitchen in her pajama bottoms and a loose T-shirt, her curly hair wild and big from the night's sleep.

"Morning," Claire said. She reached for a quick hug.

"Morning," Lilah mumbled. Her arms dangled at her sides, then she crossed them over her chest. She stood looking around, like she was confused by the daylight.

"You okay?"

"I had a really bad dream," Lilah said. "And it reminded me of something."

"What happened?"

"You were there. So was Audrey. But then you both died. It was really sad. I couldn't get back to sleep after that. I felt so alone."

There was a tightness in Claire's throat. "That's awful. I'm sorry you had such a bad dream."

"Thanks. At least it wasn't real. And anyway, like I said, it reminded me of something."

"What's that?" Claire asked.

"It reminded me of how good it feels to have family, and how much I miss it when we lose someone."

Claire's heart lurched. She instinctively reached for Lilah, but Lilah pulled back an inch. "Is this about Grandma?"

Lilah shook her head. "No. I mean, it is, but not just her. It's mostly about Audrey."

That wasn't exactly what Claire wanted to hear. It surprised her how much of a pull Audrey had created over Lilah in such a short time.

"Why Audrey?" Claire asked.

"You told her to get out of our lives, Mom. She's gone. And I really liked having her around."

Claire opened her mouth to say something, but Lilah held up a hand.

"Hang on. I'm not done," Lilah said.

Claire closed her mouth again and shifted her body so she was facing Lilah completely.

"I know you think having Audrey around is confusing, but I don't think it is. I don't think she caused our lives to turn upside down," Lilah said.

Claire couldn't help herself. She interrupted. "When she arrived, everything fell apart. I just want to go back to how it was. I want you to be safe."

"That's the thing. You can't keep me bubble-wrapped forever. At some point, you have to trust me. I know how to be safe. And Audrey isn't the one you should be blaming. You know she didn't know what was going on with you and I when I showed up at her house. All she knew was that I said I needed her. I feel so listened to when I'm with her. I feel so valued."

Claire's throat hurt now and it was difficult to swallow. "I listen to you," she said.

Lilah let out a loud sigh. "This isn't all about you."

"Okay," Claire said gently. "Tell me what else is going on."

"I don't know. It's just that it makes me happy to have more family in my life. It's always been you and Grandma and Dad and that's it. No siblings or cousins or aunts and uncles around because Dad's family lives far away and you only had Grandma. I love you and Grandma and Dad, but it's been amazing to feel loved by someone else, too. Audrey is really interested in me. She cares about me."

"I know she does." It was true. Audrey had shown so much interest in and kindness to Lilah. It had been hard for Claire to appreciate that up until now, but she should have seen Audrey for who she truly was.

"I've been thinking," Lilah said.

Claire didn't want to move or say a word to interrupt her daughter. It was rare when Lilah would open up and share so much with Claire. Claire stood still and nodded at Lilah to show she had her attention.

"I would love to travel when I get older. I'd love to see other countries. I might want to move somewhere new. I don't think Summerville is where I want to stay forever." Lilah's eyes shot to Claire's. They were wide, searching Claire for a reaction.

"Okay." Claire hoped she was hiding the pain radiating through her body. She knew this was bound to happen one day, but she always hoped it wouldn't.

"I'd love to see different places, but..."

"But what?" Claire asked.

Lilah looked down. "I don't know. I don't want to say it."

"Say what? You can tell me," Claire insisted. A pang of worry shot through her at what Lilah might be about to say.

When Lilah looked up, she chewed on her bottom lip.

"What?" Claire asked again.

"I'm worried about leaving you behind. I don't know if you can handle it."

A tingling swept up from the back of Claire's neck and across her face. How awful. Her heart sped up. Lilah was worried about her. To think that Lilah might stop herself from doing what she wanted because she was worried about her mother. She looked and sounded so much older than her years, standing in front of Claire now. It wasn't just that she was tall and getting taller each time Claire turned around; it was that she was being so mature. It nearly broke Claire's heart.

"Hey, Lilah, no. You don't have to worry about me. I'm an adult and not only can I take care of myself, but I'm fine. I'm perfectly fine."

Lilah didn't look convinced.

"I mean it," Claire repeated.

"I'm glad," Lilah said.

"But?" Claire could tell there was something Lilah wasn't saying.

"I'd like to have more people who care about me in my life. I think you should, too, especially if I leave one day and I'm not always here. Like Audrey. We should have Audrey in our lives."

When Lilah said it, the truth of it smacked Claire in the face. Everyone should have more people in their lives who cared about them. Audrey had shown up for them over and over. She was reliable in her care and kindness, and yet, Claire kept resisting. Now she couldn't think why she would ever treat Audrey this way. Her entire life, Claire had wanted a sister and Audrey had come and literally knocked on her door. Maybe Claire had resisted because it didn't turn out neat and perfect the way Claire liked her life to be. When the papers came back and said Audrey wasn't actually her biological sister, that had put up a wall for Claire, but it shouldn't have. She could see that now. She had been so stuck on it being her way, the way she thought it should be, that she had almost lost something so wonderful. And it took her daughter to point that out to her.

"You're right. I think that's a good idea," Claire said. "I can call her."

"It won't do any good." Lilah shrugged.

"What do you mean? Why not?" Claire asked.

"Because," Lilah said, "she told me she's moving."

"Moving? Where to?"

"To British Columbia. She's going across the country. She'll be in a different time zone." Lilah's lower lip trembled when she spoke, which made Claire's entire body feel heavy. She wanted to stop Lilah's tears before they even appeared, but Lilah's entire face crumpled.

"Hey, it's okay," Claire said. She moved toward Lilah, and when she reached for her daughter, this time, Lilah didn't pull away.

"I need help." Claire stood outside Greg's house, on his front porch. Greg was on the other side of the door, his brow furrowed.

"What's going on?" he asked.

"Can I come in?"

Greg stepped to the side in a jerky, quick motion and held the door open. "Of course. Sorry, come with me." He turned and motioned for Claire to follow him inside. They went to the living room and took a seat on one of his soft couches. Then he studied her.

"I don't like who I am lately," Claire said.

"Claire." He frowned. A pained expression crossed his face. "Don't be so hard on yourself. You've been going through such a rough time." He ran a hand through his hair and shifted his seat on the couch.

Claire shook her head. "That's not an excuse. Besides, I'm starting to think I've always been like this."

"Like what?" Greg asked.

How could she put it into words? Claire could suddenly see that she had been so desperate to lead a carefully organized and contained life, but it wasn't working. She couldn't control everything; she hadn't been able to keep her marriage organized into the perfect little package she wanted it to be. Now she couldn't ignore the truth about her mother and who she really was. It felt like she was losing her grip on everything.

"I don't know how to relax. Or to let myself be open to new experiences. I don't know how to leave my comfort zone. I don't even know how to let people in," she said.

Greg scooted closer to Claire on the couch. "It's hard for you. I understand that."

"I think this is why we didn't work."

He reached for her hand and squeezed gently. "Ah, I don't really know. I think we did work in our way." He smiled.

Claire laced her fingers through his. He was just being kind, Claire could tell.

"I don't want to be like this. I don't want to lose Lilah. I've already lost you."

"You haven't lost me or Lilah." Greg's eyebrows shot up on his forehead. How could he be surprised by this? Of course Claire had lost him. She had let him go because of her desperate need to be perfect.

"Can you forgive me?" Claire asked.

"Forgive you? There's nothing to forgive. What's this all about?" Greg turned so he was facing her. "Claire."

He said her name so softly, she felt such a strong affection for him in that moment. He was always checking on her, ensuring she was okay, and she had taken him for granted.

"Do you think you might be able to help? I would love it," Claire said. "I love you."

She was lucky to have Greg in her life, and had known she wanted him closer again for a while, but she had been trying to ignore it because it didn't fit into the perfect vision and controlled version of her life that she desired. But where had that gotten her? Her life was a mess. She didn't need Greg to fix it for her, that wasn't it. What she needed was to let people in. She needed to let the love in and let go of some of the control.

"I love you, too. I always have," Greg said.

Claire's stomach flipped. Imagine your ex-husband being able to make your stomach flip.

"I mean it, Claire. I haven't stopped loving you. We seemed to grow distant from one another, but I think it was just life. We were busy, you were often stressed. The space grew between us, little by little, but I never stopped wanting you in my life."

Claire's eyes welled up. "I've always loved you, too. It just took me a while to figure it out. Do you think we could try again?"

"I'm so glad you said that." Greg's shoulders lowered. "I've been thinking about it for a while, but didn't know how to bring it up exactly. I would really like that for us."

"But we'll have to be careful," Claire said. Greg gave her a look, so she added, "For Lilah's sake. I wouldn't want to confuse her."

"Of course." Greg reached for her and pulled Claire in close. She rested her head against his chest and listened to his heart for a moment, the steady rhythm relaxing her into a calm state.

"You didn't say what you need help with." Greg looked down at her intently with his gorgeous eyes and Claire could feel her pulse quicken.

She tilted her face up toward him. "Could you help me figure out how to fix things with Audrey?"

"Really? Are you sure about that? I know Lilah seems to have become attached, but that doesn't mean you have to force it."

Claire gave her head a small shake. "No, I wouldn't force it. I think it would be good to have her in our lives. Both Lilah and I."

"Even if she's not family?" Greg said.

Claire pulled away. She looked down at her knees and thought before she spoke, "That's the thing about family. It's so complicated, isn't it? I think we feel this pressure to have relationships and make them work just because we're related to someone. But I don't think all the rules around who we love and who we have in our lives need to be so defined. Sometimes it just works to have people in your life, no matter who they are." She smiled at him.

Greg smiled back and kept watching her closely, listening.

She continued, "Audrey isn't blood-related, but she's a good person, and I like her. I want to get to know her better. I just hope I haven't ruined it all by being so caught up in how I thought things should be."

"I bet you haven't. And I'm not sure what I can do, but whatever you need, I'm here," Greg said. When he took her hand again, she leaned into his body. For the first time, she let herself be in the moment and didn't think about anything else.

THIRTY-ONE

On Monday morning, Claire got up early. She made breakfast for Lilah and left some of it on the table—a bowl with dry cereal already poured into it, plus a note telling her to look in the fridge for the milk and to find her favorite smoothie already made and waiting for her in a mason jar. Lilah would be fine getting herself ready and off to school on her own. Even though Claire knew this in the rational side of her brain, she never left Lilah alone in the mornings. It was easy enough for her to be present, to take care of things and see her daughter off for the day. Today, however, she had somewhere to be. Today, Lilah would have to do it all on her own and she would be just fine. Claire was sure of it. She didn't even call Greg for backup, that's how sure she was.

The air outside had a whiff of chill to it. The first sign that fall was officially here. Claire pulled her cardigan close across her body as she went to her car. She fastened the seatbelt and put both hands on the wheel before pausing for a brief moment. This was going to be okay. It would all work out. Claire had begun to feel this since reading the letter from Veronica. It was as if things had fallen into place and a calm had come over her.

She couldn't fully explain it, but somehow it cemented in her mind that Veronica was her mother, the one she had always known. She had done something so wrong, but it was that same over-protective love she'd felt all her life, and there was something weirdly comforting about it. Claire realized she had a new kind of love for her mother. It was the kind that came with understanding just how much Veronica had sacrificed for her. It was laced with sorrow for what that had meant for Audrey, too, though. She couldn't ever make that right, but she could try to do the right thing now.

The drive was easy. Claire arrived quickly because traffic was light. She followed the directions on her phone to Audrey's house. It was like she was seeing it for the first time; a small, Tudor-style home on a quiet street. She glanced down at her phone: eight-thirty. She hoped it wasn't too late.

Claire knocked on the front door and waited. After a brief pause, the door flung open and Audrey stood there, a purse slung over her shoulder and a lunch bag in one hand, a travel mug in the other.

"Oh," Audrey said. "What are you doing here?" Her face was blank. Claire couldn't read if she was shocked to see her or not.

"I came to talk to you. If that's okay," Claire said.

Audrey's shoulders moved upwards an inch, as if her body was tightening. "I guess it is, but I'm on my way to work. I have to leave right now."

"Can I come with you? I'll drive you. We can talk in the car," Claire said.

"How will I get home at the end of the day?" Audrey asked.

Claire hadn't thought this all the way through. She rubbed at her lip with the tips of her fingers as her stomach rolled. She hadn't expected to be this uneasy. "How about we go in your car? Then I'll find my way back here. I'll take a cab."

Audrey eyed her. Claire supposed it was odd that she

sounded so insistent, that she had showed up here almost out of nowhere. It was natural for Audrey to be hesitant.

"Okay," Audrey said finally. "Let's go."

In the car, Claire settled her nerves before speaking. She should have rehearsed something. Then again, what she needed to say was really quite simple.

"I was hoping we could be in each other's lives. Like, a family maybe?"

Audrey's eyes were on the road in front of her, she didn't react and didn't say anything. Her face was blank and cold, like stone. This wasn't going to be easy, but Claire knew it was her own fault, so she continued.

"I know I've been very hot and cold up until now, but it's been so hard for me to know how to take all of this."

"It's been the same for me," Audrey said. Her voice was flat.

"I know."

They sat in silence for a moment.

"Why has your mind changed all of a sudden?" Audrey asked. She glanced sideways briefly, her eyes searching Claire's face quickly and then darting back to the road again. "I thought it mattered to you that we weren't related. I thought you wanted me out of your life and now suddenly you're showing up at my door to talk?" There was a heaviness to Audrey's voice. It was filled with hurt.

"I had a long chat with Lilah. She said some pretty honest things that made me realize I haven't been fair to anyone."

Audrey's face seemed to soften at the mention of Lilah's name.

"What is it about Lilah that you like so much?" Claire asked. "I'm her mother, so I know why I think she's wonderful. You've been drawn to her since day one, and even after we found out she wasn't your niece."

Audrey's head tilted an inch to the left. "She's an easy kid to like. She's smart and funny. Being with her —and with you—has made me feel like I have family. It's made me feel less alone. It's good to feel cared about and wanted."

It was similar to what Lilah said.

Claire put her hands in her lap and thought about how much she hadn't realized earlier. She had been so focused on her own feelings.

"But if I'm being completely honest," Audrey continued, "I could sense she would be easier to get to know. She didn't immediately reject the thought of having me in her life the way you did."

That brought Claire up short. She had been pretty bad about all of this, hadn't she? She'd had so much to deal with, it was impossible to get it all right.

"She's usually the tough one to get to open up." Claire's voice went quiet.

Audrey shrugged. "Once I started to get to know her, I thought it might eventually bring you around and we could be close, like sisters. No matter what the tests said."

Claire nodded and felt a flicker of understanding. A part of her wanted the same thing.

"What did Lilah say to you to change your mind?" Audrey asked.

"Similar things to what you said. She would like to have more people in her life." Claire turned to face Audrey, who was still focused on the road in front of her. "She wants you in her life."

Audrey blinked, like she was clearing her eyes of tears.

"I got a note from Veronica," Claire continued.

"You did?" Audrey's head snapped sideways to look at Claire and then back at the road again. "When?"

"She wrote it when she knew she was dying. Fatima found it and brought it to me. She said your father used to update her every once in a while about you. Did he tell you that?"

"Yes," Audrey answered. A frown appeared on her face.

"When?" Claire could see she was going to have to do the work.

"A little while back."

"You didn't tell me," Claire said.

One of Audrey's shoulders raised in a shrug. "How could I tell you? You've been so mad at me, you told me to never come around again."

That was true. Claire lowered her head. "I'm sorry."

They drove past common September things. Trees with leaves that were just starting to turn, kids with backpacks slung over their shoulders walking in pairs, talking and smiling, adults driving shiny cars, their faces creased in concentration, no longer relaxed the way they were when they were on summer vacation. Life was resuming for most. Life would resume for Claire eventually and she would have to learn to go with it, even as things had changed.

"When you showed up, my world was rocked. Everything I knew was turned upside down. It's been incredibly hard for me to make sense of my life."

The frown on Audrey's face deepened, but she didn't say anything, so Claire kept speaking.

"I found out my name. I was a completely different person at one point. The note explained most of the things we were looking for."

"What else did you find out?" Audrey asked. She kept her eyes on the road, so Claire couldn't read her expression.

Claire considered the question. Aside from finding out her name, she had also learned that she was mistreated and her birth parents were likely abusing her, that Veronica had given up everything just to save her, to protect her. She found out that even though everything had changed, her mother had remained the same. That she did her best.

"She said she wanted to be honest with me and with you, finally, but she knew your father wasn't well when she called him, so she wrote everything down for me. I guess she wanted to talk to you but didn't get the chance."

Audrey's face looked pained, and her body almost sagged. She nodded. "Yes. You already know I was too late when I called her back." There was a defensive edge to her voice.

"Will you be okay?" Claire couldn't imagine what this must have been like for Audrey. It had hit her fully after reading Veronica's letter; her mother gave Audrey up. The longing Veronica must have felt her entire life, the raw hunger, for a daughter that was within reach, but also unattainable. Because of Claire. Audrey must have felt that same pain for her mother. Claire wondered if it was anything close to the pain she felt from missing her father all her life. When friends or kids at school would do things with their fathers, Claire was always jealous; she wanted a dad in her life, too, but at least she had her mother. Veronica. She had been such a good mother.

Claire suddenly wanted to reach out to Audrey, to touch her shoulder and tell her something other than just sorry. She *was* sorry. She had been singly focused this entire time on herself. Her own sorrow and grief. But there had been so much of it everywhere that she hadn't been able to see anything else. Audrey had so much to grieve.

"Audrey," Claire said, her voice hoarse now. "I don't know how to say it well enough, but I'm sorry. I can't imagine the pain you've been through. To spend your whole life without your mother—" She couldn't continue.

"Thank you," Audrey answered, her voice quiet.

They drove in silence a little further. Then Audrey spoke again.

"The school's just up here." She nodded at the road ahead of her. Claire could see a large redbrick building in the distance. This meant their conversation was ending. So was Claire's chance to make things right.

"Do you think we could try again?" Claire asked, watching

Audrey's face carefully for her response. She was surprised by how nervous she felt all of a sudden.

"What do you mean?"

"Start over. Try to be in one another's lives." Claire rubbed at her forearms and tried to swallow. Her throat was dry and sore.

Audrey glanced over at her and then back to the road again. "I don't know."

Claire's stomach sank. She deserved that answer. She had been awful to Audrey.

Before she could say anything in response, Audrey kept speaking.

"We tried to make this work, but there's too much baggage. You said it yourself, we're not related. And you seem like you want to keep things the way they've always been."

That was true. Claire thought life would be easier and better if she kept within her tightly made borders. Everything was simpler that way. She had been certain all her life that what she had was more than enough for her. Lilah, on the other hand, had been trying to show her how much more was out there. She knew she had to fight for that—she knew she wanted more now.

"Lilah would miss you," Claire said. That was also true.

"I'd miss her, too, but I still don't know."

Claire looked at Audrey, at the familiar profile that reminded her so much of Veronica, and remembered how much she had longed for her all her life growing up. Now she was here, and everything had changed. But she wouldn't lose her again. "I thought that I couldn't handle change," Claire said, as she shifted in her seat to turn and face Audrey more directly. "Then I met you and I've had things thrown at me I never would have imagined could happen to my little life. And at the end of it all, I'm coming through with more than I had before. I'm lucky. I'm lucky to have you. It's like I'm just waking up now, realizing I have people around me who love me. I want that for both of us."

Audrey's eyes met hers and she seemed to relax back into her seat as if absorbing Claire's words. Claire hoped she knew she meant every single word. She *was* lucky to have met Audrey and have her in her life. Why had it taken so long to see that? Maybe Audrey felt lucky, too. Maybe that's why her body softened and a small smile came to her lips. Claire thought her expression resembled Lilah's, but that was genetically impossible. Still, there was something about their mannerisms that was familiar. She felt like family.

"I feel lucky, too," Audrey said in a quiet voice.

Claire smiled. She sat back into her seat and let the wave of relief wash over her.

THIRTY-TWO

The roads in town were quiet. September felt like a fresh start in a lot of ways, but it was also a kind of closing. The lake wasn't as busy, the shops that thrived on income from tourists changed their hours. Fewer people were on the streets. Claire breezed through town on her way home after being at the clinic. It felt right to be back at work, seeing clients and getting women ready for one of the biggest changes in their lives to come. She loved being around people who were so happy despite their exhaustion and the discomfort that came with pregnancy. These women could be having a hard time, but as soon as you told them something about how their baby was doing, their faces would light up. It was beautiful.

Claire's coworkers at the practice had been gracious when Claire had been approved to return to work. Sarah had even said she was happy with how Claire was doing. Back to her old self, she had said. Claire knew how lucky she was to be getting back into her stride, doing the work she loved so much. She wasn't going to mess up, she was determined to earn everyone's trust again.

Once she arrived at home, Claire dropped her bag at the front door and walked through to the kitchen. A couple of glasses were by the sink, a plate with a few crumbs was on the counter. The pie Claire had picked up at the bakery was also out, but not cut into yet. Good. Claire didn't want to miss out.

Voices floated into the kitchen from the back. Claire went to the screen door and found Lilah and Audrey. Lilah was wearing a hoodie and sitting cross-legged on a chair while she picked at the bowl of chips on the table in front of her. Audrey was reclined in her chair, a mug of tea in her hands. The two of them could often be found out here, now that Audrey visited as much as her schedule allowed. They both turned when Claire opened the screen door and stepped out to join them.

"Hey, Mom," Lilah said. "How was work?"

Audrey watched Lilah and smiled, then turned to Claire, waiting for her to answer.

"It was good," Claire answered. "Great, actually. I'm so glad I'm back."

"The timing is off, though," Audrey said. "It would be nice if you could come with us."

"You two are going to have the best time. Besides, I won't miss the next one." Claire took a seat. She was happy for Audrey and Lilah. They were planning an extended weekend trip to New York City over Thanksgiving—a huge deal for Lilah. Claire would have gone, she felt ready to try to dip her toe into new experiences, but she was also happy to be back at work and on call again. There would be plenty of time for her to explore, for her to spend time with Audrey. This was a unique chance for Lilah and Audrey. And, Claire realized, she trusted Audrey completely.

As if Audrey knew Claire was thinking of her, she turned her head to Claire and raised an eyebrow when she smiled. Her expression was one of hope and excitement. It was also contentment. She had Veronica's face again. It was just as Claire saw on that day back in July in the middle of town when she had first caught a glimpse of Audrey. At moments like this, it was as if Veronica was looking back at Claire. Goosebumps sprang up on the back of Claire's arms.

"Hey, is that pie in there for us?" Lilah asked.

"Yes, let me go get it," Claire said. She went into the kitchen and grabbed it along with a knife and three plates.

When she got back to Audrey and Lilah, Lilah said, "What kind is it?"

"Raspberry," Claire answered. She glanced shyly at Audrey and Audrey smiled back.

While they sat and ate pie, Claire considered how this all felt. Her world had been small, mostly just her mother and her until Greg came along and then Lilah. Now Audrey. She didn't know what it was like to have many people in her life, let alone someone like a sister. Yet, she knew it was what she had wanted for so long. She could remember distinctly longing for it as a kid. Something magical had happened and now she had everything she wanted. She knew she couldn't let that slip through her fingers. She wouldn't.

"You sure about New York?" Audrey asked as she took a plate of pie from Claire. "I don't want to leave you alone on a holiday."

That was it. That was what Claire didn't even know she wanted to hear. She had only a little family, and she had been so worried about losing them, she tried to keep them close and controlled. But Audrey wouldn't leave. She would come back. In fact, Audrey had come into her life unexpectedly. Imagine what else Claire could have if she were open to it.

After the pie had been finished and cleaned up, Claire told Lilah and Audrey she would be back in a while, left through the front door and drove straight to Greg's home.

He was there, on the other side of the door, his light hair shining, like he had just showered and let it air dry.

"Come in," he said. He held the door open and Claire walked inside.

They had been through so much, and all along Greg had been there. He knew how to be there for Claire in the exact way she needed. He wasn't there to solve her problems or take away her pain; she had to learn to do all of that herself, but he was a steady support. From that support, Claire had noticed the love she felt for him grow again. It built itself from their shared history and developed until Claire knew there was almost nothing she wanted more than to have him in her life. She had tried to create space in their marriage when things didn't go the way she expected or wanted them to go, but Greg showed her a new kind of love. It was one that could develop from their past, one that could accept there had been bumps and bruises along the way, but could still grow.

Audrey had shown Claire a new kind of love, too. It was meaningful, even in such a short time and, for a while, Claire felt she wasn't worthy. What had she done to deserve this? She thought she wasn't the kind of person who could be loved this much. But she was. Audrey, and Greg and Lilah showed her that. But most of all, Veronica had shown Claire a deep and unconditional love when her own parents had failed to, and now Claire understood the enormity of what her mother had done. Her mother had been the first to show Claire how valued and worthy of love she was. It was her legacy—and her greatest gift.

Claire reached for Greg's hand. It was familiar, the shape of it; their hands had always fit together so easily.

"I don't know how to say what I need to say," Claire began.

"It's okay." Greg smiled at her.

"I want to, though." Claire looked up at him.

"Then we can figure it out together," Greg answered.

Claire leaned into his body and felt the warmth of him against her when he kissed her.

A LETTER FROM THE AUTHOR

Thank you so much for reading *The Summerville Sisters*. I loved writing it and introducing you to Claire, Audrey and Lilah. I hope you were hooked on their journey. If you want to join other readers in hearing all about my new releases and bonus content, you can sign up for my newsletter!

www.stormpublishing.co/heather-dixon

If you enjoyed this book and could spare a few moments to leave a review that would be hugely appreciated. Even a short review can make all the difference in encouraging a reader to discover my books for the first time. Thank you so much.

This book is somewhat of a love letter to my daughters. I find raising girls is interesting and challenging and wonderful all at once, especially when you reach each new age and stage. I, like Claire, often find myself marvelling over each little thing about my kids that makes them unique and complex. When I started writing it, I knew I wanted to explore the mother-daughter relationship and the sister relationship, as well. As I get older, I realize more and more how lucky I am to have so many wonderful women in my life—my mother, my daughters, my friends. The support, understanding and love and friendship women can provide each other is a beautiful thing—and it's a story that I wanted to tell. I hope I did these women justice and I hope you enjoyed reading.

Thank you again for being part of this amazing journey with me and I hope you'll stay in touch – I have so many more stories and ideas to entertain you with.

Heather

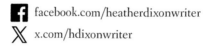 facebook.com/heatherdixonwriter
x.com/hdixonwriter

ACKNOWLEDGMENTS

Thank you first and foremost to my editor, Vicky Blunden. You are patient, attentive, caring and an expert at what you do. I appreciate each email, each note, every time we speak. And thank you to everyone at Storm Publishing who helped make this happen. You all have been a dream to work with.

To the writing community—my fellow writers, and all of the incredible bookstagrammers who show so much support. I'm forever in awe of and grateful for all of you. There are so many people I need to thank, including Bianca Marais, Karma Brown, Michelle Meade, Georgina Kelly, Lydia Laceby, Rosemary Twomey, The Cobb Salad Crew, the SPs, Mary Taggart, the Toronto Area Women Authors group, Liz Kessick, Jackie Khalilieh. Thank you, always.

To my friends—for buying my books, chatting with me about them, showing your support, inviting me to your book clubs. It has been so beautiful for me, and I am so grateful for all of you. Thank you to Derek Boyce for answering my questions about missing persons, and thank you to Sarah Branson for chatting with me about midwifery. Thank you to the hockey moms —our group texts give me life! I have a feeling they may appear in some future books. And I will always say an extra special thank you to Sarah Langley. You're one of the very best.

Thank you always to my family—Mom, Dad, Chris, Melissa, and of course, Andrew, Anna, Lauren and Paige. Your support and love have meant everything.

And finally, to my readers. I am so grateful for all of you—thank you for contacting me, supporting me, and enjoying my books.

Printed in Great Britain
by Amazon